Why are sowboys social outcasts when cowboys are the stuff of romance and glory? Where are the sowboy movies? The hand-tooled sowboy boots? Who is the John Wayne of the sowboy set?

Aimée, inspired commodities investor, pig lover, new in Chicago and lonely, is throwing a party and inviting her guests by ringing down to the pay-phone in the street below her apartment. She's already invited Phil, a lawyer and computer-whizz looking for better things . . . So when pig farmer George, on the run from the police, and sowboy Billy, on the run from the Marines, pick up that ringing receiver and the four of them get together, it only takes a few glasses of wine for them to realize that they're the perfect partners in swine . . . And before you can say *Suidic Saturnalia*, they've invented the answer to their wildest dreams: Pig Spa Island, Indonesia.

Sowboy follows the twin trails of porcine practicality and youthful idealism from the now into the future when Dan Quayle is president, the environment is falling apart, and flies can think. Must humankind die so life can live? No, thinks Billy, we can divert the momentum of history.

SOWBOY

Richard Miller

BLOOMSBURY

First published in Great Britain 1991
Copyright © 1991 by Richard Miller
This paperback edition published 1991

The moral right of the author has been asserted

Bloomsbury Publishing Ltd, 2 Soho Square, London W1V 5DE

A CIP catalogue record for this book
is available from the British Library

ISBN 0 7475 0985 9

Typeset by Hewer Text Composition Services, Edinburgh
Printed in Great Britain by Cox & Wyman Ltd, Reading, Berkshire

DEDICATED TO JOY AND GENIUS.

For
Salman Rushdie

With thanks to Captain Joshua Pryor

of China Basin Charter
1129 Folsom Street
San Francisco

PART ONE

OF PIGS

PIGVILLE

Ours is the age of transition,
if not of metamorphosis.

Billy Williams
(a.k.a. Alexander Burke)
Pigville, 1992

ONE

In June of 1992 Billy Williams graduated cum laude in history from the University of California at Berkeley, and now here he was, two months later, sweating profusely in the Indiana sun, a backpack at his feet, leaning on a pasture fence, talking to a cow. His professors had nominated him for a Rhodes Scholarship and elected him to Phi Beta Kappa, and, one imagines, because he had everything going for him – looks, health, talents both athletic and artistic, and a warm heart too – they, like everyone else, expected him to move swiftly into some responsible profession and rise quickly to its summit. Yet here he stood in cutoff military pants, cascading sweat, unemployed, on the run, provided with little but a blanket and a minimum of clothing and eighteen dollars, feeling no remorse for having frustrated conventional expectations, candidly confiding in a piebald black-and-white Holstein heifer.

'A pretty pass, eh, Farnsworth?' An odd name for a heifer, but what the hell. 'Me, that sleek and promising Billy Williams, *me*, a fugitive from justice.'

Farnsworth dropped a pie.

'My strengths are my weaknesses.'

Under his stroking hand her brow felt hard and smooth as a pool table.

'My dad used to ask me sometimes, "What have you done lately to make the world a better place?"'

Farnsworth peered sympathy through sisterly brown eyes.

3

'So, old girl, what have *you* done lately to make the world a better place? Me, I deserted from the Marine Corps.'

Graduation night, squired around Frisco by his antique godfather-and-honorary-uncle Bill – folks called him Billy to distinguish them – and later back home in Pacifica drinking after hours in Uncle Bill's saloon, the El Flaco Club, he told Uncle Bill what's happening now is the tribes of the world are melding into a single confederacy because, to survive, they must. Our refining, mutating technology, accelerating change every day, has placed the tribes in the same room and given them the power to provide a decent living for all. But the cultural DNA has not gone through harmonious transformation. Instead, it evolves like cancer and produces tumors; atom bombs, nerve gas, war germs. Ill-organized and misdirected, it's poisoning the biosphere and building mass-murder machines, exterminators, which will finish us off, sooner or later.

'We're watching a race. Arms or poison or plague, which one will win the honor of snuffing us? You know, ashes to ashes and dust to dust, if the chiggers don't get us, the skeeters must.'

Farnsworth flourished her tail.

'And look at me. I've got every gift a man could want, and more! And on top of that, I'm lucky, like my dad was. They called him Lucky Al. When the old-timers die off like he did, I'll be part of the new team. Me, if *I* don't do something about directing change, who will? Who'll replace Gorbachev and the Cousteaus? Won't be long before my team takes the field. Right now, I'm in spring training, waiting for the season to begin.'

Convinced his dedication to peace obliged him to study war, Billy, in the name of understanding, joined the Marine Corps and went off to boot camp at Parris Island, South Carolina.

That's where The Fly entered his life and changed his future.

The Fly paused on its daily round from the latrines to the kitchens and mess halls to glance down on formations arranged on the parade ground like sun-dried candy bars. All of a sudden, almost as if transformed by some higher power into a buzzing harbinger of salvation from outer space, The Fly dropped down to alight on the cheek of a skinheaded recruit standing at order arms in the front rank of his platoon near the tall end.

The Drill Instructor paced slowly before his pupils.

4

The Fly reveled in a Jacuzzi of Billy sweat.
The sun stunned all of nature into terminal silence.
The Fly stretched and relaxed in Roman luxury.
Billy perspired and itched in utter misery.
The sun baked everything, even time, into ceramic rigidity.
Slowly, Billy raised his hand and smacked The Fly.
The Fly tumbled into the dust at his feet.
The DI turned and glared.
Billy basted motionless at order arms.
The DI strode to him, gazed into his eyes.
The DI bent and retrieved the corpse.
The DI displayed the corpse in a nerveless hand.
'Boy, are you responsible for this atrocity?'
'Sir?'
The DI paced around Billy, confronted him again.
'Boy, did you murder this poor de-fence-less creature?'
'Yes sir.'
'Have you given thought to the mag-ni-tude of your crime?'
'No sir.'
'You will now re-flect upon it.'
'Yes sir.'
'We are contemplating the death of a *Fly*.'
'Yes sir.'
'Does this Fly have a mother?'
'I suppose so, sir.'
'Does he?'
'Yes sir.'
'Does this Fly have siblings soon to be in mourning?'
'Yes sir.'
'Are you aware that this poor victim of your random application
of superior force supports a wife and thirty-five children, one of
whom is an ep-i-leptic, and all of whom are now left destitute?'
'No sir.'
'What!'
'Yes sir.'
'And are you o-ver-come with remorse?'
'Yes sir.'
'What!'
'No sir; none sir.'
'You are a knucklehead.'

'Yes sir.'

'A sentimental pus-faced snot-eater.'

'Yes sir.'

'Boy, you should have sent your mother in-stead.'

The DI paced front-and-center to stand before the platoon. He drew a matchbox from his pocket and placed The Fly inside.

'We are going to celebrate the funeral of this poor murdered creature.'

He made them double-time off the parade ground and out into the boondocks where pine runts struggle to suck nourishment from dirty sand.

He reassembled them in formation.

Again he confronted Billy.

'Boy, we will hold a service, and then you will bury this Fly six feet deep.'

'Sir, it's against my religion to bury what I kill.'

The DI detailed a squad to bury The Fly while the rest stood to attention presenting arms and, as demanded, meditating upon the sacred life but so recently cut short by megaviolence.

Then he made Billy carry his rifle over his head as they double-timed back to the base, and made him trot around the parade ground for two hours, still holding his rifle at high port.

This is not for me.

It's not that I can't do it. Drilling comes easy, and so does the manual of arms. I breezed through the obstacle course, tough as it is, and it was fun. I shot expert on the range. And, smiling, persisting, I endured the aching torment of jogging at high port. They like that. They try to break you down into fragments and then rebuild you, and that pleases them, but if you don't break, that pleases them more.

They have a poetic dimension.

But it's not for me.

The next day, Sunday, hoping to devise some way to get to the post exchange, sacred precincts forbidden to recruits, Billy pocketed all his money and sat on the barracks steps looking at the company street, waiting for opportunity. A civilian pick-up truck stopped at the intersection and his mates cheered him on as he vaulted into it and lay down. The driver pulled away, and after a few blocks, parked and came back. 'Where you going sonny?' Post exchange, sir. The driver smiled a yellow smile, and ran the truck by the PX. But why jump out at the PX? Why not keep on going? Make room under this tarpaulin among the tools and boxes and crawl in. They hummed across the causeway to the mainland, and voices came, and they were past the gate, into Beaufort, where he bought a backpack and a cheap imitation Swiss army knife and a few clothes and hitched west.

'And that's how I came to visit you, my dear Farnsworth, and consult you about my new career.'

Farnsworth seems content with her present employment as a source of milk and cheese and calves for veal.

'I can't ply your trade. I'll just have to think of something else.'

The cow, Farnsworth, from under her brow, gazed out at the world as its odor came into her through wet, black nostrils. Focussing perhaps, but not naming things, birdsong and insect babble echoed dull in her head; the fragrance of grass, a new smell, Billy, bananas rotting in bogwater; no distinctions, no names for things, everything a single together, a changing atmosphere throbbing with the thunder and lightning of feeling – more usually a discomfort – a gut-quake, a milk-rush, a sting, a tail swat, no words, no thoughts, no past, no future, no now.

'I'm running from it Farnsworth, and I have no word for it; I don't know what to call it.'

Her drooling tongue hung over black lips.

'My dad used to say persistence preserves, prudence provides, and power prevails. To me that's just drawing circles. Yeah, well, at least I know what to call them, uh . . . that.'

Farnsworth lowered her head to the grass and Billy scratched her brow.

'Tautology.'

She made a rumbling cow sound.

'Sometimes what rides my back, I call indignation, or outrage, or just plain wrath, anger, but that's not it either. I don't know what to call it, or how to outrun it. It follows me like the back of my neck.' She nuzzled his wet chest. 'When words mount feelings they produce deformed offspring.' With a swish of tail, Farnsworth turned to graze, a toy of comfort-discomfort. Billy beat down some

7

tall grass and sat. Anonymous specks and flecks, some alive, itched his sweating legs. He drew a half-liter bottle of red wine from his pack, opened it, and drank to the blue sky. Ration time. He put the bottle back, pulled a choice grass-stalk, and, farmer-style, began chewing its tender end. He'd always made things happen, or so it seemed, but now what? Wait, watch the drift, see what washes up on the beach. Can't go home. Canada? Send Uncle Bill a power-of-attorney and ask him to take care of things for a while, whatever he isn't handling already. Other than the law, there's no reason to worry. Odd jobs are easy to get, and to do. I can go without food, if need be for two weeks – a month. Water's always around.

He glanced back at the fence. Farnsworth stood there, motherly, sympathetic.

'You can be the first to know. I'm resigning from the now to join the future.'

Whistling 'C. C. Rider', which he thought of as 'Easy Rider', he nested in warm itchy grass waiting for the future to come cantering down the road.

TWO

The future came rolling down the road instead. It materialized from the heat shimmer in the form of a rusty yellow flat-bed truck with Louisiana plates, an animal cage made of wire built on to the back. Billy thumbed. The truck stopped. A big solid man in a greasy T-shirt reached across and opened the door, revealing a ragged seat repaired here and there with curling silver duct tape.

'Where you going, kid?'

'Kansas City,' said Billy, wondering at another level why that popped out.

'Me, I'm going to my farm.' Billy climbed in and slammed the door with a thud and said any ride west would bring him closer to Missouri. He charmsmiled and fumbled for his seat belt until realizing it had been cut out.

'So what's your name, kid?'

'Bill.'

The truck accelerated, windows open, making a sweat-drying breeze and intensifying the fragrance of hot pasture.

'I'm George.' Crushed manure marbled the floor mat. 'So what you doing way out here in the middle of fucking nowhere?'

'I'm an adventurous traveler.'

'Too fucking hot for travel.' George seemed a crude hard sort of guy, thirty-five maybe, and his voice came loud and deep, but touched a gentle quality. 'I'd give my left nut for a drink.'

Billy drew the bottle from his pack.

'Here, have some wine.'

George raised the bottle and chugged it and wiped his mouth on his arm. His wrist displayed a wild boar tattooed over the legend

9

LEGIO DIX FRETENSIS. Mourning the vanished wine, Billy stared through the yellow crush of dead bugs on the windshield at a passing orchard. George flung the bottle out among the trees.

'So, hey, George, doesn't it make you apprehensive to pick up a total stranger like me, a skinhead who might be a mass killer, or cannibal, or something?'

George blew a pink gum-bubble, sucked it back in.

'You want a job?'

'I could use one.'

'I don't know if you'd want this one.'

'Right now George, anything short of selling used toilet paper's okay by me.'

'Yeah, but I don't know.'

'I can quit.'

'So you can. I always do. Why keep a job forever?' He ran over a flat rabbit. 'I worked as motorman on a New Orleans streetcar. Played the horses, won, quit, bought my farm, and here I am.'

'And you'd hire some punk skinhead right off the road?'

'For this job the pay's ten percent of our monthly net, all you can eat, and all the wine you can drink, starting in twenty minutes. But don't expect no Châteauneuf-du-Pape, 1788. Okay? And, yeah, one more thing. You get a shack with locks on the doors. So how about it?'

'Done! Shake on it, and then tell me what it is, and if I don't like it, I'll quit.'

'My farm's a pig farm.'

'Somebody's got to raise the people's pork.'

'The music might make you fat.'

'I'll chance it.'

'Well, like you say, you can always quit.'

'So what's the deal, George? Can't quit before I start.'

'Man Friday to the pigs and me. Includes clipping tusks and tails. And vaccinating and chopping the balls off adolescents.'

They rolled through the greens of Indiana summer, between forests of corn, by some walnut trees, and turned into a driveway to pass beneath a plywood triumphal arch inscribed:

LEGIO DIX FRETENSIS

SWINE RANCH

G. Baxter. Prop. &

Praefectus Castrorum

10

'Why do you call it that?'

'It's a long story.'

'I'm your man Friday. You can tell *me*.'

'Can't. Story's too fucking *long*.'

'*Praefectus Castrorum?*'

'That's my title for formal occasions.'

They crunched along the graveled driveway around some walnut trees into a parking area and stopped. Standing on a grassy slope across a brook were clusters of automobile bodies with no doors, no engines, no frames or wheels, all inhabited by hogs and their families.

'Pigville, son. Pigville.'

Pigville began at a wallow by the brook and went about one hundred yards up a gentle slope, by the auto bodies into an apple orchard, the whole being enclosed by a barbed-wire fence. Loudspeakers placed on poles among the bodies diffused soft chamber music. On the windshields George had painted white letters, phrases, but not RUNS GOOD, $99 DOWN. The closest windshield, that of a chancred brown Buick, proclaimed:

IMPERIOUS CAESAR, DEAD AND TURNED TO CLAY,
MIGHT STOP A HOLE, TO KEEP THE WIND AWAY.

and on a crumpled Toyota:

MAY NOT IMAGINATION TRACE THE NOBLE DUST
OF ALEXANDER
TILL HE FIND IT STOPPING A BUNG-HOLE?

'Those substantial, polychromatic pigs over there are Duroc-Jerseys, and the elegant animals, the ones with the classy profile, are Hampshires.' Billy tried to imagine being the servant of huge, gross Durocs, and their aristocratic Hampshire companions. 'Ain't they fucking lovely? Them Hampshires make a real high-grade carcass.' They were black with a white section extending from their backs down over their fore-trotters. They looked like police cars. 'And them other sweethearts, the Durocs! Best lard breed there is. Saw one in a carnival weighed almost two tons!' Their colors ranged from light golden-yellow to mahogany-brown. 'The ideal is deep golden-yellow inclining to cherry-red.' Several met

11

that standard of Duroc beauty. Show hogs perhaps. 'Now that the farm is running smooth, and I have you to help out, my only worry is we're close to town – too close – and not very popular. We ain't appreciated. Not at fucking all! Greedy speculators are moving in. Want to build condos, right here! They're trying to annex our neighborhood to the town, change the zoning from Agricultural to R3, and run us the fuck out!'

'That's going upscale, boss. Progress! After all, ours is the age of transition, if not of metamorphosis.'

George flashed a glance of savage rage, chilling Billy's urge to tease him. Billy beamed charm at George. George led the way up a path to a wheelless bus. The DONT TREAD ON ME snake flag drooped from a pole set by the central door. Above this entrance spread a sign saying G. Baxter, Praefectus Castrorum, Office and Residence. Stepping in, Billy saw George had cut two doorways into the far side of the bus and welded the rear end of a dead Winnebago camper to each, giving his quarters a square U-shape and himself a bedroom, a bath, and a kitchen, the bus itself being reserved for dining and receiving. An antique map of Prussia embellished the bedroom door. It showed Swinemünde and the River Swine, thirty-five miles north of Stettin, now all swallowed up by the Polish ham system. The walls displayed framed centerfold pin-ups in full color torn from *The North American Hogman's Journal* and *American Porker*. From a place of honor, framed in false gold, snarled an S. Clay Wilson comic of 'The Hog Riding Fools'. Next to the stereo system and the rack from which one could select cassettes to play to the pigs, Billy saw an elaborate weight-and-feeding chart, correlated with types of music and items of diet. And, over the desk, printed on parchment:

> To be truly successful in
> The swine business one must
> Like it,
> Put his heart into it,
> Yes,
> And live with it.
>
> John M. Evaard, Professor of
> Animal Husbandry, Iowa State College

12

After showing him around the place, George motioned Billy to sit on an old auto seat, and put a Fats Waller piano rag on the stereo. He wrote a number on the feeding chart, then, taking two mugs from a shelf, went to an old-fashioned office-style water cooler. It bubbled and burped as he filled the mugs with white wine. He offered one and raised a toast. 'Hey, sowboy. Here's to you, and here's to me, and should we disagree – To hell with you and here's to me.'

'Here's to the boss swino.'

'Yes,' said George. 'Swino. The public perceives us swinos as more loathesome than the scabiest wino, and I shit you not. High fucking time we did something about it!'

He told Billy doctoring the image of the swineherd's profession is at once appropriate and necessary. What is it about hogs that makes social outcasts of those who keep their company? The associates of cattle are the stuff of romance and even, as with bullfighters, glory. Why not boarfighters? A much worthier contestant! Hogs are attractive, bright, clean. Their powerful intellect eclipses bovine wit. What do cowboys have that sowboys don't? Why is the hog, noble beast that it is, censored from the history of the American West? Why don't stores display hand-tooled sowboy boots? Where are the sowboy songs? Why no 'Lone Sowhand from the Rio Grande'? No 'Sowboy's Lament'? Why aren't sowboy skills celebrated at rodeos? Why no John Wayne of the sowboy set? 'We're misfits! Outcasts! The cowpoke's a hero, the sowpoke's a fucking joke! Yet – and Bill, I swear this is as true as shit comes from assholes, one-fourth of the meat consumed in You-Es-A comes from pigs. Ninety million pigs live in this country. The weight of America's pigs is equal to that of the American people!' Why are the custodians of these sensitive and useful animals calumnated, slandered, libeled, maligned, and reviled? Why is hog nurture a disgrace? The cattleman is respected; the hog man, despised. Cattlemen's associations are honored. Swinemen's associations meet secretly in the shadows of shame. 'Is that justice? I ask you, Bill. Is it?'

'Indeed it's not,' replied Billy, thinking of Farnsworth and his brief moment as cowboy.

'Sometimes,' said George, as he stripped the wrapper from a new lump of gum, 'I suspect hogs are as smart as I am. They have a refined appreciation of music and a developed sense of form and color. Now that you're helping with the work, I'll be

13

able to devote more time to their education. As they say, we humans use everything but the squeal. Me, I'm a hundred percent. I save the squeal on tapes, to study, to edit, to play back to the squealers. I'm learning their language. I think I can see into their minds. I'm teaching them to read poetry. I take the very best ever thought and said – as seen from their aesthetic and ethical bias, of course – and write it on the windshields for them to contemplate. Not bad, eh?'

He gave Billy a two-liter wineskin full of Chablis to keep in his shack and carry around on the job. Then, with a sweep of his hand, he gestured toward the front row of windows and the view they revealed: a panorama of polychromatic auto bodies, black-and-white Hampshires, and colorful Duroc-Jerseys.

'What do you think of my agricultural architecture?'

'Makes a pretty picture.'

'Picture! Hell! It makes money!' He displayed an old catalog describing the Iowa Moveable Sunlit Hog House, a handsome, practical – and expensive – accommodation, rendered superfluous for him by the auto age. 'The name of the game is profit. The name of profit is weight. Weight is money! Fat is money! Lean is money! Money! That's the only reason for this enterprise, for any enterprise. Money! And don't you forget it!'

THREE

Billy had spent the summer of '9l in Monterey, two hours south of Pacifica, going to music clubs and working on a squid boat, and now, in defiance of all probability, the summer of '92 had carried him from Parris Island, South Carolina, to an Indiana pig farm. In the morning, still half drunk, reflecting on this wonder, Billy chugged an eye-opener, slung his wineskin, breakfasted with George on baked apples, pork chops, walnuts, and sow milk, and went to work. His first duty – quotidian chore as George put it – would be to hose the pigs and their dwellings. Here in Pigville, George explained, because he believes sado-maso systems breed content, he'd established a social order of dominance-submission, of strength over weakness, a hierarchy of might-makes-right. 'It's the clean and happy hog who fattens fastest.' Would he put *that* on a windshield, or did he keep his philosophy of rule secret? 'We castrate them so we can terrorize them – I mean govern them – easier.' In consistence with this method of dominion, Billy was to start at the top of the social scale with the home of number-one hog – Big Daddy. Billy began his day by dragging a hose from a tap by the wallow, up the slope into Pigville Heights, to the carcass of a pearl-gray stretch-limo with blind windows whose windshield displayed $E = mc^2$, emblem of supreme power.

Big Daddy lay in the back, by the TV, yawning and scratching. His head rested on a cushion marked INDIANAPOLIS SPEEDWAY, 1991. A lordly, well-groomed Hampshire, Big Daddy, the only adult aristocrat with testes, father of all the

15

young aristos in town. From his lodgings wafted the fragrance of some subtle perfume. Abruptly, the gentle birdsong of a dawning summer's morn ceased as Pigville's loudspeakers burst out with the 'William Tell Overture', thus shocking the pigs awake for another feeding day and making Billy as nervous as a volunteer fireman who can't start the truck. Big Daddy uttered a rasping growl of protest and stood. The music slid into mind-soothing musak, 'Moonlight Cocktail', 'Begin the Beguine', 'String of Pearls'. Billy hesitated in apprehension at squirting that formidable black-and-white whose minions were now moving into the orchard to feed on the night's windfalls. A fence barred them from one section; a gate implied they were at times admitted. But, evidently, not often, for the ground was blanketed with rotting apples. Billy and the city father glared at one another through the open door of the limo. 'You won't like me, Pops,' said Billy. 'We humans taste like pork.' No Passover there! he thought, remembering George's story about the pubescent pig who'd eaten his own balls a moment after George had cut them off.

Billy squirted the boss.

The boss loved it.

And so, in turn, did the others.

They all came running to Pigville Plaza for their bath, and snuffed approvingly as Billy went up and down the streets, from auto body to auto body, washing away the night's excrements, leaving their houses squealy-clean.

At noon, Billy found himself perched high in an apple tree at the orchard's edge, waiting for George to come save him from an angry purple sow squatting at its base. Ranged on the street below, on the windshields of a file of dead Toyotas, he saw a series of phrases, constituting what George could remember of Australia's favorite folk poem, a doggerel concerning a job interview. The leader of the Sydney crime syndicate – The Push – is questioning an applicant for employment, Foreskin Ned, the Bastard from the Bush:

> Would you bust the heads of tourists?
> Would you give up work for good?
> Would I bust the heads of tourists – ?
> Me fucking oath I would!

16

Would you live on gin and whiskey?
Said the Leader of The Push;
Why, I'd live on crime and murder!
Said the Bastard from the Bush.

What were the pigs expected to learn from that?
Doubtless, it contained a lesson of some kind.

Would you curse your dear old mother?
Would you slap her in the moosh?
Would you rob your dear old mother?
Asked the Leader of The Push.

Would I rob my dear old mother?
Would I slap her in the moosh?
Why! I'd knock her down and fuck her!
Cried the Bastard from the Bush.

Instead of being busily engaged in his work, why is Billy nesting high in an apple tree waiting to be rescued? First, because it's noon, and he need not be on the job until the garbage trucks arrive from town, and, second, because he fears this fierce and angry distaff Duroc. After hosing the pigs and their living quarters, and doing some cosmetic raking in the streets, he'd had nothing more to do until the trucks came but drink wine and walk around, observing, socializing. At Pigville Plaza he'd spied a cute cherry-red Duroc piglet and teased it and romped with it and picked it up to cuddle. Suddenly, from behind, came a gasping snorting sound, and there stood good old mom, all quarter-ton of her, infuriated, and he dropped piglet, and bolted, and came to rest in his treetop, whence he could take the long view.

Right now, had it not been for The Fly and PX lust, he'd be on Parris Island, dining family-style with his platoon in their mess hall, passing around the salt and the pepper and those big shiny pitchers of milk, and his imagination would be making stoic anticipations of the afternoon's impending torment, a batallion review, hours of marching manual and of standing motionless at order arms, all under the sun. Instead, in the fleetest sprint of his life, he'd accomplished the impossible by outrunning a hog, a feat of which his DI would have been proud, and now here he sat, in the shade, enjoying a luncheon of apples and wine, reading wisdom from windshields. Even if the Corps employs Sherlock Holmes and the FBI and all the rest of the alphabet soup of federal police to hunt me down, as long as I'm here I'm safe. With wonder he reviewed his lucky escape the memory came of a TV special he'd seen at Uncle Bill's El Flaco Club. It showed several hundred young men in Pamplona, Spain, running before the bulls. Each year, said the TV, to inaugurate the bullfight season, the street leading from the stockyards to the bullring is flanked with strong fences. Days before the main event, everyone in Pamplona and for miles around quits work to drink wine and party. The whole town goes crazy. Car-ni-*val*! The big day comes. He who enters the street is in the game. The bash before the bulls is as easy to join as the Bay to Breakers Run or the Big Sur Marathon. The season's bulls are loosed. The men run. Bulls pursue. The bulls wound or kill enough runners to make things interesting. It's a male poem, a perfect sport, better than basketball, better than football, better than rugby, better than soccer, better than hockey, better than the Corps, better than war. It's *the* perfect sport, Billy decided. It's in absolute congruency with the nature of spirited young men. No rules, no practice, no coaches, no teams, no varsity, no uniforms, no equipment, no umpires, no referees, no leagues, no stats, no stars, no pros. Beaucoup vino. Admiring ladies look on gasping, shrieking, yelling, and proud parents cheer. Perched there in the crown of his tree, Billy vowed to make the Pamplona Run, and soon. What a scene! The mad rush. Lads falling to the sides, running up the fences, gored sometimes, on occasions crushed beneath swift gray hooves, exiting right and left as the bulls stampede in to the ring.

Could they run before boars? Chaos! Mayhem! Massacre!

Here comes George. He looks upset.

'Goddamn it to hell! Why the fuck you getting the pigs all shook up? Some fucking sowboy you are! You're about as useful as tits on a bullfrog! They sell better brains than yours in the butcher shop!' He shooed the sow away. 'Okay, come down from that goddamned tree.' Billy slid down and faced him. 'Now, Bill, understand, it takes a long time, a long apprenticeship, experience, thought, hard study, to make a good sowboy. You don't work up to journeyman in a day, no sir! I don't like to yell, but you got to use your head. You got to remember our job is to maximize *weight*. To do that, we harmonize

18

science and art, as well as costs allow. Engrave this on your mind: *Flesh* is *money*. You say it.'

'Flesh is money.'

'That's better. Now keep thinking it. At birth, pigs weigh less than three pounds. Yearling Maryland #1 boars can weigh seven hundred pounds. Hogs can grow to over two thousand. We humans, we weigh less than ten pounds when we start out, and some few of us grow as heavy as me, two-fifty. So you see, hogs can get eight times as big as I am. And they do it faster. A pig can gain two-and-a-half pounds in a single day. But that's under the best of circumstances. Our feed could be better – who wants to live on apples and garbage? – but it's free. Our shelters are good. We have good water and we keep things clean, though that's not as easy in winter as it is now. Those are the givens. We cannot make meaningful changes in them. What we *do* control is art. We can form the pattern of stimuli they receive, use the multimedia approach to shape and direct them toward the maximization of *weight*. For different results, a different style of art, built around a complex of different themes. You agree? I knew you would. If we upset the pigs, make them nervous, they may only gain, uh, say one pound a day. Imagine, in that case, how much money is lost. One-and-a-half pounds times three hundred and twenty pigs times the current live-weight price in Indianapolis. That's big money! You notice I've thought of almost everything. Take the poetry. Death is the main theme. Why? I want them to get used to the idea and accept it. I don't want them fretting about their fate. And I think they know what *that* is. They have a sense of predestination I reinforce with my windshield precepts. Now that you are here, I'll have time to paint murals on your shack, on the auto bodies, on plywood secured to the fences. I'll tattoo some of the Durocs. I think they know what Weird has in store for them. I want their fate to seem as natural to them, as inevitable, as our rendezvous with the atomic flash does to us. I want them to submit to their destiny, not question it, because if they question it they might become nervous, ulcerous, hyperactive, and lose weight. They might even do something to change their situation. Think of George Orwell's *Animal Farm*! Nobody's going to sing 'Beasts of England' around here, not while I control the music. As it is, the citizens of Pigville accept their destiny. They know at eschatology's end lies the trip to Indianapolis and the rites of the slaughterhouse.

19

It's their kismet; it's their limbo, the unavoidable and inevitable end of the trail of life, and that's that. God created them without souls, so for them there is no afterlife. It's not my fault. It's not their fault. Nor is it the fault of the meat packers in Indianapolis. It's as God ordained. With art we make them accept a most profound truth: for them, and I express it in our idiom, there can be neither Superpig nor Savior.'

He blew a pink gum-bubble and his voice assumed a truly intimate tone: 'So, Bill, it follows, at all times you think *art*; you think *weight*; you think *money*. Art. Weight. Money. The holy Trinity of the sowboy and of the hogman.'

FOUR

A pad of paper in his hand and a pencil behind his ear, Billy came out of his shack and sat down on its rough wooden steps. Feeling himself submerged in the orange light of sunset, he looked though the barbed-wire fence, across the wallow surrounding Blood Creek, and up the slope at the flaring colors of dwellings, of inhabitants, as the sun declined behind the ridge and the speakers broadcast a baroque piano concerto George had selected as vespers for Pigville.

His imagination drifted back to former times when this slope, and the slope at his left beyond the drive where George's bus stood, had been the pasture and orchard of the farm across the road, and this shanty the home of the hired man. And he daydreamed further back, to ancient days, before the Civil War had christened Blood Creek, to when Pigville had been part of the great, virgin forest, stretching continuous and cathedral-like from Maryland to Kansas, home to parties of traders and hunters, some, perhaps, his ancestors.

He'd been here six weeks, long enough for his hair to grow back, and to think things through. Time to write Uncle Bill.

An occasional flash of fear blazed across his firmament as he went through the daily routine of this strange place. Like the cow, Farnsworth, he had the gift of living in the now, of never worrying, but he could not escape the intrusion from time to time of a sudden shock of awareness of the danger his Fly-driven spontaneity had produced. If, or more likely when they caught him, a court martial would convict him of desertion and sentence him to Portsmouth Naval Penitentiary, one of the horrors of the world.

Sunset had faded to firefly time. I'll be a firefly among fireflies. I'll be a firefly who shows no light. So hang on here for a while, reason it out, earn my keep, decide what to do – then go for it! Australia? Canada? A new identity? Surrender myself to ... the Marines? The police? A senator? I'm Lucky Al's son, and the family luck has always been part of me, so in luck I'll trust, but I'll give it all the help I can. Australia? A senator?

Luck had presented him with the perfect hideout and the ideal companion. George had no social life, no sex life either, unless clandestine, with some pig. He only went to town when absolutely necessary. Crude, a simpleton, yes; yet for all of that, the *Praefectus Castrorum* of the *Legio Dix Fretensis* Swine Ranch appeared to be extremely well informed and knew so much about history in the sense of past gossip as to seem to have lived through it. George existed within some twisted, sunken fantasy which Billy sensed, and of which he saw flotsam, and, through momentarily clearing water, an occasional fragment, but which on the whole constituted a mystery as profound as that presented by the depths of the canyon in Monterey Bay.

Monterey Bay. You can plunge down more than a mile before touching bottom.

Monterey Bay. Uncle Bill had always called Billy a water baby, and that was true enough. Since childhood he'd been a male naiad. 'Me, George, I ain't no sowboy. I'm a merboy.' He scuffed at the ground with his foot and listened to a lullaby coming through the loudspeakers. Maybe Australia. Yes, Australia; surfing, swimming, scuba, sailing, and beach people who share that mistress. He picked up his writing pad and went inside and lit his kerosene lamp and found himself near the center of soft, yellow light, a surreal illumination for a surreal situation. But not nearly as surreal as the dim half-known world fifteen miles due west and more than a mile straight down from the sunlit daily life of Calle Principal and Alvarado Street. If he had an ambition to match those propelling his classmates toward success, whatever that is, it was some day to explore the depths of Monterey Bay and learn its secrets.

Billy searched around in the shadows of his one-room villa and its lean-to bathroom, found his shirt and buttoned it against the evening's chill. So, yes, write to Uncle Bill.

'Twice as idealistic, twice as practical.' Billy spoke his private motto, and thus evoked the guardian angel of luck.

Consider it carefully. The feds might be watching Uncle Bill. So seal the letter and enclose it in a larger envelope, one addressed to Uncle Bill's bar manager, Heather, the woman who in his early adolescence had introduced him to sex. Get George to address it and mail it from Indianapolis to her house in Daly City. A letter from Indiana addressed in George's hand to Heather at home should do the trick. He sat on his cot to write, as he'd done so often at his dormitory desk in college, but then in a brighter, whiter light. Back in the far-off days ending this spring, when life unrolled on the Berkeley campus of the University of California instead of on this Midwestern pig farm, Dwinelle Hall and California Hall and the Undergraduate Library and Larry Blake's beer cellar and Sather Gate had seemed as naturally familiar a setting for his daily activities as George's bus and the wallow and the apple orchard and the feeding ground and the auto bodies and Pigville Plaza did now. From the Charybdis of college images, the swirling memory-slides, one flung out and stuck: a blonde in shorts riding through the class-change mob, *uphill*, on a motor-driven skateboard.

Graduation had made him a Berkeley alumnus, an Old Blue in search of a new future.

Portsmouth Naval Penitentiary.

The thought struck him with arctic windchill shock.

Folly!

No. Not folly. Perhaps he should have gone about it differently, but it had been the right thing to do.

FIVE

Billy began with the beginning. He wrote Uncle Bill that he had deserted from the Marine Corps, asked Uncle Bill to take care of all of his affairs, which mainly meant the house his father had left him, and to keep his eyes open for signs of feds snooping for news of their quondam marine. He reread. It seemed so factual, so common; a newspaper report about somebody else. He tried again. He could not get the feeling into it. So he left it the way it was and footnoted it.

Uncle Bill, there's a lot more to it than that, and I wish I could convey it to you through words, as if we were seated at your bar together, looking out the big window at the beach, late at night, alone and really getting on to the same wavelength, but we're not, and I can't.

Believe me, it's a long cold way from life to the paper.
Yes. Now, something easy
Describe my day.

Existence here, Uncle Bill, is routine, healthy if not whole-some, and safe for me.
Mornings after breakfast – George cooks all the meals and I wash the dishes – I hose the pigs and their living quarters and do some light raking. Then I weed and hoe and water the vegetable garden behind George's place: two camper bodies welded to the side of a dead bus. After lunch, I make suggestions about

24

the images on the plywood panels George has been painting. When wired in sequence to the orchard fence along the crest of the ridge above Pigville they will compose a mural of pigs going to and through the stockyards and the slaughterhouse, thence into cans or refrigerator trucks and onward into pans placed on fires or in ovens whence their charred fragments pass into serving dishes or sandwiches and are consumed by eager eaters who transform them into energy, human fat, or excrement. Thusly, George will keep their futures ceaselessly before them, together with the implied moral he has painted on to the windshields along every street: EAT, SLEEP, AND BE MERRY, FOR TOMORROW YOU MUST DIE. Believe me, Uncle Bill – all this is enough to make me think the vegetarians are right when they say, 'Meat is murder, cheese is theft, eggs are abortion.'

Afternoons, except Sundays, I receive the garbage trucks from town. They dump into a fenced-off field right by the main gate of Pigville. With the scraper blade on our tractor, I spread the garbage around. Then I admit the pigs. In the evenings, after the pigs have dined, I doze the leftovers into a deep ravine adjacent to the feeding grounds. At twilight, George and I like to sit on the verge of the ravine with twenty-twos, and drink wine and shoot rats for the pigs to eat on the morrow. All in the interests, one might say, of five pounds of food make one pound of meat. With the help of our rifles and a young Hampshire George named Sir Ronald after our knighted ex-president and trained as a rat-retriever, the rats find food the pigs can't reach, and deliver it to them. The members of the rat colony work for us, Uncle Bill. They give their lives that we may prosper. George calls the dump his Sanitary Landfill Site. He thinks this will help if he has to face an inquisition of town planners. Hundreds of birds live here at the landfill site. They're big, fat, white and slow birds, clumsy as the pelicans you and I have laughed at so often. Even though it would be more appropriate to call them sanitary-landfill-site birds, they're just plain dump birds to us. Bill, really, you'd love to see them struggling to rise into the air! Talk about stout birds! George is very fond of them. What the pigs miss and the rats don't find, the birds eat. Consequently, our dump stinketh not. It's picked clean. We buy abandoned cars from the police, cars they can't sell anywhere else. Every now and then their tow truck brings us one. George and I butcher it with crowbars and a torch. The body goes to Pigville; the rest goes mainly into a huge pile of engines, frames, doors and wheels we're rearing on the crest of the dump. This Acropolis, this alp of iron, is George's savings account. He takes pigs to market weekly and returns with more money than he needs. The scrap is destined to be rendered into pig iron as he plans someday to cash it in at the steel mills in Gary. As for the tires, they are the substance of a companion peak we are raising, one which will remain here 'til Doomsday.

So that's about all there is to my regular duties: light chores and art criticism. When George goes to town, I select the music. Some things I play make those hogs sweat! I'll stir them to revolt if I can. Coming back from town yesterday, George ran over a neighbor's dog, Waggles. He crushed Waggles flat. We laughed about using a big envelope for Waggles's coffin, then we sailed his remains to the pigs. The farmer from across the road came inquiring after his dog. We lied, and he left.

I haven't seen any money yet, but I have plenty to eat, chiefly pork and sow cheese and English walnuts and vegetables and apples. George has a meat grinder, so sometimes we have hogburgers. I get all I want to drink just so long as all I want is water or white wine. George buys it wholesale by the hogshead and keeps it in the cooler. I've worked my way up to where I equal George's daily consumption of one gallon plus. We talk about everything. Although a bit of a dunce, George has amazing depth. Sometimes he seems to me an embodiment of history. He knows a lot about literature, the stories anyway, and he's an amazing linguist. Philosophizing, yarning, fantasizing, George and I, we often drink ourselves to sleep, and I wake up raw-eyed, on the floor of the bus. When I came to this morning, I found a poem laying on the Volkswagen seat I use for a bed table. I think I wrote it. It's an artifact of yesterday, like my finger- and toe-nail clippings in the weeds by my steps. Sipping wine, holding the poem, I sit on the steps, in the shade. It's warm already. The day smells of heat to come. I gaze along the drive to where it fords Blood Creek and beyond at the garbage feeding ground and George's alp of rusting iron and tire hill. My steps are battered and worn, split and rotten. So is my poem. At breakfast time, carrying my poem, I follow the scent of frying

26

bacon to the bus. 'It ain't poetry if it don't rhyme,' says George as he crumbles it into the stove. We walk outside. Already, the sun broils down. 'You flush the pigs yet?' I say no, and he tells me to skip it for once. 'I hate Sundays. We don't have to worry about garbage trucks, true, but we have to give the bastards real commercial feed. Three fucking tons!' He popped a pink gum lump into his mouth, and smiled. 'Maybe not today. Today, we party.'

He fetched an electric amplifying horn from the bus and with a thunderous SOOOOOeeeeey SOOOOOeeeeey SOOOOOeeeeey, he called the hogs. They began emerging from their auto bodies and running down the slope, through the wallow, to pack up against the fence. 'First, I'll make my announcement.' George motioned me into the truck and we drove about three hundred yards from the parking area through Blood Creek Ford to the main gate of Pigville. George mounted the hood. He turned up the volume and called again. Pigs came running from everywhere. George stood there on the hood, erect, surveying his audience. As you may have guessed, we were still drunk from the night before. He called for silence. They hushed. Their anticipation focussed on him. He then – and Bill, this is the honest-to-God truth – he then made a *speech* to the pigs.

'My friends. As your guardian and mentor, as your *Praefectus Castrorum*, I have convened this popular – pigular – assembly to inaugurate the Hog-of-the-Month Prize Competition. Citizens of Pigville, you will participate in a monthly evaluation determined by a one-hundred-point scale analytically defining our ideal. Prizes will be awarded in the categories of boar, sow, gilt, castrato, shoat, weanling, suckling. The title and grand prize go to the overall winner: The Hog of the Month. Each winner will receive a month's supply of scientifically blended feed; each winner will appear on community television. The photograph of each winner will be placed on temporary display in Pigville Plaza. The name of the grand prizewinner will be inscribed upon the permanent Hog-of-the-Month roster. He or she will receive a brass nose ring, a blue ribbon of honor to adorn it, and, for a whole month, the very best gourmet food money can buy. Today, we shall hold a Hogfest to celebrate the opening of the contest, the addition to our staff of William Williams, our new sowboy, and the completion of a community television system which, henceforth, will play constantly in Pigville Plaza during daylight hours. Now, if you will be so kind as to follow me, we shall proceed to the Plaza where I will post xerox copies of the contest criteria. That accomplished, we shall retire to the party orchard and get all fucked up and raise hell!' He paused, then said: 'A healthy mind in a heavy body! Let that precept be our guide.'

His words produced a medley of grunts and squeals. Or was that my imagination? But there's no denying those polychromatic Durocs and handsome Hampshires seemed pleasantly surprised. George and I went in the main gate and, after he secured it behind us, led the procession to Pigville Plaza. George posted his norms. Then he activated the TV, a giant screen elevated on a ten-foot pylon at the bottom of the piglic square. Awed into silence, we all stood there admiring the TV's flashing colors. George adjusted it and an episode of what George called 'The Young and Brainless' began to unroll. Smiling, he went on to tell me he believes the total lethargy the TV will produce in the pigulation can, if his figures prove correct, create seven hundred and forty-three extra pounds of weight daily. 'It's almost as good as nailing their feet to the floor, like the French do to geese to produce pâté de fois gras.'

As we led the way to the party orchard and its deep blanket of fermenting windfalls, George told me pigs get drunk on rotten apples. I asked if the same pig could win the grand prize, month after month. No problem there. No sir. The nose rings would prevent winners from rooting up lesser nourishment than that provided by their deluxe prize food. When that food was gone, they'd be in ideal condition, especially now that TV would render them comatose. Pigs of the Month would then be awarded free excursions to Indianapolis, to the stockyards, where he'd sell them at a premium. In the orchard, outside the fenced-off party area, he posted more copies of the One Hundred Suidic Points of Perfection. Much as emotional advertising inspiring self-contempt produces muscle builders and aerobic dancers obsessed with shaping their defective bodies toward congruency with an ideal, so would these criteria inspire the pigs toward self-improvement. In the larger sense, he favors incest as a means toward this end. He breeds brother to sister, sire to

28

daughter, dam to son in the endless struggle to incarnate the ideal. I enclose a copy of its definition for the edification of the regulars at the El Flaco Club.

SCALE OF POINTS — FOR Hampshire	Perfect score
General appearance:	
1. Weight, 170 to 200 pounds, the result of thick cover of firm flesh	6
2. Form, long, level, smooth, deep	10
3. Quality, hair fine; skin thin; bone fine; firm covering of flesh without any soft bunches of fat or wrinkles	10
4. Condition, deep, uniform covering of flesh, especially in region of valuable cuts	10
Head and neck:	
5. Snout fine	1
6. Eyes full, mild, bright	1
7. Face slim	1
8. Ears, trim, medium size	1
9. Jowl, light, trim	1
10. Neck, medium length, light	1
Forequarters:	
11. Shoulders, free from roughness, smooth, compact and same width as back and hindquarters	6
12. Breast, moderately wide, full	2
13. Legs, straight, short, strong, bone clean, pasterns upright; feet medium size	2
Body:	
14. Chest, deep, full girth	4
15. Back, medium and uniform in width	8
16. Sides, long, smooth, level from beginning of shoulders to end of hindquarters. The side at all points should touch a straight edge running from fore to hindquarter	10
17. Ribs, deep, uniformly sprung	2
18. Belly, trim, firm, thick without any flabbiness or shrinkage at flank	10
Hindquarters:	
19. Hips, smooth, wide; proportionate to rest of body	2
20. Rump, long, even, straight, rounded toward tail	2
21. Gammon, firm, rounded, tapering, fleshed deep and low toward hocks	8
22. Legs, straight, short, strong; feet medium size; bone clean; pasterns upright	2
Total	100

SCALE OF POINTS — FOR Duroc–Jersey	Perfect score
General appearance:	
1. Weight, score according to size	6
2. Form, deep, broad, low, long, symmetrical, compact, standing squarely on legs	10
3. Quality, hair silky; skin fine; bone fine; mellow covering of flesh free from lumps and wrinkles	10
4. Condition, deep, even covering of flesh and fat over all parts of the body	10
Head and neck:	
5. Snout, medium length, not coarse	1
6. Eyes, full, mild, bright	1
7. Face, short, cheeks full	1
8. Ears, fine, medium size, soft	1
9. Jowl, strong, neat, broad	1
10. Neck, thick, medium length	1
Forequarters:	
11. Shoulder, broad, deep, full, compact on top	6
12. Legs, straight, short, strong; bone clean; pasterns upright; feet medium size	2
Body:	
13. Chest, deep, broad, large girth	4
14. Sides, deep, lengthy, full; ribs close and well sprung	6
15. Back, broad, straight, thickly and evenly fleshed	10
16. Loin, wide, thick, straight	8
17. Belly, straight, even	4
Hindquarters:	
18. Hips, wide apart, smooth	2
19. Rump, long, wide, evenly fleshed, straight	2
20. Ham, heavily fleshed, plump, full, deep, wide	10
21. Thighs, fleshed close to hocks	2
22. Legs, straight, short, strong; bone clean; pasterns upright; feet medium size	2
Total	100

Some beauty contest, eh? Imagine using the same standards for the Miss America competition!

I'll write you later, Uncle Bill, and tell you about the party when I see you. Man alive! What a blast! Ain't nothing on earth like a Suidic Saturnalia!

SIX

George strode to the gate of the party orchard. Beyond it, a dense layer of hot apples in all stages of fermentation lay sweating and sweltering in the sun. Their sweet, rich odor wafted through hundreds of trembling snouts. He turned to Billy, grinning so widely as to expose a gold tooth Billy had not seen before.

'My boy. We can take pride in our apple crop, fresh or fermented. I never use spray, or powder, or chemicals in any other form. My apples are the epitome of natural.'

The squirming churning hogs shuddered and gasped in anticipation of frustration relieved. The very model of Freud's pleasure principle in action.

'No sir. I don't poison my apples before I deliver them to the consumer. They are true health food, and can, in fact, by themselves provide a balanced diet. Fret about worms and fruit flies? Not me, buster, not me. Worm meat and fly larvae are pure protein – healthful food supplements.'

George opened the gate. Boars, barrows, sows, gilts, stags, porkers, weanlings, and even sucklings stampeded, all three hundred and twenty of them. No teetotallers in this crowd! As soon as all the suidae were safely inside, George swung the gate shut. Leaving Billy there to chaperone, he drove back to his bus, and thrust several cassettes into the player: Wagner, Rolling Stones, Scruggs & Flatt, Grateful Dead, and set it to repeat. The 'Ride of the Valkyries' burst out of the speakers loud enough to make continents drift. George fetched two gallons of applejack brandy from his private stock, selected two beer mugs and two bread pans, filled a big thermos with ice, and drove back to the party. Already, the weather had cooked up to one hundred degrees in the shade. George and Billy stripped off their shirts, flung them into the truck, and went inside the party orchard. George filled the mugs. Flaunting the boar guarding *LEGIO DIX FRETENSIS* on his tattooed wrist, he raised a toast.

'*Cogito, ergo sum.*'

'I think therefore I am,' Billy translated as mugs clicked.

Poto, ergo sum!' said George, dedicating another.

'I drink, therefore I am.'

'You better believe it, and get ready for it, because you're sucking white lightning.' He led the way up the hill. Happy hogs grunted and chirped. 'Our two generals expect their perks. You know, mission and command merit special privileges. That's what life's all about.'

'Really?'

'Yes. As long as I maintain command over my two generals, and they maintain command over the pigs, I have only to give them my missions, and they carry them out.'

George and Billy went to the top corner of the party orchard where Big Daddy, generalissimo of all the pigs, sat conversing with a huge golden-yellow hog, Father Duroc, who, like George and Billy, was one of the few uncut adult males living on the ranch. The two commanders groveled up to the feet of George, El Supremo of Pigville, and rubbed their snouts in the dirt. He told Billy to place two pans before them and fill them with brandy. He told Billy to leave the bottle, and then he led the way across the party orchard to the corner by the gate where they sat on a boulder in the shade of a tree to drink and to rest and to enjoy the downhill view of sun blazing off the many-colored auto bodies.

'In the winter,' he said in his rough voice, 'you see snow outside their homes, but not inside.'

From their vantage, Billy observed that a thundering torrent of Wagner music plus a rush of booze can definitely rowdify the most civilized of swinish communities.

'As with the Roman army, Bill, it does the hogs good to shed discipline every now and then and let themselves go. Fools feast and lords misrule at the Suidic Saturnalia!'

Our rat-retriever sat down beside us.

'Hello, Sir Ronald, how they hanging?'

That, thought Billy, was unnecessarily rude.

'Hello yourself,' Sir Ronald snorted.

George gave him a gulp of brandy, extending, no doubt, a privilege commensurate with his philosophy of command.

'Hey George, I read in the paper that once pigs taste blood they go hog wild for more, shift into a regular *meat frenzy*. Well, if they love meat so much, why don't they forget apples and eat us?'

'That kind of shit irks me. Say something bad about cattle, and the beef lobby pee-are men are all over your ass like flies on death. But just you say something bad about hogs! The papers print it and TV pushes it and everybody believes it. Say something good? Forget it!'

'Are you saying they'd rather eat us than apples?'

'Wouldn't you rather eat us than apples?'

'George! Sir Ronald here could make party hors-d'oeuvres out of us in seconds.'

'Yes, but he won't. Those pigs won't eat us because they like us and trust us. It's, well, it's what I call an extrasensory ethic, a perception of kinship with all life, especially with us.'

They drank and meditated within a warming womb, and drank some more.

'George, I been thinking, it's like, well, I guess, for *eight thousand years* we've been breeding hogs as food for us. They embody our plan! Hampshires are British innovations, and Durocs were invented in *New Jersey*. We've formed swine to meet *our* meat-frenzy ideal, to satisfy *our* garumba. We've gained their confidence. We've charmed them! They trust us. *Trust* us. We created them to eat. As *food* for us. And we *do* eat them. Their only hope for immortality is to become canned ham! You and me, we live high on the hog, don't we? We live on them, and we live as long as we can, and have all the fun too, and most of them, even though they can live twenty years, most of them we kill at the age of six months! I know they're not all dumb, not *that* dumb. Some of them must see through our bullshit, and believe in eat-the-eater. And you say don't worry. Don't fucking worry!'

'Tomorrow, while they're sick and weak, you and me, we'll cut the balls off the pubescents and clip their tusks.' He stroked Sir Ronald's head. 'Ain't that right, pal?' Either Sir Ron did not remember, or purposely remained indifferent. 'My mother was a ball-cutter, Ron. It runs in the family.' His voice was beginning to slur and blur. 'As a child, I lived on a farm.' Had George ever been a child? 'Mater used to yell at pater and tell him in different ways how much she hated men. She hated *me*. Imagine! Wonderful, loveable me! Men, she'd say, looking at me, men always tramp into the house with manure and straw sticking to their feet.'

He took Sir Ron by the jowls and looked him in the eye. 'And you know what? I'll tell you in case you haven't guessed. Understand, both of you, Ron and you too Bill, I *do not* give a shit, not really, about *anything*. I never have, I never will, and I don't now. I am the soul of utter indifference, the heart of absolute insouciance. So fuck you. Fuck the world. Fuck the cosmos. Fuck them all, fuck them all, the long and the short and the tall. Fuck all the sergeants, those optio bums; fuck all the corporals and bugger their sons! For we're saying goodbye to them all/as out of the shithouse we crawl/there'll be no cunt or cookies/for fart-sniffing rookies/so cheer up me lads/fuck them all!/There's a troopship just leaving Bombay/filled with time-expired men/the generals and colonels/are riding up aft/the corporals and sergeants/are out on a raft/so we're saying goodbye to them all/as into the gutter we fall/just to be funny/we'll fuck the old gunny/so cheer up me lads/fuck them all!' George spit out a giant green-veined hocker that splatted on the boulder and began to fry. 'We wanted the army/to come to Tulagi/but Douglas MacArthur said no/ He gave as his reason/it wasn't the season . . .' He was singing now, and Billy sang along and Sir Ronald tried his best and Billy poured more drinks, for Sir Ron too, and fed them to him.

Billy wassailed his comrades. 'Do you suidae know we're all outcasts, fucking outcasts! But George, Ron, believe me – Today's misfits are tomorrow's fit-fits. Right, Ron? You understand? Sure. I knew you would. We're in society's swino class, but we swinos got our pride. You fucking-A! We swinos have been kidnapped. On to the ship *Titanic*. The berg. The hogs don't know it's there. Everybody's berg. Or their own special berg, the slaughterberg, either one. Not until they see your murals. They don't know. But *we* know. *I* know. I know our berg is there. Why? Because we built it. It didn't just naturally float down from the icecap. Shit no! We built it. We put it there. And now, maybe, people are chipping at it. But nobody's *un*building it! Fuck no! Instead of taking the bergs away, they keep building more and setting them out there, dead ahead, and nobody on the bridge tries to change the course! And people say Billy-be-practical (like us). And what-you-going-to-be-Billy-when-you-grow-up (like us)? And why-are-you-pissed-off-all-the-time (not like us)? So, George, Sir Ronald, believe me, I don't give a fucking shit fucking either!'

Billy pulled off his shoes and threw them over the fence into the regular orchard. George put an arm over his shoulder, the other around Ron's neck. Sir Ron was singing. 'Riggidy dig dig! Riggidy dig dig! It's the Cin-cin-nati dancing pig!'

'You know what, George? I feel safe around here.'

'Ain't you still scared of being eaten?'

'I don't mean that. Guess I should have told you before. I deserted from the Marine Corps.'

George blew a pink gum-bubble and popped it.

'You don't say!' He sucked the gum back in. 'Tell me about it.'

Billy told him the whole story, and, as it babbled out, he heard his sober voice within saying, cool it, telling George could be a fatal mistake, but glossolalia had gripped him, and he kept on blurting.

George seized him by the shoulders and stared into his eyes. 'Boy, you ain't as safe as you think.'

Not any more, thought Billy, as he blabbered on.

'Shut up. Shut up and listen to *me* for a while. Gotta tell you something! Okay! I ain't myself these days. I really need a drinking pal, and now I got one. And I appreciate it, you bet I do. So listen to this shit.' George told him the speculators had hired petition-circulators, and, at two dollars a signature, had caused thirty-five percent of the registered voters in the town and fifty-eight percent of the voters in the unincorporated township to sign a petition asking that a small segment of the township, one including the pig ranch, be annexed to the town. The county commissioners had approved the annexation. The evening George squashed Waggles, he'd been on his way back from a town council meeting where annexation had passed the first reading. 'And tomorrow night those bastards are having their regular monthly meeting and the second reading is on the agenda and it's going to pass and we'll wake up Tuesday morning as citizens of fucking Clown Town!'

'What then?'

'Me and you and Sir Ron and all the rest lose our home.'

34

'They all do anyway when you take them to Indianapolis.'

'The town is going to zone our area R3, but that R don't stand for suidic residences, for sties, you better fucking believe it don't. As of Tuesday we're out of here.'

'Really?' George could have said so sooner. 'And then?'

'The law will seize me. The law will have my body.'

'No shit!'

'You can just hit the road.'

'I'd rather sit and hang around/the Picadilly Underground/ and live off the earnings/of some high-born la-dy.'

'Shut up Bill!' He squeezed Billy's shoulders. 'Listen. Waggles, that butt-sucking dog, Waggles, belonged to the fucking neighbor what circulated that fucking petition around here! Yes! The day I crushed their mutt, I was coming back from town thinking about the council meeting, and it dawned on me my case is totally fucking *hopeless*. And there was that pus-sucking Waggles in the road, and I chased that bastard with my truck, and got him too, by God, snuffed him, and on purpose, you can bet your ass on that! No remorse here, boy, and the only regret is that he wasn't twins so I could kill him twice! I'd like to kill all the dogs in the world, the fucking cats too, and eat cat for lunch like the French do, and every night have dog *à la Chinoise* for dinner. The Chinese eat dogs the way we eat pigs. I mean, dogs are a good crop in East Asia, domesticated prey. So I crush that fucking Waggles and we throw him to the pigs. We feed one food crop to another! Okay! Two Cub Scouts, punk kids from across the road, see the whole thing. Those two bastards saw the family dog eat blacktop, and they watched his blood spin off my wheels. And so they came in here and spied on us! If I'd known it, I'd have told the hogs to eat *them*. Wouldn't you know. When we tossed that Waggles carrion to the hogs, the little shits were watching. Just my luck!'

'George. Me and Sir Ronald here, we truly do not give a shit!' Billy stripped off his pants and threw them over the fence; he stripped off his underpants, and threw them too. 'I do not . . . give . . . a shit! How about you two swinos?' George stripped off too and flung all his clothes over the fence. That the two of them were gorged on brandy and it was about a hundred and ten in the shade made it easy. Billy put an arm around George's shoulders and they tried to stand and they slipped on the boulder slimy with fresh hog piss and fell down and got up on their hands and knees and crawled through soft hot apples and other yielding débris over to Sir Ron and met him eye-to-eye as he made a syncopated squealing sound and George said, 'You're laughing at us, you porcine twit!' He kissed Sir Ron on the bristling jowl and Sir Ron shook his head, eyes wild, confused. And then Billy was nose-to-snout with Sir Ron, telling him a joke.

'Okay, Fatso – we're in Cape Town, South Africa, on a pier, watching a shipload of grunting, squealing hogs come in. An Afrikaner standing next to us says, "Ho ho! Look there! A shipload of American immigrants!" "Ho ho," says I. "And they've learned the language fast, haven't they?"'

Sir Ron chirps delight, but maybe more on account of a pile of luscious-looking apples he's found than of the joke.

And now George and Billy are hand-and-kneeing around, socializing freely with guests who are mainly on all fours too and doubtless feeling soft stuff underfoot, but no, they don't have feet, just two hard toes at the end of each trotter, cloven fossil feet, so they don't feel much. Could George really nail their hooves to the floor? He'd been talking about a weight maximization experiment. 'Guess what, Sir Ron. In German folklore, pigs are thought of as lucky animals along with rabbits and foxes.' By now the three comrades are crawling into an open space with blocks of rocksalt and a TV perched on a tall pylon. 'Flies bring bad luck.' Pigville Plaza! Billy's hand closes on something soft. A glance at George.

'Hey, what's this?'

'Pig shit. That's pig shit.'

'Hey . . . this?'

That's your wineskin. If you weren't wearing that wineskin you'd be bareass naked.'

'And this?'

'Banana slug.'

'Oh fuck. This?'

'That's a hypatica.'

'A what?'

'Hypatica.'

'What?'

'An ethnic blue flower.'

'Here, Sir Ronald, a blue flower. Come on, pal, don't eat it.' Oh well. Whoops! Now Billy's lying flat, wallowing in soft stuff.

You can tell a man who boozes by the company he chooses. And Sir Ron got up and slowly walked away. 'Fuck you, Ron!' George? 'George! Don't let me pass out here. We gotta get out of here before they eat us.'

SEVEN

The next day, after running the pigs out of the party orchard, they clipped tusks and cut testes, and then slid back into the old routine of wash, rake, weed, hoe, water, and spread, a monotony broken a fortnight later by the arrival of a four-door Nissan Maxima behind a police tow truck. The driver, whom George called Tom, a fat, weary, middle-aged sergeant with a slack but kindly face, dropped the sedan off in the parking area and accepted George's invitation to come into the bus for a drink. Billy stayed outside to make the Maxima ready to butcher. He jacked up the back and set it on blocks. A rust-scabbed, peeling imperial-yellow, the body, a *pig*ment which would best blend in at the end of Pigville's main street, Appian Way. But what differences did appearances make now? Pigville was doomed. Soon he'd be loose on the road again watching the colors flash by in random order. The Nissan had grown so hot you could barbecue pork chops on top and roast corn inside. Unslinging his wineskin from the aerial stub where he'd hung it, Billy tilted his head back and after raising the skin to arm's length, he squirted Chablis into his mouth. Sparkling in the sun, it sure looked like a stream of piss. What to write on *this* windshield? George was running out of ideas. He saw no humor in Billy's suggestion they switch to pig Latin. But, so what? Why care? What does it matter? Roasting as it was in the oven of Indian summer, their apprehension of the imminent fall of Pigville made them too lazy to work. Drink wine until the deluge. But they felt their responsibility to the pigs, so they worked anyway. Without us, thought Billy as he struggled to break a lug nut loose, who'll keep the pigs clean? Who'll connive their garbage? If we don't, who will? Reminiscing about the pig party, that coarse farce, he smiled. He'd mined his conscience in search of a vein of guilt, but could not find a single black streak, not in his recollections of life at the Suidic Saturnalia. Day after day in the party orchard, more apples fell to earth. Nobody'd tried to eat him, either. In response to the new threats to Pigville security, George had begun to train Sir Ronald as a watchhog, to make of him a guard even more formidable than your basic rottweiler. They'd given him the run of the ranch. They served him deluxe pigfood. They let him sleep in the bus and use the shower. Day and night those Cub Scouts lay out there somewhere, watching, building a case for the District Attorney. So George believed. Those relentless Cubs had vowed to avenge the family dog. That's what George said. Paranoia?

Billy stood on the lug wrench and jumped and the lug ground loose. Always before this he'd managed to avoid meeting the tow-truck drivers.

'This here's Tom,' said George, 'the only true friend we have.' The policeman smiled. 'Tom, this here's Bill. Helps me out with the chores.'

Hoping his sweating palm would not reveal his state of mind, Billy shook hands with danger.

At least hair now shrouded his skinhead.

'Doggone if it don't look like you'll be in our jurisdiction soon. I came out to tell George things are going to be changing around here, and I wanted him to know in advance.'

'Yeah, Tom came out special. He don't usually drive the truck.'

'You a stranger, sonny? Don't believe I've seen you around here before. I'd have noticed a nice-looking young feller like you.'

'I'm from California.'

'That right? For years I've been promising myself to go out there and have a look, and this year by gosh I'm going to do it.' He sat up on the Maxima's hood. 'What town you from?'

'Uh . . . Monterey.'

'Is that a good place for a vacation?'

Billy answered yes, and all the while he was talking about Monterey and Carmel and the rest of it, he was feeling badly about having lied – and having to lie, and nervous about being such a bad liar.

'How'd you happen to end up in our neck of the woods?'

'Uh well, you see, it's uh . . . when I got out of college I decided to hitch to New York and see the country. And, yes, you might wonder how I got so far off the highway. Me, sometimes I wonder that myself.'

Tom sighed, and lit a cigar, his weight denting down on the Maxima hood.

'Son, if I was a young feller again, and had it all to live over, I think I'd hitch around the country, and go to college, and maybe to France and England, too. Like my father used to say, Too soon old and too late smart.'

The next week it rained, then turned sunny and crisp. That morning, early, George and Billy and Sir Ronald the rat-retriever went out to the Sanitary Landfill Site with a big shoulder-bag and their twenty-twos, and a shotgun. They slew a few rats. Sir Ron fetched the bodies and piled them by the bag and Billy suggested they add a rat mountain to their alpine range of tires and iron.

'Now,' said George, smiling wide, 'for the next order of magnitude.' He spilled an avalanche of moldy English muffins out of the bag, pumped a shell into the chamber of the shotgun.

'Okay, Bill, sail one up in the air in front of me.'

Soon Billy was tossing English muffins skeet-style and George was blasting them out of the sky. 'That'll give them little titheads something to think about.' Alarmed dump birds writhed aloft and planed to the apple trees. 'Your turn, Ron,' said George. They tried to snug the shotgun up against Sir Ron's shoulder, but he hoofed them away. 'Well, what do you know? Sir Wimp here's afraid of guns.' Maybe that was because when he was younger, George had cut his balls off. The morning after the party, when they'd castrated the hung-over pubescents, George had let them eat their own balls. 'Waste not, want not.' He referred to this delicacy as mountain oysters. 'My mutilating them is nothing compared to their crime. What could be more depraved than self-cannibalism?'

George tossed the shotgun aside. He was a storm cloud, about to release a patter of tears. 'Early last week, when you were cultivating my garden, Tom came back in a prowl car. He gave me a ticket for misdemeanor cruelty to animals! In two weeks I have to appear in court!' He took the shotgun and blasted a dump bird out of the sky. 'That cur's ghost'll hound me for fucking ever.'

He offered Billy a turn with the shotgun, but Billy demurred.

40

Instead, he passed his wineskin around. Sir Ron had learned to love bad Chablis. Sir Ron chirped happily as he raised the skin aloft between his foretrotters and squirted a long stream into his mouth. 'He's becoming a true swino, George, let's give him his own private bota-de-vino.'

'As soon as he does me one favor.' George stroked him affectionately. 'Don't he have a beauty of a back! He's about ninety-five on our hundred-point scale. Look at that back! So smooth, so straight, so well defined.' Sir Ron smiled. George liked playing to his vanity, but in all truth it wasn't hard to do because he was indeed one of the BPs – beautiful pigs – so fashionable these days. Could George really get him to earn a personal wineskin by eating those nasty Cub Scouts? Tough old George sniffed and his eyes moistened. 'Let me tell you, Bill, when I saw Tom coming up the drive in a prowl car, I knew we'd been annexed.' He stood. 'Put the rats in the bag. We're going back to my place. I have something to show you.'

Once in the bus, George went to his desk, took out a letter from the town's public health officer, and three hundred dollars in cash. He gave Billy the money, his first wages, then showed him the letter. It said keeping pigs within the town limits is unlawful so George must dispose of the pigs in seven days, or else. 'We ran out of time yesterday.' He kicked the wall. He put Mozart's *Don Giovanni* on the Pigville sound system. 'I think they're coming today to move us out.' George went on to the porch, and returned with the DONT TREAD ON ME flag, then led out to the parking lot where he tied the yellow banner with its rattlesnake rampant to his truck's aerial. 'And I'll bet those shit-faced bureaucrats ate bacon for breakfast and right now are daydreaming lunchtime ham sandwiches.' He took some polish and a chamois skin from the glove compartment. 'That fucking Waggles! In his lifetime he must have digested ten tons of pork!'

'So what we going to do?'

'We're going to show them ours is a proud profession.'

They washed and waxed and polished the truck and its cage, then the tractor.

When they'd finished, George spoke to Sir Ronald, who'd been watching, but not working.

'Goddamnit pal, you got to help me and the sowboy.'

Billy and Sir Ron and George climbed into the truck, and, immersed in the solemn chords of Mozart, drove into Pigville, to the Plaza, where scores of hogs sat rapt before the TV watching a game show. George switched it off, eliciting grunts of angry protest at being brought back into the real world. The three comrades clambered up on top of the cage, and stood erect on its plywood roof.

George, his *aides-de-camp* at his sides, called the hogs. As they came running, he spoke quietly to Sir Ron, who had now waxed intent, alert. 'Don't forget to tell them, Ron, if they promise to help us, we'll open the party orchard.' He turned to his grunting, chirping audience, and hushed it with a level gesture of his hands. When the pigs had quieted, he muted the music, and made a short speech about suidic rights and the sacred duty of defending them. He gave the floor to Sir Ron.

Sir Ronald had scarcely begun to speak before cries of passion came winging back from the audience. Although given in Afrikaans, and consequently unintelligible on its surface, as the speech went on, as sentence mounted on sentence, an edifice rose. Billy felt himself in the presence of a great communicator; he began believing himself an auditor of a lordly address, a participant in a truly historical moment. Emotional! Willful! Inspirational! Transformed, transported, aroused to an intense awareness of solidarity, of honor outraged, the suidae grunted and chirped and squealed their unified devotion to the defense of Pigville. A cyclone gust of clacking swept over Billy as applauding trotters, responding to Sir Ronald's peroration, composed a gale of sound that did not subside when he sat down. Deeply moved, even though he'd understood but a smattering of words and phrases, Billy clapped and wept while by gesture and command, El Supremo, the *Praefectus Castrorum* of Pigville, face stretched into a gold-tooth grin, quieted the aroused suidae.

'My friends,' said he, 'in honor of the profound dedication to the defense of ourselves, our loved ones, and our community we have so proudly expressed here, in recognition of our vows of mutual support and of our commitment to the common good, and in witness of the love for one another we so intensely share, I shall now open the party orchard.'

Joyful cries burst forth and followed George to the party gate which he flung open. The three comrades stood aside and watched the pigs bolt in to slobber and wallow in a rich accumulation of fermenting windfalls.

'Their enlistment bounty,' said George.

George, Billy, and Sir Ron strode back to the bus where George plucked a cassette from the rack and thrusting it into the player caused a German drinking song to erupt from Pigville's speakers. A police car, a black-and-white, turned in from the drive and stopped in the parking area. 'Hey look,' cried Billy, 'a mutated Hampshire!' George led Ron into the Winnebago bedroom. 'Wouldn't you love to live in a body like that?' Ron assented. 'If we win today, I promise you, I'll get you a genuine cop-car body and I'll weld it to the south end of my headquarters bus.' He closed the bedroom door and stepped out on to the porch to greet his friend Tom, now in uniform, and a civilian clad in a stylish gray suit.

Tom introduced the stranger as the Indiana State Swine Commissioner.

The swine commissioner gave George an executive order from the governor issued under his emergency public health powers.

George scanned it and passed it to Billy.

The document declared that the pervasive squalor of the *Legio Dix Fretensis* Swine Ranch created an unacceptable risk of hog cholera and, consequently, it ordered the proprietor, George Ahasuerus Baxter, to remove the pigs forthwith, or suffer the consequences.

'What's the or-else this time?'

'Mr Baxter. Are you going to move your hogs out today?'

'As you well know, properly disposing of all these porkers, that's a very complicated undertaking. Shit! I can't just turn them loose!'

'Mr Baxter, the deadline for complying with the municipal order in this matter has passed. The hogs are still here. Obviously, neither one of you has made arrangements of a substantial nature to remove them. And so therefore we have made our own. *We* will take them away. We will deduct the expenses of disposing of them and your fine of one thousand dollars from the proceeds of their sale.'

George showed his side teeth like an angry dog.

Sergeant Tom rose up from where he'd been sitting.

'I'm truly sorry about this, George, but the DA upgraded your misdemeanor charge. So, er, Mr Baxter, I have a warrant for your arrest on a charge of felonious cruelty to animals. I also have a John Doe warrant for the arrest of your assistant as an accessory.'

He turned to Billy.

'Young man, what's your last name?'

Billy gave his father's last name. 'Burke.' It was his real name, but he'd long used the name of his stepfather.

'And your social security number?'

'I don't have one.'

'Son, we all have one.'

'No sir, not me. I've never had a job. Went straight from high school to college.'

'You work here?'

'Yes,' George interrupted, 'but he's not an employee. He's a junior partner and need not get a number until he files his first income tax return.'

'Gentlemen, you understand, I'm writing all this down.'

'Sir,' replied Billy, 'I'll tell you whatever you want to know, and I hope you believe me. After all, according to the law, I only have to tell you my real name and, perhaps, my address, which is here.'

'Not for long, I'm afraid.'

Billy strode to the bedroom door. 'I guess you'll have to arrest the other assistant too.'

'You have a helper?'

'Yes, my colleague, Sir Ronald.'

He snatched open the door and in came Sir Ronald, who dashed outside to rub against the beautiful aristocratic dream-house police-car body.

George stepped to the porch and called him back inside.

Sir Ronald came trotting – all three hundred pounds of him – and as he came inside, the visitors stepped back against the bedroom door under the map of old Prussia and Ron lunged at them and the commissioner bumped the wine cooler and it toppled and crashed. George said something in Afrikaans and Ron put on the best show of constrained ferocity yet presented anywhere in the Indiana theater-of-the-real. The visitors' feet crunched broken glass as they sidled through a pool of cheap Chablis toward the door.

'You better run for it,' said George.

And they did. They fled to their car and sped away, Sir Ronald in pursuit.

Shaking his head and burbling mirth, he returned.

George stroked his brow. 'Well done! And I say so formally, in my capacity as your *Praefectus Castrorum*.' He gave Ron a bowl of brandy, and as the noble Hampshire slurped it up, he snapped a

44

new cassette into the sound system. 'Gentlemen, I think it's time to show the flag.'

The three comrades walked outside as dirty boogie began pulsing from the speakers. A rumbling humming noise swelled in from the road.

'Sir Ronald! This is it! Get Big Daddy and Father Duroc! Call out the forces!'

Billy ran off with Ron to open Pigville gate, and dashed back to George as Ron rushed inside to muster the Pigville militia. 'Ron's Run,' said Billy, 'will go down in history along with Sheridan's Ride.'

'The bastards!' cried George.

Slowly, cautiously, along the driveway came a procession, led by Tom's police car carrying the swine commissioner.

For a moment, George seemed irresolute.

'George, at a time like this, remember, Some things are too serious to take seriously, and too funny to laugh at.'

'They're going the whole hog!'

And indeed they were. Behind Tom's car came another cruiser followed by press and television vans, cattle trucks to carry off the pigs, and a bulldozer to push the auto bodies into the ravine.

'Wait there!' George marched back to the bus. Presently, he reappeared, clad in a dazzling armored kilt and breastplate, the battledress of an optio of ancient Rome's Tenth Legion, *Legio Dix Fretensis*, first cohort, as indicated by the sky-blue horse-like mane bristling from the center of his helmet and the blue field on his oblong shield, blazoned with Jove's thunderbolts. He gestured with his short sword. 'You follow me in the truck.' He strode to the tractor and as he sprang into its seat his armor clanked upon him.

What was Rome's Parris Island like?

They started their engines. The speakers burst out with taped war-squeals melded into 'The Yellow Rose of Texas' and everything began to throb in resonance.

George lowered his scraper blade and moved into the driveway; Billy followed, the don't-tread-on-me flag, snake-crossed, billowing from the aerial.

The suidae, all thirty-five tons of them, the cavalry, came dashing through Blood Creek Ford toward the fray, Father Duroc in the lead. Warhogs can outrun any warhorse ever bred! An Indiana

Pamplona in the making! The commissioner's face, behind its windshield, expressed a mixture of admiration and fear of the approaching swine.

Tom seemed stoic. He turned aside to avoid George's scraper blade, angled now to clear the way.

With a tremendous thud, flesh on metal, the furious porkers collided *en masse* with the procession. Vehicles backed and turned and impacted. George advanced in the tractor, brandishing his Roman sword as he plowed the opposition aside. Chaos! Cacaphony! Pan-demon-ium! The Yellow Rose of Texas! the yellow DTOM flag! The brave TV cameraman taping from the roof of his van! The shriek of swine! The horn-bray of car and truck! The clash of steel and thump of flesh! And then the police began shooting; pistols, shotguns, assault rifles. They blasted pigs, not people. Sir Ron fell, weltering in gore. Father Duroc absorbed the contents of a Uzi and fought on. Snorting rage, keening defiance, pigs by the score fell to earth, but, despite this lethal fire, they did not lose heart, but kept on denting vehicles and smashing windows as they raged and struggled to get at the invaders. Looking back from the calm heights of Later, Billy felt proud of his brothers, those embattled fellow humans for sustaining the dignity of their kind, for recording the event on video to serve as inspirations for future generations. As for the hogs! Noble! Brave! Courageous beyond words! An honor to their homeland and to their forefathers. There they lay on the sanguine field, the gasping wounded, the gory dead, having met an early Indianapolis, another Waterloo, martyrs to the suidic spirit, writhing in a blood wallow sanctified by their bodily fluids. Theirs, the heart of glory! The soul of valor! Blood Creek reconsecrated! A new Verdun! They shall not pass! *Ils ne passeront pas!* And all because of the assassination of Waggles. From the smallest seeds mighty trees do grow. They lay there, those rude citizens, self-sacrificed for their city, for the motherland, dead and dying that Pigville might live, if not in fact, in glorious memory.

It made Billy proud to be a sowboy.

On arriving at the grand portal, the triumphal plywood arch admitting to LEGIO DIX FRETENSIS SWINE RANCH, G. Baxter, Prop. & Praefectus Castrorum, George waved Billy through with the truck, then turned his tractor to block the way. He snatched out the distributor wires, slid in behind the truck's wheel, pushed Billy over into the shotgun seat, and sped off.

Billy looked back for a last view of the Summer of '92. It was to remain in memory a broken image in black-and-white, Hampshires, Holsteins, and police cars, all seen together in the silence of freshly fallen snow.

PART TWO

OF MONEY

SOWGIRL

Sensuality and kindness
must unite and dominate
the future.

Philmer P. Swait
Chicago, 1992

EIGHT

Aimée glanced from her vanity mirror to the crowds five floors below. How could anyone sympathize with a street named Wacker? A drive, that is. She smiled at herself in the vanity mirror. Did she really look like Maeve, the lady on the Irish one pound note? Jamie thought so. She gazed down at the people moving along the sidewalks of East Wacker Drive, by the public phone booth, her secret power. They'd all peered into their vanity mirrors this morning. She made a vanity face at herself and then, studying sidewalk faces with her 20-20 eyes, she transferred the interesting ones to her mirror, and imagined being them, or having them as companions, and then she imagined what they'd seen gazing in their morning mirrors.

How many of them keep china pigs on their dresser tops?

She stroked the pig Jamie had given her and imagined Jamie ambling down there in the Wacker crowd, in his smiling, hockey way.

And so, as they say, they're made in Heaven, or is it Japan or West Germany, love affairs and pink-and-white china pigs. Transferring another face from the street to the mirror, she wondered if this one could replace Jamie's in the boyfriend department. Every ending is a beginning. She glanced from the pig to the book she'd been reading, *Even Cowgirls Get the Blues*. How about us *sow*girls, Tom Robbins, how about us? She pictured Tom Robbins's face in the mirror. As she'd never seen a photo of him, she had to invent it. Because all of his book had passed through his head, he must look as nice as his book is. He most likely looks like Jamie.

And Jamie's back in Montréal at school, and I'm here in Chicago to put my money to work.

She'd earned it – if that's the right verb – through an innovation she'd made in the health industry about the time she'd met Jamie in London – Ontario. Jamie had made her a plant doctor, *Bot.D*. They'd printed an impressive degree conferred by the imaginary School of Advanced Botanical Studies, and hung it by her real bachelor's degree in a fancy office she'd rented and furnished with her savings. Using advertisements aired by chiropractors – chiroquacktors as she called them – for a model, she bought radio spots urging people to bring their sick plants to the plant doctor for outpatient or inpatient treatment. Her first client trusted her with an ailing rhododendron, which she cured. She soon built a thriving practice, and, eventually, moved to the center of action, Toronto, and began betting her profits on American commodities futures.

And Jamie? Saskatchewan born, British Columbia bred. She'd been a London cocktail waitress and Jamie had come in for a beer. He'd just walked from Cleveland across the Lake Erie ice to Canada, and Greyhounded from Port Stanley to London.

Love at first sight.

Made in Canada.

Aimée, Aimée, shrivel it back down to the truth.

Jamie'd only walked about half-way, fifty or sixty kilometers, when helicopter police – no, police in a helicopter, Hell-i-cops – had seen him and snatched him up to frustrate the fulfillment of his romantic dream.

The truth, Aimée, the truth.

Jamie came to a mile-wide stream that seldom freezes over, and the helicops brought him back to the old home country where it's winter all the time and everything is second class, like the tinny red mailboxes, and the crime stats. Even in Toronto, where the action is, they never get their share of murders.

She poured a glass of scotch, and looked down again at East Wacker Drive, and at the public telephone, reposing clam-like in its transparent shell: 424-3192.

It's almost time for the party.

She'd only been in town for a week and she did not yet know anyone she liked.

She could cruise Captain Streeter's Bar, just down the street, but all the young people there were randy idiots.

And now, evening rush-folk, anxiously treading the Wacker-walk beside the river.

Time for the party.

The don't-know-anyone-in-town party.

Her glance roamed around her studio apartment as she tried to imagine two hours hence, and who would be there.

Plenty of food, plenty of booze, plenty of ice.

She lifted the pinkly sexless pig and looked it in the eye.

'Sowgirls never get the blues.'

Yes!

She dialed 424-3192.

The commuter current streamed by the public telephone. Keep on ringing. Somebody, eventually, would take the bait. There! A middle-aged man, blazer, slacks, tie, stepping into the shell and lifting the phone.

'Hello. I think you have the wrong number.'

'I have the right number.'

'You have a problem? Can I help?'

'Look across the street, fifth-floor window, I'm leaning out, holding my phone.'

Stretching the coiled wire, he backed out for a better view.

'I see you!'

'I see you.'

'You in trouble?'

'No, no. I'm a stranger in town, and I want to meet some nice people, and so I'm having a party starting now, and you're invited.'

'What a delightful idea! My name's Phil.'

'Come on up, Phil, and help me add to the guest list.'

'Well, doggone.'

'I'm Aimée, my place is 507. I'll buzz the door.'

'Okay, Aimée, here I come.'

She watched him trot through Wacker traffic accumulating behind a light.

And then, there at her door, stood a smiling Phil.

She poured him a drink.

'I should be on my way to Wilmette, but what the hell, trains run all night.' He combed fingers through his hair. 'This is fun! I'll phone my wife and invite her, if that's okay.'

'Sure, Phil, invite her.'

He called.
'Here comes Jenny.'
Aimée raised her glass.
'To Jenny.'
'She'll be here in about an hour.'
They both sat down by the window.
'Your turn, Phil.'
'Okay.'
Phil dialed 424-3192.

At the edge of his ranch, George wheeled a screeching left into an overgrown lane going along his fence line and they bumped and slid to the woodlot behind the orchards where he'd stashed a getaway car. Stroking its rust-chancred hood much as he'd stroked Sir Ronald's brow, he said, 'Built this baby out of parts. It's even got Indiana plates, but don't ask where I got them.' He opened a back door and took a Chicago Cubs cap out of one of the cartons he'd packed in the back along with some suitcases. He tugged the baseball cap down on to Billy's head, then took a false moustache out of a carton and glued it to Billy's lip. 'Skinhead in, shaghead out.' He packed his armor and dressed in a sports jacket, red shirt, and slacks, admired himself in the rearview, and then inspected Billy. 'That moustache looks good with your hair. Right kind, too. I cut some off your head last night when you were asleep, and you never missed it! Ha ha!'

They drove to the country road at the far end of the lane, passed Farnsworth's pasture where Billy caught a glimpse of her, and stopped for gas at a crossroad station. A sweating fatboy wearing nothing but bib-overalls pumped it. George skirted around the town and drove through Indianapolis to Chicago.

'Well sir, it's goodbye Eden, hello Chi.'

'Wonder what they'll do with my snake flag.'

Billy was new to Chicago. They came in on Interstate 55 whence George rapturously admired the Sears Tower, the world's tallest building, visible for miles. To Billy it seemed a lofty, concrete cage. As they approached, the skyline of cages rose higher and higher, to predominate over the flat insipid supine ex-swamp once fed by a seeping river Indians knew as the Checagou, Onion Creek, which some three hundred years ago was discovered and then scorned by Louis Joliet. 'Imagine all that action, George, all those people. I'll bet there's a million who go to work there every weekday of their lives, and they sit for seven hours doing their quotidian chores, talking on phones, peering at green screens, and passing papers around.' He watched George unwrap some gum. 'What they're doing, can they possibly believe in it?'

'Does the Devil have scales?'

'All that effort, all that dedication, yet they don't make anything useful, or grow anything you can eat.'

'If they all stayed home, and we used them buildings for hogs, the world would be better off. Sties like that! I bet we could raise hogs by the million!'

'Take them up and down in elevators, clean out with sprinklers and fire hoses.'

'Yeah, boy, they ain't completely useless. You can't raise corn in them, or fucking dumb-ass cattle either, but hogs, yeah! Except you can't open the windows.'

George drove down into what seemed to Billy an endless maze of streets, all very much the same. Eventually he parked in front of the YMCA. 'We'll stay here. It's cheap and clean.' Billy peeled off the moustache and dropped it into a sewer. George registered them, and then, after driving through more streets and across the Chicago River, George led into a saloon called Captain Streeter's and they sat at the bar. After some argument, the barmaid brought two water glasses brimming with cheap white wine.

'I've always liked this place. Everybody who comes in here is big.'

It was, indeed, true. The place seemed the habitat of football and basketball players.

'I hate runts.'

George, thought Billy, the Fates decree our ways will soon part.

'I don't like cripples either.'

'George. From the long view, our relationship reminds me of Prince Hal and Falstaff, if you know what I mean.'

'I've heard of Shakespeare.' He showed his side teeth. 'Trouble with you is, you think other people don't know nothing.'

They slid back into silence. Billy studied the tattoo on George's wrist, *LEGIO DIX FRETENSIS* guarded by a wild boar. Only it *wasn't* a boar. 'Hey sport, your tattoo. That's a sow.'

'Don't you think I know it!'

55

'But you call it a boar.'

'So I was drunk and the artist played a joke on me. If I could catch that son-of-a-bitch, I'd . . . I'd fucking *blind* him, like the Byzantines blinded the Bulgars.'

'Sounds like it was your idea.'

'Fucking-A.'

'Our relationship, George, I think it's more like the Gilgamesh Epic. I'm Gilgamesh, and you're Enkidu.' Billy glanced at the faded blue tattoo. 'Or maybe – may the gods preserve me – or maybe I'm Barney and you're Fred Flintstone.'

'Let's go.'

They crossed to the river side of the boulevard, passed a public phone in its shell.

The phone was ringing.

George stopped.

'Come on, let's go back to the Y.'

George stepped into the shell and lifted the phone.

'Yeah!'

Silence.

'Hey! Anybody there!'

'Yes. And I'm inviting you to a party. Look up across the street at the windows of the fifth floor. Guy in the blue blazer, holding the phone, that's me, Phil.'

George stepped out to look.

'I'm George.'

'So come on up, George, and bring your baseball pal, too. We have food and drink and music, and good cheer.'

'Broads?'

'Well . . . maybe.'

'Okay. Here we come.'

'Apartment 507. I'll buzz you in.'

Answering their knock, Aimée walked with Phil to open her door. They'll think we're a nice, sophisticated, yuppie couple, except Phil's older than me by more than an acceptable yuppie margin.

She invited them in.

She looked at the newcomers, then at Phil.

The three of them, they surely are different.

Phil is my slickest uncle.

This big one must weigh more than my refrigerator.

And the young one, he looks much bigger up close than he did at a distance, probably because he's so well proportioned.

'I'm Aimée, and this is Phil.'

'This is Bill, and I'm George.'

Billy tipped his cap.

She motioned them to sit at the table, and while fixing drinks, explained that Phil, too, was a guest. 'My name, Aimée, rhymes with day, or fey, or say, so you *may* remember it that *way*. Phil and Bill rhyme, so that's easy, but what rhymes with George?' She served him first. 'I don't know what to rhyme you with.'

'I'm always left out.' He looked at Billy as Aimée sat down. 'Take off that cap. Don't you have no manners? There's a lady present.'

'These days,' said the lady, 'men wear hats inside. You're downright old-fashioned.'

'That's the truth and a half.'

He told her they'd just come up from the south, that he seldom visits Chicago and Billy'd never done so before.

'Nor have I. I'm from Canada, I'm an investor, and I was born on Easy Street,' which was true enough. 'My dad was in real estate. He laid out five streets, and the one where he built the best house – our house – he named Easy Street.'

'They called my dad Lucky Al. Our answering the phone, that goes to show luck still runs in my family.'

'I'm in computers,' said Phil. 'I'm from Oak Park which means I was raised with the ghosts of Frank Lloyd Wright and Ernest Hemingway.'

'I'm in swine, myself,' said George. 'And Bill here's a sowboy.'

A happy shriek burst out from Aimée and she embraced Billy and kissed his cheek. 'A sowboy! Fantastic!'

'I'm more of a merboy,' he said, blushing.

'This is made in Heaven, or maybe Japan! I was just thinking of myself as a sowgirl!' She led them to her dresser by the window where they admired her china pig. 'All right, George, you phone for the next guest.' George dialed 424-3192. The Wacker-walkers had thinned out now. The phone rang and rang without result. Who'll be next? In the days of yore when people still hitchhiked frequently and she was very young, she used to fill her van with hitching strangers, like a city bus, and always felt comfortable as soon as she'd made the second pick-up, because they were strangers to one

57

another as well as to her, and, consequently, would and did behave themselves. 'Keep trying, George.' She went back to the counter to freshen their drinks, and George's voice sounded, but she did not catch the words, and she looked out the nearest window and saw a woman slam the phone into its cradle and pace furiously away.

'I'll tell you what, gents. We'll have a dinner party, just us and my trusty microwave.' She prepared lamb chops and potatoes for her trusty microwave and began making a salad. 'Dinner will be ready right on time for Jenny.' Her phone rang. 'For you, Phil.'

He conversed in low tones and hung up.

'Sorry, no Jenny. We thought her mother would sit with the kids, but the old gal has to go to a meeting.' He lit a small cigar, then crushed it. 'Trying to quit.'

Aimée made him agree to stay for supper. She put a record on her stereo, soft music George said would make them fat, and soon, thanks to her trusty microwave doing its stuff while George was explaining to Phil how you must guard against sows crushing their young, she had the food on the table. George was saying that because there are six to twelve piglets in a litter, a good adolescent sow – a gilt – must have at least a dozen prominent, evenly spaced tits. 'Me, on my ranch, I owned *thousands* of tits, more, even, than the Ephesian Artemis had, and now I don't own any.' Aimée looked at him, then at Billy, and then at Phil as she served them and poured out wine, and again she was struck by how different they seemed. She felt suddenly aware of her breeding instinct, and she opened to it, and felt a surge of temptation to try them all, to see how close anticipation would come to realization. George is the kind of guy who'd go to a restaurant, and eat the menu. He probably thinks Hitler's Nazis were just a bunch of noisy boys. George. He'd be a vigorous, direct, bruising lover, but with a gentle dimension, and fun to try. Bill would be smooth and comic and imagine things like drinking champagne from creation's tenderest cup, and he'd fly through her memory as a kid brother, a swan diver in lavender briefs, springing off a cliff to plunge down toward a foamy cloud. Phil – Philmer P. Swait is what he'd said – would be formal yet laughing as he steps out of his boxer shorts and stands there sturdy and smiling and waiting for her to come to him. She'd tease him by calling him daddy, and he'd like that, and he'd put some smooth jazz on the stereo, and they'd dance and glide and eventually reach the bed. Music. Bill would like rock'n'roll

58

and call it abstract expressionism, a thought she'd believed until this moment was entirely her own. 'Do you sometimes think of rock'n'roll as abstract expressionism in music?'

'Not when I play. I have a lute at home. When I open the floodgates and my feelings rush out through the strings to, yes, express, water music happens, and when I feel like storm, I finger-pick my Pete Seeger banjo, and blast down all the coconut trees.'

'I thought you'd go for rock'n'roll.'

'That's old stuff. That's raw energy. When I'm blowing raw energy, I blow it through my banjo. Bluegrass.'

'Old stuff!' Her girlhood had throbbed to the sounds of Rolling Stones and Led Zeppelins and Jefferson Airplanes. 'And you don't like it.'

'I don't play it, not on a lute, a banjo, but I open to it. I wear a Deadhead sweatshirt.'

'You were born in 1970. Right?'

'Right. The year Nixon broke the constitution by invading Cambodia.'

'I'm the old-timer here,' said Phil. Rock'n'roll makes me think of '68 and that riot at the Democratic convention.' With a hand he brushed his hair back, fine and light-brown, and exposed a scar. 'My souvenir of the '60s.'

'Made in Chicago?'

'Made in Chicago.'

'Out of yesterday comes today.'

George stood and walked behind Phil. 'You've got an interesting head, and I'd like to feel it.'

'Feel it?'

'Yes. I'm a student of phrenology. I can read disposition and character by feeling heads. It's like braille.'

'Jesus, George,' said Billy, with an open-hand gesture, 'all the time we've been together, and I never knew you're into phrenology.'

'A lot of things about me you don't know.' He stepped behind Billy. 'I've felt your head before.' He laid his open hands on Billy's scalp and began kneading and probing. 'When you were fucked up and passed out.' He looked at Aimée, then at Phil. 'Marry the brain to the body. Marry the brain to the skull. Marry the skull to the flesh. Marry the flesh to the brain. Connect them dry bones to wet meat. I'm no chiropractor, not me. I'm a phrenologist, and I understand this shit, bet your sweet ass. Nobody believes in phrenology any more. You say quack quack, I know you do. What *you* know about it? You don't know shit, that's what! I really *do* it. And I learned it from the great practitioners. The masters! I look for self-esteem. I can magnify it. Just by tapping around with my hammers. Self-esteem, it's there in the head! America is supposed to mean self-esteem for everybody. Canada too. That's what they're supposed to be about. And not through mission and command, either. No way!'

'Does it work on pigs?' asked Billy.

'You fucking-A! That's why I understand them so well. And that's why I understand you.' He was rubbing and probing Billy's head as he talked. Would he produce his hammers? 'Sowboy Bill here has the same configurations as Alexander the Great.'

Aimée stood, saying, 'He *looks* like Alexander the Great! Like a coin from twenty-two hundred years ago my parents gave me, Alexander's profile, taken from life by Lysippus, as Alexander sat in his studio!' She fetched the coin from her jewel box. Billy was blushing bright. She held it next to his profile. 'Amazing! Look at that!'

'My dad used to say I resemble the Nathan Hale statue in New York City.'

'That's modeled on this coin. My parents told me nobody knows what Nathan Hale really looked like, except a few descriptions in words, so the artist modeled that statue on Alexander.'

'Alexander was blond, not light-brown like me.'

George went back to Phil and felt his head.

'Another pagan.'

'We're all pagans here,' said Aimée.

Phil brushed George's hands away and leaned back. 'You know, friends, right now we're in a time of profound and accelerating change. Technology, sure. But the flip-side is myth. We're in transition from tribal myths to a shared myth for the world tribe, for everybody. The revolution is transforming the illusions we live by. What I'd like to see is a marriage between the pagan and the Christian, not Old Testament Christian, but the Gospels. I mean sensuality and kindness must unite and dominate the future.'

NINE

When dinner was over, and they'd had their brandy-coffee, Phil excused himself, shook hands all round, and Aimée went with him to the door. 'Phil. I want to see you again. I'll phone you.' He smiled and gave her his card, and, accepting it, she said, 'I'm here in Chicago to play the casino from inside, and I'd like to have access to your cool and experienced head.'

'And I'd like to have access to yours. I'm in midlife crisis, looking for a new career.'

Phil backed into the hall. Billy tugged his hat on and snapped up the visor. 'Guess we better go too.'

'No. Please stay. Something I want to talk over with you guys.'

As Phil closed the door behind him, George snatched Billy's cap. 'You ain't outside. Act civilized.'

Aimée sat down at the table and poured brandy into snifters. 'George, what does civilization mean to you?'

'Civilization is when everybody has good plumbing.' He raised his snifter to eye-level and peered at it contemplatively. 'Plumbing. I mean no dirts, no rotting fluids, no piss, no shit, no cunt juice, wet or dried.'

'Is that all?'

'It's one hell of a good start! If you know anything about the old days, and I've lived in them, believe me, if you've ever experienced a lesser level of civil-eye-*fucking*-zation, you know progress starts with keeping things clean.'

'I'll buy that.' She looked at Billy. 'From now on I'm calling you Alexander.'

'Good idea. I need an alias.'

'Alexander. Have you ever walked from Cleveland to Canada on the Lake Erie ice?'

'No, but I'm game.'

'I believe it.'

'Is that what you want us to discuss?'

'No.'

'How are you going to remember my new name? It's even harder to rhyme than George.'

'Menander. The ancient Greek from Alexandria who invented bawdy farce.'

'I think God deserves the credit for that.'

'Indeed He does, but He has to share it with man and woman.' She assumed her serious face, and spoke in her business voice. 'I'm considering a big move, and I'd like to talk it over with people who have no part in my life, folks who can view it all objectively but I'll never have to see again, not unless I choose to.'

'And that's us, eh, sweetheart?'

'Yes, George, it's you, fallen right out of the sky into my life, like a meteor, like an airplane part.' She fetched the china pig from her dresser top and set it on the table. 'This swinish centerpiece is our common denominator.'

Yes, Aimée, so it is, and now be candid, be perfectly frank, tell them everything and see what they think. 'I'm like Phil. I'm looking for a new career.' Wrong place to start, Aimée, but that's part of the reason for telling them. Telling is organizing, and, organized, I can see it whole, add it up. 'The plant doctor scam, I made a lot of money on it, enough to send my pal to college in Montréal, McGill, and for me to accumulate enough to invest, to gamble, to recycle. I have a bachelor's degree in botany, and I'm good at it, and I worked hard, and I did cure people's pet plants, I really did, and it made them happy, so I like to think my business was no more of a scam than what's practiced by dog-and-cat doctors.' Now, I'm tired of it. 'Let others do it.' And they are, copying me. 'So I started studying the futures market, wheat and corn and soybeans, and studying the world political-economy which, along with crop sizes and such, determines prices. And whenever I thought I'd found a number of factors conjoining in a vector pushing prices up or down, I'd buy or sell contracts on the commodities market, through the Board of Trade here in Chicago, and from the start, I regularly won more bets than I lost.' That's enough details; they have the point. 'So I saw a real hot opportunity in soybeans, and bet all my money, about one hundred grand, going with the minimum margin, and came out with four hundred grand, and built that up, and did two more all-or-nothings, and six weeks ago I hit big on wheat, and now I'm sitting here on top of seven-point-seven millions of dollars, US dollars, and that's why my pal gave me the china pig.'

'Pig?' asked Billy. 'For your money wallow?'

'My ice-walker pal thinks trading in hog-belly futures, sides of bacon that is, symbolizes the spirit of Commodities Casino, so he gave me the pig to celebrate my lucky September hit.'

'I've hit on foreign currency deals there,' said George.

'No shit!' Billy stared at him. 'I thought you were just a street-car motorman transformed into a hog farmer.'

'Rancher!'

'So, boys, where do I stand now? I'm still winning money on the market. True. But the time has come to make the next move. And here you sit, ready for me to throw ideas at, and see where they bounce.'

'Or stick,' said Billy.

'The other people I've met in Chicago, my broker, his contacts, the gents down at Streeter's, they're all advantage suckers, no romance, just greed, squalid career builders, no sense of public service, futures and stocks, out for the bucks, suck old-lady blood and pop pension-fund pimples, get big money, big power, and get the girls and boys of their dreams, never age to forty, turn into George Bush and live happily ever after. I can't tell them any of this. And I don't. I just pick their minds. I'm a hen, picking corn out of shit. You follow me?'

They do.

'What's my idea?'

Pause for effect.

'I want to buy an island, maybe ten square miles, off the coast of Africa, or maybe in Indonesia, or the Philippines, and build the pleasure dome of my dreams, a romantic spa for romantics, a Pugwash conference for composing the world-tribe myth. Yes. But I need more money. I can get that by incorporating. Incorporated, if I lose I'm not lost. Incorporated, I can sell stock.'

Elbows on the table, she knit her hands together and rested her chin on them.

'Before I can look for investors, I have to know exactly what I want. I have to finish the picture, *trompe-l'oeil*. What I can see now, looming in the mist, is a theme resort.' They look interested. 'But I need a theme. Something new, truly unique, that would be ideal.'

They sat in silence.

'Big game won't do, because they don't let you hunt big game any more, not in any way you can rely on.'

George gazed down at his feral sow tattoo. He flushed with excitement. 'I've got it!' he cried. 'Hogs! Fence off the wild part of your island and populate it with pork. Wild boar! *Sus scrofa!* Not razorbacks, the real thing! We build a dream castle, with gardens, everything, even phony peasants' huts. Thatched. Pay enough bucks, Mr Bourgeois, and you can live your aristocratic dream. Sporting girls and ballet boys. Ass-sucking servants. We import European wild boar, fence off their range, let the guests hunt them. Yes! And the menu! Feature boar, in all its forms, all the recipes. I know how they prepared it for Domitian Caesar, his favorite dish! Boar throughout the ages! Hog Park! There's your theme. *Sus scropa!*'

'Well, maybe.'

'If you go for hogs, I'll put in the bucks.'

'This lady's a sweetheart, George. Don't bullshit her.' He turned to Aimée. 'Look at him. Tell me, does this guy look like he controls big bucks?'

'I'm the richest guy in the world.'

'Bullshit.'

'I'm the Wandering Jew.'

'Sure, sure.'

'I own the biggest account at US Trust! The biggest of all!'

'Of course you do, George.'

'And six Swiss bank accounts!'

'Easy does it, George.'

'And countless bars of gold.'

'Really?'

'So, sweetheart, how much do you need?'

'Eighty mil, US, ought to do it. The rest we can borrow from banks.'

'You go for hogs, Aimée – I'm your man.' He held his arm out to her displaying his tattoo. 'When it comes to hogs, I speak from experience.'

'I don't doubt it.'

'I'll be *Praefectus Castrorum* of the spa. I deserve no less.'

'True enough. He was *Praefectus Castrorum* of Pigville.' Billy told her about Pigville, its rise, its eventual decline and fall, and how progress and greedy developers had undermined it. 'He's been around the block a few times.'

'Tomorrow,' said George. 'Right here. I'll be back here at three p.m. with eighty mil. I've made some good investments in my time, you better believe it.'

'George. Also bring the rest of my pay.'

'I'll have to think about that.'

'Think about that?'

'Yes. I have to be certain of your loyalty.'

'He was boss and still owes me part of my pay. He was *Praefectus Castrorum* of the whole farm, of me as well as the pigs.'

'Ranch,' said George. 'Ranch.'

'Okay, George. Ranch.'

'No matter how the details work out,' said Aimée, 'I'm going to sell stock to the public. Even if we don't need the money, it's a good form of advertising. Get people talking about the spa. But I won't sell too many shares. I'll keep the power.'

'What do stock and pigs have in common? Give up? You water both on the way to market.'

'In Delaware, where I'm going to file the papers, it takes three to make a corporation. So I'll put you in as incorporators, and . . . I'll call it Z E U G M A. Yes. A zeugma is a figure of speech in which two basically unrelated ideas are connected by some superficial syntactical similarity. As in: George roared off in a rage and his Buick. What superficially equates us – what we have in common – is pigs. My piggy bank here will be our phantom logo representing that ethereal line where hogs and money meet.'

'I like your attitude,' said George. 'Z E U G M A it is.'

'We can invent the acronym later.'

'But I can't see you holding all the power. How about the pigs?'

'Power to the pigs? No. Some stock, perhaps, just some, to the pigs. To those hateful, arrogant young brokers. Okay. Here's the fantasy. A Wild Boar Spa. Done! A fancy pig farm. Sorry, George, a righteous ranch. So be it! So now – imagine this scene. George comes here tomorrow, or maybe to Captain Streeter's, at three.

65

He brings the bucks in a bag. And, George, don't forget Alexander Burke's pay. From now on, we'll call him Al for short. Don't forget Al's pay. I'll get a lawyer to write up some quick corporation papers. We breathe life into ZEUGMA. We embody a legal fiction. It's a joke. We leave the whole thing out there in fantasy-fiction land. We let the word get around. We spend serious bucks on public relations. We sell shares. We don't build a thing, not a thing. We put our gold pile into an independent foundation. We reimburse ourselves. We bankrupt. The foundation gives all the plunder to Amnesty International, Greenpeace, Sea Shepherd, and the Cousteau Society, and dissolves itself.'

George sprang to his feet, his side teeth bared. 'The hell we will! We'll fucking *do* it. We'll *build* Hog Spa Island. We'll build it with two-fisted tender care, and in the future, thanks to us, the great day will come when pigs and people will lie down together in peace and harmony, you better fucking believe it!'

TEN

Well, this is one of those days beginning yesterday. Aimée looked out at the Wacker-walkers, and then at her reflection, imagining various ways of adjusting her appearance to the future, humming 'What a Difference a Day Makes'. Banal, but true. What part would today's script ask her to play? Dressing for the street is guessing what the future holds, and so is making-up for the street. Which costume? Which face? Chic, or fun? If they're coming at all, George and Alexander, they'll be here in about an hour. So, Aimée, go down to Streeters and sit out of sight, in the back, so they'll have to hunt for you.

If they do hunt for you, it could mean they're serious.

Serious!

Pig Spa Island!

Why not? As good a way as any to work on her ambition to form a worldwide myth suited to now, one romantic enough to give meaning to life in the world-tribe, and yet at the same time consistent with probability, and even, perhaps, reality.

Whatever that is?

A new myth for a new world gestating in the new technology.

A trendy hog wallow will do as a place to start . . . sculpting a new myth around the armature of new facts.

Right, Aimée? As in London – England. In the course of a few decades the facts of going from here to London have changed, haven't they, Aimée? I can join the Wacker-walkers, take the El to O'Hare International Airport, and jet to London in a few hours. Not so long ago, it would have been a cab to LaSalle Street Station, the 20th Century Limited to New York City, the *Queen Mary* to Portsmouth, and a train to Victoria Station.

A week at least.

A century ago? Same route, more time.

Two? Canoe. New Orleans. Sailing ship. Coach to the George and Vulture.

Old myths rule new facts.

So, Aimée, make up, and dress up, for your part in the new myth, an as-yet unwritten play, one which in the manner of Plautus, or Menander, you will explain in the Prologue.

At three p.m. At Streeter's. The Prologue shall begin.

She painted her eyebrows silver.

And the costume, Aimée, the costume?

The audience is mired in old myths.

And dressed in money-drag.

I shall be clad in sensuality and kindness.

She phoned Phil at his law office, but he was out.

The new myth is lived in comfort.

She put on a white sweatshirt, a beige skirt, beige-and-white running shoes, but no hat for George to snatch, and then she slung her shoulder-bag and walked down five flights of fire stairs and out of the lobby, joined the flow of Wacker-walkers, and eddied out of it, into Streeter's.

She found a booth in the back, not visible from the door or the bar, and ordered her favorite myth-lubricant: brandy. It could silence numerous voices of reality, but not the one saying it was her time of the month. Aimée, think of it as a reliable connection to reality. The curse. Ameliorated by new facts. The curse! Her mother's voice reminded her to look at the shiny side. Yes. I'm a link in the progression from amoeba to whatever will evolve from us. The farthest past and remotest future meet in me. I transform past into future. In me, time metamorphoses! So let that give direction to my Pig-Spa Power.

Women are the links of the life-chain; men are barnacles growing on the links.

Up until their brains introduced the era of genetic control.

She raised her glass to toast to herself. '*Novus mythos seclorum!*'

'*Nova insula porca,*' said a beaming George, in a trombone voice.

Billy stood next to George, carrying two suitcases and dressed as before in cutoff military pants and T-shirt, but hatless. He sat in a chair across from Aimée and motioned George to sit by him, saying: 'I'm glad we found you, Aimée. When you didn't answer your door, and I didn't see you out at the bar, I began to wonder.'

George, still standing, again used a brazen voice. 'Well, sister, is it pigs, Pig Island, or ain't it?'

'Sit down.'

He sat.

'George, tell me . . . What do you do when you have to be a gentleman?'

'Pretend I'm somebody else.'

'Try.'

This time he chose a softer voice. 'Is it Pig Island, or ain't it?'

'It is.' She'd been to a lawyer that morning and had some rough corporation papers drawn up for filing in Delaware, the easiest, sloppiest state. 'And to show my good faith, here are preliminary papers of incorporation.'

His back to the room, he set one of the suitcases on the table of the booth, then the other. 'Here's the dough.' He dumped one out, releasing an avalanche of packets of thousand-dollar bills. The money drifted into a pile, upsetting Aimée's drink. 'Three cubic feet of thousand-dollar bills equals twenty million. I had them flown in from Switzerland.'

'I accept the gesture as your act of good faith,' said she, stacking the coveted portraits of Grover Cleveland back in the suitcase, 'but I don't think you should carry this around with you.' Maybe it really will work out. 'Wait there.' She stood. 'I want to call Phil.'

Fortunately, neither the waiter nor anyone else had seen the money. 'Aren't you afraid to carry that stuff around?'

'I ain't afraid of anything.'

'Or to let Alexander carry it?'

'Him? Run? Just let him fucking try it!'

'George. In this town, they'd kill for just one of these bills.'

'Nobody can kill me.' His voice softened. 'Give me your hand.' Why not?

He filled it with quarters. 'Play some music. Something you think savage suidae would appreciate.' He smiled up at her. 'I like your style, sister. Should have done this long ago, built a proper spa, but, well, it's so easy to let the days slip by.'

She sat down again. 'You know why I like this place?' She told

69

them the first time she'd come in she'd asked the manager: Who was Captain Streeter? And you know what? He said Streeter, Captain George Wellington Streeter, a Union veteran of the Civil War, noticed a shallow area of the Lake, now filled in, had been left out of Illinois and USA, and Canada too, in the maps and treaties, so Streeter claimed it as his own country, and made himself chief of it. 'Imagine! He started his own country!'

Sweat it down to truth, Aimée. Not his own country. No. His own district, as in Washington DC. And in the war, he was a common soldier, not a captain.

But, what the hell. They like the idea as is, Aimée. So let it stand.

'You look at contradictions. *For* them, I mean. For the point of paradox, the line of yin–yang, like Streeter did. He lived in his private country years and years while his breakwater caused the Lake to fill it with sand. Streeterville, that's what they call it now. A part of downtown Chicago. The place where opposites meet. The neglected vacuum. Pet plants. Hog Spa Islands. Why hire professional killers to slaughter pigs for the rich when you can get the rich to pay big bucks to slaughter the pigs for themselves?'

'So,' said Billy, 'we'll get the rich to butcher them, too.'

'Yes! And cook them, and serve them to the poor.'

George reached into the suitcase on the table and stripped out an engraving of Grover Cleveland. 'Drinks for the house!' he cried in his brazen voice. 'In memory of Captain Streeter!'

'No,' said Aimée.

'Drinks for the horse,' said Billy to the waiter. 'He wants to buy drinks for his horse.'

'The hell I do! Set up everybody, and tell 'em it's on George – George Wellington Streeter, *Praefectus Castrorum* of Streeterville.'

'What!'

Billy leaned back, laughing. 'It's on Captain Streeter. Captain *George* Streeter.'

So stand up, Aimée. Get moving. Get Phil into this. We need another hitchhiker in the Pig Island van. With quarters, she bribed the jukebox to play top-forty dance music, then went outside to her lucky telephone shell.

'Sure, Aimée. I'd love to! I'll be there in a few minutes.' Phil's voice had a genuine love-to sound.

She went back to the table. 'What color are your thoughts?'

70

'Color?' George chewed the edge of his thousand-dollar bill. 'What kind of shit is that? Color!'

'Color. As in greening.' As in the next item on the agenda: Keep the hitchhikers in their place. 'As in Al's pay.' She snatched the banknote and gave it to Billy.

He laughed and pocketed it. 'If you're going to call me Al, I have to ask you, What did you do today to make the world better?'

'Collected your pay.'

'Thanks, Aimée, for preserving the sanctity of wages.'

'Wages!' said George. 'Ain't nothing holy but money.'

He seems, nevertheless, willing to let that scrap of money go. He's blowing an enormous, pink gum-bubble, styling like a baseball pitcher on TV. We wait for the pop and suck, which he accomplishes with the finesse of a twenty-game winner. 'What else do you believe in, George?'

'I believe in pigs.'

'I believe we're even crazier than Captain Streeter.' The thought was hers, but the voice was that of a smiling Phil. He seated himself, immaculate in his downtown uniform of blazer and quiet tie and pastel shirt and gray pants. 'Pig Spa Island! The heart of Madness, the soul of Folly! Yes. With us people, when the body's fed and dry and warm and rested – when it's content, life becomes a struggle among illusions. Yes. Among men enslaved to gods – field hands or house servants or suck-asses in some Heaven; among those becoming gods – presidents or proprietors of countries and corporations; and among those crushed down so low in this life they yearn to follow gods or be gods in the next. So people play their appropriate parts in the grand drama of illusion.'

'And,' said Billy, 'nowadays, all those different dramas are playing on the same stage.'

'That's why I believe in pigs.' Elbows on the table, George gestured with open hands, palms out, and spider webs seemed to lace between his fingers. 'I love what I can trust. Money and pigs. People are hypocrites. Every fucking one. People live balancing their realities and their illusions, which is about as hard to do as pour five gallons of piss into a one-gallon bucket. Basically, pigs and people ain't that different. They like the same food; they like to booze and live the lazy easy life; and, stressed, they get ulcers and croak with heart attacks. What pigs don't have is illusions. No myths, no legends. No heroes or celestial lies.

No flags. No tribes. No hymns. No anthems. Just down-home up-front appetites. No troubles but lice, worms, and mange. People! Two-faced, split-tongued, double-thinking hypocrites! But hogs! A million pounds of meat and not an ounce of hypocrisy. They're realists and I trust 'em. Society! The company of men? For a true comrade, give me a Superior Certified Meat Sire any day!'

Speak up, Aimée.

'Nonsense! In your version of This-Little-Piggy-Went-To-Market, all the little piggies go to market.'

'And why the hell not?'

Phil smiled and replied. 'That's better than feeding them roast beef, or going wee-wee-wee all the way home.' He ordered a drink. His face is too fat, but he has lovely deep gray eyes. 'Pig Spa Island,' he said in his lawyer voice, 'founded by Dr Dada and Alfred E. New-man. Our suidic tropical isle embodies the spirit of utter folly. I like the idea. It's going to be fun. And it might do some good, too.'

They all clasped hands on the table.

In wassail, they dedicated their joint venture to Hilarity and Genius. *Hilaritati Ac Genio dicata.*

George showed Phil the money.

'Looks like we can dispense with credit cards.'

George squeezed a packet of currency in his powerful hand, making it writhe, thus establishing mastery over one hundred thousand dollars. 'This is shit you can rule.'

'That's true. Credit cards can rule you. They are downright Faustian. When you sign for one, you sign a pact with the Devil. You can have anything you want now, in exchange for your soul, payable later.'

Get practical, Aimée. Make them talk business.

'Now that we've agreed to do it, it's time to draw our plans, time to sketch out how we'll build and launch the good ship *Zeugma*.'

'When the fucking Vikings launched a new ship, they rolled it on logs into the water, and between each log they laid a trussed captive, for lubrication, for Odin and Thor, and to show the color of their thoughts.'

'Yes,' said Phil. 'And one reason they prevailed over so many civilized people is they never washed and never wiped. These days, one must be subtle.'

They retired to Aimée's apartment, where they spent the evening making plans and eating sandwiches and talking philosophy. Eventually, they agreed to reconvene in the morning.

'We'll meet here at ten a.m. Then, for an eye-opener, I'll take you to the Chicago Board of Trade to see the money frenzy.'

After they left, Aimée, yawning and stretching, stripped off her clothes, folded them, and slid naked into bed. As she drifted into Dreamland, she sensed, quite independently of all their talk, the whole ZEUGMA thing felt right. Yes. It's true. It's as George said on his way out. Words on feelings are like flies on meat.

ELEVEN

In August of 1968, after being beaten to the ground in Old Town, Phil, fallen to the nadir of his eighteen years, his scalp seeping blood, crawled among feet and legs and twisting torsos into a Rush Street alley. To that night he attributes the kindling of his interest in law as a complement to his lifelong romance with theoretical mathematics. Certainly, he thought, it had precipitated his hitchhike to San Francisco, his Beatle hair adorned with Bandaids instead of flowers. So what happened to that Phil, the real Phil, the passionate lover of clean cool math, he who lived by selling the *Berkeley Barb* to folks alighting from cable cars on the turntable near Fishermen's Wharf, the Phil who spent most of what he earned on food, which every Wednesday he and his pal made into sandwiches and gave away to the swarming young people who passed by where they sat on the sidewalk of Haight Street, near Cole?

Where is that Phil today?

So what do I want?

Not this.

Nor, in Aimée's exquisite expression, to be a barnacle on the chain of life.

Schwein, Porque, Swadey, Pige, & Hogg. And Phil. My firm. And me telling Aimée that Jenny's my wife. Next to Phil's office door, another, a partner's, labeled in gilt letters, like those of all the partners, Jennifer Alison Swade (What happened to the *vitch*?), Attorney-at-Law. Looking at the gilt letters, gilt meaning having the appearance of gold, he sometimes thought of guilt, deriving from what they did to the public for their corporate clients, and then one day, while preparing a case about hog futures, he'd seen the other meaning of *gilt*: a young sow who had yet to give birth, and from that – from gilts and guilt – flowed his fanciful name for the firm.

And so he'd phoned Jenny, partner not wife, from Aimée's, and invited her to the telephone party. What emerged from that? Nothing less than her usual yes–no.

Jenny'd been at the police riot too.

She was already a law student.

In his office bookcase, occupying an entire wall; in it, along with all the elegant law books, bound in leather (pigskin?), with their solemn gilt titles, those tomes nobody needs any more, because of his computer programs, he kept the volume which now lay open before him, a coffee-table format photo-essay about the Democratic Convention, Chicago, 1968, which had fired his interest in politics and the law.

And so now, Phil, at forty-two, you go with Aimée (née Amy), Alexander (né William), and George Baxter, the most improbable George Baxter on earth, to visit the Chicago Board of Trade.

CBT, like meat-packing and railroads, Chicago quintessence, commodity pits, a unique tourist attraction. And, thought Phil, they've always attracted me, but, somehow, I never got around to leaving my calling card.

Sandburg and Dreiser – that firm had done so scores of times.

The scene on the trading floor of the CBT is said to be wilder than Wall Street, more frenzied than any rodeo yet produced or ever imagined.

The pits of the CBT, where bulls gore and bears claw, are the arenas of the food wars, whence basic food prices emerge.

As in the cost of the bread Phil and his pal – her name was Jenny too – had used in the sandwiches they'd given away free to the Haight Street hippies in '68.

That, also, had been a dramatic scene, a unique tourist attraction.

'Yes, Jenny, pal Jenny, not law-partner Jenny, my mu-mu and beads Jenny, and me, your pal, Phil, the software genius, destined to be an attorney-at-law, bound to a different Jenny. Big law firms don't have to shepardize to find precedents, not any more, not with Phil's programs around. You want precedents? Past decisions?

75

Favoring either side of the argument? Both sides? I can find them. I do find them. Me. The same Phil who lived in a crash pad on Page Street, and transformed underground newspapers into free food, and dialed POP-ACID when he wanted the time.

Now, it's POST-MAN.

He punched out LAW-YERS to see what would happen, and a grandmotherly voice said the prefix had been changed to 708.

SOT-YERS.

I'm forty-two. Forty-two! Aimée is thirty.

In '68, she was *six*.

And I turned eighteen.

Just before the draft lottery began and weakened the resistance.

How much of my idealism was altruism, how much of it my alibi for dodging the draft?

He stood, smiling, and adjusted his tie.

Off to the money frenzy.

Take them some food.

Bologna-on-white.

Baloney-on-white.

Legal size.

With my pals Aimée (Amy) and Bill (Al) and George-fucking-Baxter.

Aimée. She knows where brains pay off. Not manufacturing, but health. Not stocks; commodities. And now she's sailing our imaginary good ship *Zeugma* to the best port of all, the capital of the greedy moniers.

Realty City.

Partner Jenny went to law school. Pal Jenny went to the San Francisco Art Institute. In the men's room she'd hung a checklist, naming eleven males blessed with sexy buns, and, for the fun, fucked them all.

She thought my buns too fat, but liked me anyway.

She was raped, hitchhiking, picked up on Van Ness Avenue, and the next day, in a seminar, told the story, and called it a romantic adventure.

These days, in various media, you see her sculpture pictured and reviewed.

And in 1968, Aimée'd been six, and learned about Vietnam and

Chicago and Haight Street, San Francisco, from TV in London – Ontario.

And Bill, not as yet conceived, had grown up to work on a Mount-a-ray squid boat sailing over the giant rays one mile deep in Monterey Bay.

And that's beginning to lead to Georgesque humor from a Georgeoid sophisticated by Oak Park, mathematics, Haight-Ashbury, and law school: Northwestern, night.

Ray, ray, don't bite me.

Ray, ray; okay, okay,

Today's the day,

To observe the money frenzy.

As he stepped out of his office, he made a judgment: This is for the last time.

As he went by the computer room, he passed partner Jenny.

'Catch you later, sweetheart, I'm on my way out.'

And that is the fucking truth.

I am on the way *out*.

For fucking good!

Stet!

Stare decisis.

I've plenty of money.

I'm rich enough to have a chauffeur and maids if I want them.

And more money flows in from my software copyrights.

So, off to the feeding frenzy in the food pits,

Go I,

Metamorphosed from participant to observer.

And I'll be true to my old self,

My true self,

Whatever that is.

Down in the elevator, out of the lobby.

And the air smells cool and fresh.

An east wind off the Lake.

He flowed with the current of people along Michigan Avenue, toward the Loop.

I'm on the road now. I've started on a trip. Honor forbids me to turn back. All that money! Three cubic feet of thousands. Counterfeit? My one-way ticket on the Pig Spa Island Tour presented and punched. My boon companions, three utter strangers. Can this

77

be all coincidence? Is it a scam? Three cubic feet of thousands. Starring Grover Cleveland. *George*. Heir? Dope Dealer? Am I to be a founding father of Pig Spa Money Laundry Isle? That phone party. A phony? A way to catch a sucker? Hire a private eye. George? Eight cubic feet of contradictions. No classifying him. As a talesman, make the pre-emptive challenge. As a witness? Friendly/hostile. A crude sophisticate. A cruel compassionate. A greedy munificent. A cunning naïf. Call the next witness. Bill. Bill is *too* easy. Innocent. Able. Independent. A prototype of sensuality and kindness embodied in self-reliant strength. What accident made George and Bill companions? Lovers? Impossible. Convenience. Bill is hiding from something. Pigville was his safe-house. Evicted, he seeks another. Can his sweet surface hide some awful crime?

And Aimée?

Creative. Efficient. Complex. Quite charming. Self-contained. Brilliant.

Trustworthy?

And last night I dreamed of stripping her and dancing with her to stereo jazz, turning and gliding, and then rolling on to a huge white cloud-bed and slow loving and kissing and fucking the night away.

Three witnesses. All enigmas.

Off into the unknown with three enigmatic comrades.

So? I've accepted the case. I'm ethically committed. So forget behind and look ahead. No more Schwein, Porque, Swadey, Pige, Hogg & Scam. I can afford it. Two-plus decades of self-betrayal equals a forty-two-year-old adolescent ... and enough money invested to feed on forever. At forty-two, it's back to '68 I go. Who'll greet me, who'll need me, when I'm sixty-four? So how soon will I be saying Far Out and Out of Sight? Will men become Dudes and women, Chicks? When will colloquy revert to Rap Session? Will superior change into Righteous? No matter what, I'll hold the line against Groovy.

Even at eighteen, Phil had firmly refused to say that word.

As he walked through Streeterville, toward the river, he pictured Captain Streeter, whose fierce independence had created what locals call the most valuable piece of real estate in the world. Imagining Captain Streeter striding ahead, abruptly it was George instead, and it *was* George, dressed in boots and a blue Civil War cap who strode ahead until, on arriving at the Michigan

78

Avenue Bridge, Phil paused to admire the ranks of gigantic buildings standing across the Chicago River. What stunning, powerful architecture! Nowhere else on Earth is there a view like this! The river and its bridges made him think of Paris. The Seine, too, had once flowed between foul marshy banks. But with the stone-banked river and ornamental bridges, the resemblance stops. Paris is Paris. Chicago, Chicago. Both, of a size; each, unique. He smiled at the memory of the phantom Streeter-Baxter, now vanished on the other side, and marveled at yesterday's fortuitous juxtaposition of improbabilities which had caused him to cross the river and go to a meeting and leave the meeting just in time to walk by the telephone shell and be stopped by the ringing, as if he'd sensed it was the call from his kismet for which he'd been waiting so long. And now a series of events is in train and I am riding on it to . . . Pig Spa Island? Aimée has money. That studio apartment on Wacker Drive must cost a fortune. Never go back to the office? Be practical. Return tonight, late, and gather my papers. This afternoon, as a sequel to the CBT's pits, find a new office, one worthy of our venture in show business, and work out the details of our incorporation.

That Illinois state building!

What an architectural wonder!

Anyone confronted with this view of huge, muscular banked cliffs and buttes can see why Chicagoans are in love with architecture.

From here you see amoral might, beautiful in its way, at once a hope and a menace.

If George were a building, he would fit.

Bill and Aimée, as buildings, belong in New York.

A tour boat passes below.

From it Midwestern folk observe their Onion River Mecca.

He crossed the bridge and walked to Aimée's, arriving at a prompt ten a.m., and his three colleagues came down to meet him in the lobby, and they taxied together to the corner of LaSalle and Jackson, and went into the Chicago Board of Trade. They rode a fast, crowded escalator to the fourth floor where a sign threatened a thousand-dollar fine as punishment for jumping the spinning turnstiles, and kept on going to the fifth, the observation gallery.

There, below, on a rectangular floor big as a hockey rink, more than a thousand people – many coded by the color of their coats: blues, yellow, greens, bright reds predominating – surge and eddy and flow, run and jump and elbow, wave and yip and bellow, while the colors form shifting patterns and densities, in all, a tremendous turbulence producing such din as to penetrate into the gallery through the thick glass windows spanning its open side.

'People have lived with pigs for ten thousand years,' growled George, 'and this goes to show the sons-of-bitches haven't learned a fucking thing.'

The rushing churning waters swirled around a number of octagonal islands: the pits, ziggurats, four steps up on the outside, four steps down on the inside, suited to cock- or bull-bear fights, stages for shouting, gesturing traders, each wearing his initials on a badge, buying and selling futures contracts, flashing open hands, palms up palms down, beckoning, waving away, extending fingers to show the quantity and price offered or taken, and at the same time shouting it out, while messengers and runners snatch slips of paper from them or off the floor where they've been dropped and dash to the phonedesks at the sides of the hall and hand the papers to frenzied clerks who report the transactions to the brokerage offices.

Aimée pointed down at the largest pit. 'That's for soybeans. They may be doing my order right now.'

'Where the fuck are hogs?'

'Not in this floor show. Meats are dealt at the Mercantile Exchange.'

George stuck a pink lump of gum to the window. 'So that's how they set food and feed prices. I'd love to go down there and kick some ass.'

'What they're doing is more like buying and selling insurance to restrain wild price changes.'

Across the top of the big wall and over the ends stretched a huge electronic board listing commodities and currencies. It flashed prices and exchange rates and codes as it flared in spots everywhere at once with the prickly, measly, poxy eruptions by which it presided over pandemonium.

Thinking of the Grateful Dead, Billy stared in wonder at this energy storm. 'Amazing! Each guy gets one life, and of all the things they could do, some of them choose to spend theirs in this . . . these tornado pits.'

'It's not like that at all, Bill.' She gazed down on hysteria. 'Few people truly choose how they spend their lives. Not even me.'

80

'I walked out on my law firm today.'

The boon comrades went to the door and back down to the lobby. Aimée led the way in to the Ceres Café where they were seated at a table. 'Boys, they say by doing all the dealing in public, which is the why of this bedlam, food prices are set by show-and-tell democracy, where everyone can watch.'

'I don't believe it.'

'Nor do I, Phil. It's their myth, not mine. I thought a touch of the CBT would set the proper mood for our business, you know, serve as the Prologue of our as-yet unwritten ZEUGMA play. With the taste of the pits to flavor our thoughts, we're ready to compose.' She glanced at her fingernails, imagining claws, and back at her friends. 'What goes on down there, so many layers, strata. The big traders play and bluff like professional gamblers with an unlimited deck.'

'Let's begin,' said Billy, 'by agreeing on a title for the play.' He glanced at Aimée, as if for confirmation. 'How about ZEUGMA Tour Associates?'

'No no, no, Bill, no.'

'Why not? We have to tell people what we do.'

'No, sir. We don't want to define ourselves by what we do, at the moment or eternally, any more than I want to define myself by what I do, instead of being *me*.' Whatever that is. Have I been listening too trustingly to talk-show psychologists? 'If I were truly to believe I am a lawyer, I could not have walked out on my practice today. No, don't do it Bill, don't define yourself. Me, I'm no longer functioning as a lawyer, but I'm still Phil, I'm still here.' So what's this *Phil*? Jill? Shill? 'As a lawyer, I'm real. I belong to the Illinois and the Federal Bar. But that is a limited identity, for that I have limited liability. It's one aspect of me, embodied and confirmed. We're about to join our four together as one. It's a trick, like the Trinity. We're about to create a corporation, but not in our own image. Leave that to egomaniacs like Commodore Vanderbilt, or the Almighty. A corporation, in law, is a fictitious person. We can name our Baby, Quadrinity, as seems to be theologically fashionable. But we don't want to define Baby – soon like Athena to be born full-grown from our heads – by what Baby does. No. We'll give Baby a name open to anything. Yes. How about ... ZEUGMA Theme Group? ZEUGMA Theme Group can do anything at all.'

'That's it, Phil! All business is ZTG's business.'

Billy-boy has a quick mind. ZTG is the second level of acronym – the first level, what ZEUGMA stands for, is a fact as yet revealed to none.

'Bullshit. It's been revealed to me.'

'Tell us.'

'Zzyzyptic Executives' United Gilt Meat Association. That puts us last in every phone book in the world, including Germany.'

'Indeed it does, but it's too precise.'

Eventually, they agreed on ZTG.

And then Phil posed the questions. How much money do we need? How many shares of common stock do we issue? At what par value? How many shares do we give to ourselves, free? How many do we put on the market? How many do we keep unsold in reserve? Do we issue preferred stock? If so, how much? At what par? Will we sell bonds? How many shares of marketed stock does each of us buy? How do we apportion the free shares? One free for each one bought? How many do we give to Alexander? To stay in power, when electing directors we must vote for each other, so how do we grease that in the by-laws? What *are* the by-laws? Our fiscal year is when to when? 'And *cetera*, and *cetera*, so let's go find an office now, and discuss the questions while we're looking.'

'And the guts of it,' said George, 'of ZTG, is we have to trust each other, totally, from farrow to finish.'

'What's that?'

'You don't fucking know what *trust* is?'

'By farrow to finish,' said Billy, 'he means from birth to prime condition for market, when the backfat thickness is at its best.'

Looking at George, that powerful, yes, frightening enigma, aware there was no going back, only ahead into the unknown with these three strangers as companions, Phil suddenly felt as if in going for the sweet, he'd stuck to the flypaper.

He waited, after they left, to tell Aimée he had no wife, that Jenny was his law partner.

TWELVE

By midnight, they'd roughed out some of the answers, and, thanks to a stroke of good luck, eased along by George's cash and Phil's knowledge of real-estate agents, they'd leased the forty-seventh floor in the tower of a post-modernist building in the Loop for one year. Private offices and conference rooms already were in place by the windows; the best of these enjoyed magnificent views of the Lake. It would not be difficult to remodel them or to enclose work spaces in moveable partitions. The computer room would occupy the back corner, as seen from the entrance, and accounting, and the art department, and other necessary functions would be located in the central area. 'Yes, Bill, you're right. We don't need the whole floor, but I took it so the elevator would open on our receptionist.'

Their taxi had dropped George at the Y, and taken Aimée home, and now it sped toward Phil's office, where Billy and Phil would begin moving Phil's books and papers and other essentials to the ZEUGMA Theme Group's new world headquarters.

'Aimée likes to call you Al. Should I call you Bill or Al?'

'It's up to you. But if you decide on Al, every now and then I'll have to ask you: What did you do today to make the world a better place?'

'Okay. Al. It's a deal.'

'What did you do today to make the world a better place?'

'I stopped using my gifts to help rich corporations fuck over the people.' Even though the '60s are before his time, at twenty-two, this young man is *still* in 1968. Can I get back? 'At your age, Al, I was in law school.'

'Are you saying I should go to law school?'

'Oh, no – not at all.'

'My grandfather was a lawyer, but my father went to sea.'

No need to shine a light on the irony for him to see it. No need, either, to remark the beauty of the architecture as we approach the Loop with our first load. While crossing the bridge, Alexander glances at me, a thin, merry smile lighting his face, and then back at the water.

'Do they really dye the Chicago River green on Saint Patrick's Day?'

'Yes sir, green.'

They worked until about five in the morning when all Phil's papers and books and boxes stood piled around them in Phil's new private office. 'My partners are in for a surprise.' The cab driver came in with a case of beer they'd told him to fetch. They offered him one, which he declined on religious grounds, and watched him cross the shining empty floor to the elevator and vanish inside. Billy watched the doors close behind him and sat down on a box. 'We live in our past.' He smiled up at Phil, who was leaning against a window. 'You know, it seems to me the old is fading, and the new forming, and we live in both at once.'

'You feel that too, do you? For me, the old is represented by the crime of the century – the two World Wars, the cold war and the Gulf War – and its consequences. All of them are phases of the same atrocity, of which Korea, Vietnam and the Gulf were late manifestations.'

'You were wounded, right here in Chicago.'

I hadn't thought of it that way before. But I suppose I could be regarded as a wounded veteran of the struggle. Me, an old *veteran*. 'Al. You are a son of the post-war world.'

'I hope so; I'm trying to make that true.'

'And so both of us have to do our best to make the phase-out of the old and the phase-in of the new flow harmoniously, for if cacophony prevails, so will our mass-murder germs and gasses and machines.'

'All . . . right!' Billy sprang to his feet and squeezed Phil's hand.

'You're speaking my thoughts! It seems arrogant for one guy to try, but if I don't, who will? And now there's more than one. The ZEUGMA Theme Group, which could be millions.'

And that, Phil, is the theme you've had in mind all along. Can learning be the process of becoming aware of what you knew all the time? Alexander, this smiling young man, who is he? Can he truly be as good as he seems? The Billy Budd of the 1990s? Not possible. Why not? Cold beer and a warm cozy room high in the sky and fierce arctic winds outside clean windows, and this companion, and a future of bright hopes, not a bad place to be at forty-two.

'You know, Phil, since early August, I've been alone, or with George. It's nice talking with somebody else for a change, especially you.'

'Where were you before August?'

'As my dad would say, that's a long story.'

'Why don't you ever tell folks about your mother?'

'I can't. I don't remember her.' He drained his can and tossed it out on to the floor and it bounded and clattered right up to the elevator door. 'My dad, I always think of him as Lucky Al, was almost sixty-four when I was born. That song! Me, *I* greeted him when was sixty-four. He'd been seeing my mother. She was twenty-eight. And when she realized I was on the way, they decided to make her husband think he was the father.' He popped a can. 'It feels like I'm talking about something I read in the paper. Yeah. My mom and her husband were killed in a car wreck when I was still an infant, so Lucky Al brought me to Pacifica, near Frisco, where he lived, and told everyone my mom and dad had died in a wreck, and that I was his *great*-grandson.'

'So you're a love child.'

'Yes. Are you?'

'No, not much love, and no siblings, either. Mine was a commonplace high-bourgeois childhood played out on the stage of Oak Park, a hypocrisy wallow, except when you wallow that means you like it. I don't think they liked it. Some thrived in it, but not them. I don't think they like anything. They shit all over me for standing against the Vietnam War. Now they see their error but that's just a detail. They haven't changed at all.'

85

The last time I opened my feelings like this was in 1968 to my pal, Jenny.

'Lucky Al told me he'd reared me on two principles. Never lie to a child. And teach the child how to work, to use tools, to grow up without blocs. People use blocs to control children to rationalize their own weaknesses and anxieties. Blocs are inherited. And what did I inherit? Al's house, and the lucky family heirloom baseball. In 1915, Rogers Hornsby hit it into the bleachers in Saint Louis and Al's grandfather caught it, and handed it to Al with a smile Al said he could see in his mind like a photo. Yeah. It has red lacings and smells kinda greasy. My dad was supposed to become a lawyer, and he almost went for it, except that he'd been elected president of his high school in the Missouri town where he lived and went to the Scopes trial and came back and praised Darrow and evolution to a school assembly and the principal kicked his ass. So he hitched to New Orleans and found a job on a Lykes Brothers' ship and years later he helped organize the National Maritime Union. During the war he was torpedoed twice. And he made the Murmansk Run twice. Because the casualties on it were about thirty percent, he thought three trips would be pressing his luck. And Lucky Al, my dad, stood against the Vietnam War from way back when the French called Indochina the Big Cheese, because there was enough graft for everybody.'

And now Alexander stretches and yawns and squirms sensually on his box seat and smiles.

'Tell me, Al, what do you really think of Pig Spa Island?'

'I'm along for the ride.' He held a hand up, palm out, in an inadvertant sell-five gesture. 'As George said, we have to trust each other from farrow to finish. You've heard my farrow. So now for what may be my finish.'

He hesitates.

'In August I deserted from the Marine Corps.'

Now he tells me about Farnsworth and The Fly, and I tell him he joined and deserted for the right patriotic reasons and I should know because I dodged the draft for the right patriotic reasons, I hope.

'Phil. I'm *scared*.'

'You wouldn't be human if you weren't.'

'Portsmouth Naval Penitentiary is as bad as Auschwitz. Phil, I know responsibility comes with the act, and I'm not saying poor me, but I also know I could not stand prison.'

'Did you desert because boot camp was too tough for you?'

'No, Phil. Nothing was real bad, and a lot of it was fun. The marching manual, and the obstacle course, and the rifle range, and hand-to-hand stuff. Man, let me tell you, I always avoided fights before, but doubly so from now on, because I can't draw the line. It's not-at-all, or one-hundred-percent.'

'Never lie to your lawyer.'

He looked hurt.

So, Phil, tell him you believe him. That made him feel better. And you *do* believe him.

'George said never tell anybody, ever, for any reason at all, and now I've told you, but I know it's okay.'

'You told George?'

'Yes.'

'Have you told anybody else?'

'No.'

'Well, don't. Not even Aimée.'

'All right. Not even Aimée.'

'Who else knows?'

'My Godfather, Uncle Bill. I wrote him by a circuitous route.'

'Anybody else?'

'Not anyone I can name.'

'Think.'

'Well, yes. The records of the Corps. And, I suppose, the FBI.'

'Where have you used your social security number?'

'Other than to enlist, just once. To pay taxes on what I earned the summer of 1991 working on the squid boat.'

And now all the particulars. Details of enlistment. Places lived. Schools. Expose the whole paper trail. Not bad. A path, not a freeway. 'From now on and forever, your name is Alexander William Burke. Which is what it really is, anyway. Write your Uncle Bill. Tell him. If no one's come checking by now, we can bet they won't come later. He can tell people you were discharged for a heart murmur. Beyond that, he should clam up.'

'Honest Phil, do you really think you can do something?'

Me, I've never hacked into computers for fun. I don't think it honorable or ethical, or moral. But in this case, in the interests of world peace, why the fuck not? I can't make it any worse for Alexander than it already is. It might even work. 'Tell you what, Al. I'll try a little hacking. Slip a virus or two into their myth.'

PART THREE

OF WORLDS

ORDO NOVUS SECLORUM

Breed, nest, and survive to breed
and nest again. That's what it's
all about. Everything else is
illusion, delusion – romance.

Aimée (Amy) Jones
Nemausus (Nîmes), 1993

THIRTEEN

Billy turned his back on frosty windows to glance around his private office and out the door at the first workday of 1993, Tuesday, 5 January, the grand premiere of ZTG's workforce in action. Since I read the history of its tradition in *Bohemia, Then and Now*, I've thought myself a bohemian. What a change! Me, Bill Burke, in a suit instead of a Deadhead sweatshirt, and wearing a tie! Some bohemian! Al refused to own a suit. Said suits affect character for the worse. But this is not a suit. No. It's a dark brown pinstripe costume to wear on stage, as required by my part in the play announced in the dramatis personae of the play-bill, my office door: A. W. Burke, Director.

Aimée and Phil had also been cast as directors. And so had George. The articles of incorporation provided for one more director, *ex officio*, the chief administrator. At ten a.m. they would interview the two remaining candidates and decide which one of these to entrust with disciplining details and making things happen. Phil had organized ZTG on the council-manager model of city government. Policy would be made by the directors, four of whom were to be selected from the owners of common stock, and the fifth, in deviation from the model, would be the officer, who, as with a city manager, would be responsible for executing policy. The boss of the Board of Directors, selected by the owner-directors from among their number, would preside over meetings and be ceremonial and titular chief.

Because George had invested twenty million dollars, they gave the job to him, and included his choice of title in the by-laws.

The chief would not be a Head, or a Chair. No. On George's door in gilt letters the play-bill announced: G. Baxter, Praefectus Castrorum.

How do you act out *that* part?

What an amazing change of fortune! From a fugitive on the run, almost broke, clad in shorts, hungry, soaked in sweat, so frustrated by futile hitching as to confide in a cow – to this! Cast in a leading rôle in an ad-lib write-it-as-you-do-it play, dressed in an expensive suit, preparing to assess and judge two potential general managers. And worth two *millions* of imaginary but potential dollars.

To capitalize at two hundred millions, they had authorized issuance of two-point-five million shares of common stock, par value one hundred dollars each. Of these, for starters, they would sell 1,225,000 shares outside and 275,000 to themselves: 200,000 to George, 60,000 to Aimée, and, to Phil, 15,000. Half a million would be held in reserve for future scamming. Half a million more they gave to themselves, free: 200,000 to George, 200,000 to Aimée, 80,000 to Phil, and 20,000 to Alexander William Burke, Esquire. Until outsiders bought in, George owned the controlling interest, but his colleagues formed a majority of the board. Should he sell shares so as to name new board members, the old ones could use his money to buy themselves out at an immense profit.

Money.

Uncle Bill used to say, 'Billy. Imagine you have a million and don't have to worry about money any more. What would you do then? Well, that's what you really want to do.'

He gazed around his fancy furnished but undecorated office, and at the snow blowing outside where the homeless are. Money. He thought of his stock, worth anything between nothing and millions, and from that thought came a rush of passion. Money means comfort. Independence. Inducing people to do what you want. Sure. Power. But none of that produced this hot feeling. An urge struck to run through the building. Tell everyone to take the day off. Invite the homeless inside to get warm. It's true, what Aimée says, true. Most of the tenants of the big Loop buildings – of all such buildings – are like us. All they have is offices, alive with people cast by personnel into conventional bit-parts they've been schooled to assume and, as in Stanislavsky theater, become. Out there in the wilds, far from the world's center at State and Madison, are smaller nodes whence representatives of the Head Office emerge to penetrate along web lines into society. Here, in these towers, a bank, an insurance company, commercial and interstate realtors. Law firms. Ad agencies. Architects. Publishers and psychologists and manufacturers' agents and scores of other concentrations of folk who don't make anything or grow anything, and like us here at ZTG, don't do much but administer themselves.

Hanging his jacket on the back of his chair, Billy slackened his tie and sat down at his desk, suddenly aware of the smell of new furniture. Bacon and eggs would be better. In truth, all these offices administer more than themselves. We do too. Or we're starting to. Phil went to Actors Equity and hired some trustworthy professionals to start hot rumors about our stock offering. Public relations and the ad department are working on a propaganda campaign to sell the stuff. Phil is going to inaugurate the sale at a classy banquet to be held for prospects at the Palmer House. As for the right island? We've all begun the search.

Billy leaned back in his chair and looked out his door at the action, people hypnotized by computer terminals; others, brisk, swirling about among the props, carrying papers and cases and objects, and he remembered the beer can bouncing and clattering across the shiny empty floor from Phil's office all the way to the elevator.

This building!

The Loop!

Our environment is us.

We *should* keep pigs in our empty space.

He set his radio to a classical music station and opened the folder containing the applications of the two finalists to be interviewed. There'd been three, until a private detective Phil had hired investigated the man's vitae and disclosed a tendency to exaggerate past employment and training. The two survivors passed the private-eye truth test, and, at least on paper, seemed superlatively able to do the job. So I'll listen, and observe, and keep my mouth shut. Phil and Aimée, and George too, know more about this than I do, so I'll be silent and alert and, as for my choice, we shall see what we shall see.

His door clicked shut.

Aimée!

A joyful smile spread over her and she cried out, 'Happy New Year, Burke!'

They embraced, and he felt elated, and then densely horny, all these futile months of hand and dream, and he blushed, and she perched on his desk, swinging her feet, kicking heels against it.

'I'll sit and chat with you for a while before we go do the interviews.'

'Love it.'

Standing there directly in front of her he became aware of a flush and rush and a huge aching hard-on.

'Looks like I get to you.'

'Yeah, yeah, yeah, you do.'

She grasped him. 'You're a big boy, Burke.'

He drew away and sat down. 'Sweetheart, I want you to come to dinner with me tonight.'

'All right! I'd love to dine with Alexander the *Great*.'

'Me, I'm still at the Y. I have my own room now, where I can jerk-off in peace, but I hate it.'

'So?'

'So, say *your* line.'

'Move in with me.'

'Love to. After dinner, Streeter's, we'll go up to your – our – place for dessert.'

'And practice figurative expressionism while marinating in rock'n'roll.' She picked up the applications and leafed through them while he struggled for self-control, only it was more like swimming. 'Alexander.' She glanced up. Slate-gray eyes. 'Looking through all the applications, these two and the rest, I see promising people, good-looking too, if you can believe their résumés and photos, and I wonder what happens to all the hot young idealists like you and me, the valedictorians and summa cum laudes and Phi Betas and Rhodes Scholars and Mensas, the hopes-of-the-world, the hope of the world, who should be leading the way to the big changes in time to finesse self-genocide. Where the fuck are they?'

'Same place we are. Here in this office building, working some selfish scam.'

'Except here at Zed-Tee-Gee, what we're doing, you and Phil and me anyway, is trying to get the old order to metamorphose itself.'

'And *that's* what you want to begin at Hog Spa Isle?'

'Yes. The first of our coming attractions.'

'You're not in it for money and power?'

'Fuck no!'

'Compared to George, you're going to be one hell of a *sympatica* roommate.'

'It's almost time. Let's go chat with him.'

They walked across the busy floor, nodding and smiling at people, and passed by George's glassed-in reception room, upstage for the lush blonde George had caste in the rôle of his court chamberlain, and went into an unmarked doorway and along the corridor leading to the private entrance of the huge, posh office of the *Praefectus Castrorum* of ZEUGMA Theme Group, of all its personnel and projects and property and investments. George rose and came from behind his desk to greet them. He embraced them both. 'Sure looks like we got the show on the road!'

He plucked three glasses from a cabinet and carried them across to his cooler, a big green-glass bottle inverted in a frame, filled with the best Chablis, and marked in flowing script: *CARPAE VINO*. It bubbled and burped as he filled the glasses. He offered the first to Billy. 'Kiss this, sowboy.'

'No thanks. For what we're doing now, I have to be sharp.'

Aimée smiled and waved hers off. A frosty window, big as the one in the Board of Trade gallery, spanned the wall behind George, and the wall over the cooler displayed his map of old Prussia, showing Swinemünde and the River Swine.

Beaming joy, Billy put an arm over George's shoulders and hugged. 'Sure beats a dead city bus.'

'Fucking-A.'

'Now folks'll respect the boss swino.'

'*Praefectus Castrorum!*' George was beaming too. 'I'm going to get me one of them little pet yuppie pigs they breed in China.'

'I'm moving out of the Y – and in with my favorite Zed-saying Canadienne.'

George clouded. 'The bitches always get you in the end.'

Phil came in, and they set three more chairs behind George's desk, so they'd look like an appelate court. Billy perched on the back of one, his tie still loose, and said, 'I'm the kind of guy who judges others by himself, which I guess is childish, or maybe, I hope, childlike. And I've never hired anybody, or looked for work, either. My fishboat job came from conversing with folks in a bar. So I'll let you guys do the talking, and after telling you what I think, I'll go along with you.'

'Same here,' said Aimée. 'I've dealt with beaucoup clients, and some business people, but the number of folks I've hired, eh, you can count on one hand. Other than a plant doctor and a grain gambler, all I've been's a student and a cocktail waitress, and I sailed as crew on a boat once. There's *my* résumé. Reviewing it, I see you guys should ask the questions, and me, I should listen, so I shall.'

Phil sat down in his place, and yawned and stretched. As always, he wore a blue blazer and gray pants. 'The big thing to remember is we're looking at attitudes while seeking substance. People's public attitudes usually conceal what they truly are. Today, we're in power, so they'll Uncle-Tom us, if we let them.'

George dropped into his chair, and Aimée and Billy sat in theirs. George polished his watch on the tweedy sleeve of his sports jacket. Refreshing his memory, Billy glanced at the names of the prospects. They were about to choose between C. P. Post III, and Janet Ma.

'No broad can handle this job,' said George. 'So far as I'm concerned, this interview's a formality.'

Aimée made a face.

'I'm going to call both those bastards in here at once.'

'Why not?' said Phil. 'Sounds like fun.'

'Yes. Both of them. That shit-sucking crotch-licking MBA, and that cuntless slant-eye.'

He spoke into the intercom, and immediately his sexy blonde chamberlain ushered them in and left them standing before the chiefs of the ZEUGMA Theme Group.

C. P. Post III, and Janet Ma.

That shit-sucking crotch-licking MBA, and that cuntless slant-eye.

'I am the *Praefectus Castrorum* of this outfit, and I will ask the questions.'

Post seemed typecast, in George-Bush style, for the rôle of CEO. Ma stood tall and slender in a severe gray dress.

'Get chairs for yourselves.'

Post fetched two chairs, and seated Ma, who regarded him with contempt.

'Post. I'll begin with you.'

George went to the cooler and filled his glass. He offered wine to his victims, and they demurred. He sat heavily and leaned back. That woman, Post seemed to body-say, my competitor, is not half the man I am. Aimée smiled at her thought. George glanced at the applications clamped to his clipboard.

'Harvard business school grad, ain't you?'

'Best training in the world.'

'For sophisticating greed.'

'For cost-effective administration.'

'Your physical duplicate, Post, existed twenty thousand years ago. He couldn't read or write, and when it got cold, he wore a bear skin. If he were coming here to be interviewed for this job, what would you tell him to wear?'

'The same thing I'm wearing.'

'Could he do the job?'

'Impossible.'

'Are you loyal and trustworthy?'

'Just try me.'

'Are you truthful?'

'I hope you don't doubt me.'

'Are you truthful?'

'I try to be.'

'Are you?'

'Sure.'

'So when I question you, you'll tell the truth?'

'Of course.'

'Post, what kind of music will you use to keep our wage-slaves lean and alert?'

Aimée began filing her nails. Here comes the fun! Who is this guy, really, and why does he want to work with us? George told him music will be playing on the floor at all times. C. P. Post III. His voice and style resemble Phil's, and he's about the same age, only he's dark-haired and slim-hipped, and blundering around the music barn like a brain-damaged horse.

'Get to the point. What kind?'

'Classical, Mr Baxter. Classical.'

'Classical! Musak for imperial courts and yuppies.'

'Top-forty.'

'And what foods will we put in the lunchroom and vending machines to keep our peons lean and alert?'

'I'll consult a professional dietician.'

George riffled the application papers.

'If you're so fucking hot, how come you need a job?'

'I was leveraged out.' Annoyance began to show in his voice. 'They're bringing in a new team.'

'Are you well informed?'

'I like to think so.'

'Can hogs grow to weigh a ton?'

'Oh, yes.'

'Wrong.'

'I don't know much about hogs.'

'Are you willing to learn?'

'Whatever.'

'Yesterday, I read about a Normandy hog weighing fifteen hundred pounds. It's four feet tall and ten feet long. Do you consider yourself the equal of a noble animal like that?'

'*I don't compare myself to hogs.*'

'Don't wet your pants.'

'What!'

'What do you think of Alexander's father, Philip II of Makedon?'

'Who's that?'

'What of Victor Hugo?'

'One of Germany's greatest.'

'You ever studied windshields?'

'We going to make windshields?'

'Have you studied windshield poetry?'

'Windshield poetry?'

'Have you?'

'Can't say that I have.'

'Would you let a woman keep you, would you give up work for good?'

'You can't be serious.'

'Would you live on prostitution, would you rob us if you could?'

'Certainly not!'

'Would you kick your dear old mother? Would you smack her in the moosh?'

'My mother and I get along very well, thank you.'

'Would you knock her down and fuck her, and suck her greasy tush?'

'You know I wouldn't.'

'Would you?'

98

'I'm not like that.'

'I don't know what you're like. Would you?'

'Now look, George. We're a team. We'll be working together.'

'You will refer to me as Mr Praefectus Castrorum. Do you understand?'

'Yes.'

Listening to George left Aimée smiling through and through. His mother! Would Post knock her down and fuck her, or not? Measured by money and status, what would his price be? Would he charge extra to suck her greasy tush, or would he throw that in for free? Some interview! Let George do it – a much wiser motto than hitherto apparent. George turned to the other candidate.

'Janet Ma, you have a master's in history?'

'Yes, Stanford.'

'With a minor in economics?'

'Yes, economics.'

'Are you loyal and trustworthy?'

'Yes.'

'Truthful?'

'Yes.'

'What would you tell your ignorant troglodyte bear-skinned duplicate to wear to this interview?'

'A pig skin.'

'Not a bear skin?'

'No. A pig skin.'

'Why?'

'Because I recognized your Normandy hog.'

'Not mine. Captain Streeter's.'

'Yes. Captain Streeter's. That white hog was the star of the traveling animal show he started when he came back from the Civil War. He billed it as a white elephant.'

'How did *you* know that?'

'Shortly after I moved to Chicago, I read his book, *Captain Streeter, Pioneer*, published here in 1914. Why? I was curious about the stories I'd heard about Streeterville, and about the bar, too. So last week when I got the call about the interview I reread Streeter's book, because I think his attitude derives from the same source as the ZEUGMA Theme Group's does.'

'Don't you think we're a bunch of pus-drinking Money Hogs?'

'No. But I remember them. Streeter gives a third of his book to denouncing the Money Hogs who run our country as betrayers of the pioneer spirit, and he dedicates his book to future generations, hoping they'll reject the Money Hog mental-set and be good Americans.'

'Why do you want to run ZEUGMA Theme Group?'

'I think civilization stands on the edge of self-destruction, of nuclear suicide, because the Money-Hog mentality prevails, and is taught everywhere, on TV, in ads, in magazines, to the younger generation. The public interest – what Streeter remembered from boyhood in backwoods Michigan and called Pioneer Co-operation – must hold dominion worldwide, or it's *finito la commedia*. I think you – all of you – have the imagination, the commitment, and the resources to do something about it, and that doing something about it is ZTG's *raison d'être*, and so I want to step in and help.'

'So what the fuck you got against hogs?'

'Nothing. I like hogs. Real suidae. Compare me to them, any time, but not to the metaphorical kind.' She opened her purse and from it drew a pen and a dollar, and where it declared IN GOD WE TRUST she inserted an L into GOD. 'IN GOLD WE TRUST. That's the truth, or closer to it, anyway. Hypocrisy!' She passed the bank note to George. 'Most of us don't really believe in God – me not at all – so printing this on our money is a lie. In Streeter's time it wasn't on the money, or in the pledge of allegiance, either. In Gold We Trust. Sure. When we wallow with Money Hogs.'

'Yeah.' He returned her dollar. 'Do you believe in the equality of the sexes?'

'I do.'

'And it makes no difference if a person sprouts or splits?'

'Relative to ZTG? No.'

'So you and C. P. Post III should be treated the same. Right?'

'Sure. The same.'

'In all respects?'

'Theoretically, yes.'

'How would you approach this job?'

'When engaged in administration ... excellence, rule through the force of virtue, is achieved by emulating the North Star.'

'What the fuck does that mean?'

'I remain in my place. All others move around me.'

'Ma, what kind of music will you play to keep our office-slaves lean and alert?'

'By music, we don't mean classical or country, jazz or top-forty. These are only externals.'

'What kind, Ma?'

'Can I control the office-slaves by music? Can I reach the sky by stairs?'

'And what do we feed them?'

'Do not do unto others what you would not have others do unto you.'

'What about Post's dietician?'

'It's better to light one candle than curse the darkness.'

'What do you think of Philip of Makedon?'

'I've yet to meet a man as fond of excellence as he is of outward appearances.'

'So what the fuck is excellence?'

'Be humble at home, public-spirited at work, loyal to people and to truth, and when among barbarians, do not vacate these principles.'

'Would you let a woman keep you, would you give up work for good?'

'Continuouus readaptation to suit the whims of others undermines excellence.'

'Would you live on prostitution, would you rob us if you could?'

'Who is not reliable is useless. How far can you drive a car with no tires?'

'Would you kick your dear old mother, would you smack her in the moosh?'

'The best are wholly at ease; the worst, always on edge.'

'Would you knock her down and whip her, and suck her greasy tush?'

'Set the example, then invite others to follow.'

'What?'

'Why use a cannon to kill a chicken when you can wring its neck?'

Looking furious, George sprang to his feet and pounded his desk.

'I know what you're doing! You're making me interview Confucius!'

'Not entirely true.'

'What *is* entirely true?'

'When I converse with my student I am in conversation with my teacher.'

George strode around the desk, and towered over her. Chopping the words, he said: '*Goong Hi Faht Joy.*'

'What's that?'

'Chinese.'

'I don't know Chinese. I'm an American.'

'Knowledge is knowing one might not know what one knows.'

'Indeed it is,' she replied, smiling.

The smile reflected in his face. '*Goong Hi Faht Joy* – Happy New Year!' He embraced her. 'Baby, you just got yourself a job!'

FOURTEEN

Janet Ma pushed her plate aside, bare except for duck bones and red raspberries from the sauce. In the jargon of art critique, hers had been a manneristic dish, a pretentious degeneration from roast duck rich with natural gravy. Her four colleagues, and their banquet guests, some two-score of them, mainly over-the-counter securities dealers and brokers, seemed content with what they'd ordered from the Palmer House menu. Can we soon say as much about what they'll select from the mono-dish ZEUGMA TG menu? Wine waiters move about freshening glasses. In the jargon, this event qualifies as a performance piece with dimensions in the surreal. Welcome to the Plunderbund Convention! On a small stage a string quartet is playing the music of good digestion. Public relations scams, advertisements, and a shiny prospectus, along with actors and private detectives – all of them working together at channeling dreams and energies into Greed Canyon – had produced this pool of prospects. She caught a sex smell by her side. Alexander. Smell no evil. Not on the job. Cajun catfish, savored and eaten, had set him at ease. He avoids Chicago grease food. He has the looks, and the idealism, and the courage of Alexander, but he's four inches taller and devoid of intense ambition. Why did management choose white flowers to ornament our tables? Our Purity of purpose? Thanks to the adverse balance-of-trade and its rebounding dollars, the Japanese and other aliens may have bought so much of America by now that nothing's left in the store but lottery tickets and ZTG stock. Dessert came and went. A fluffy meringue seemed favored. Sweet and without substance, like our securities.

Janet Ma rose to her feet and tapped glass for attention.

'It's my honor, on the first business day of spring, 1993, to welcome you here on behalf of the Board of Directors, to break bread with you, and to share with you a rich investment opportunity for yourselves and your clients. I now take the pleasure of introducing a prominent member of our board, a man known to many of you, who will flesh out both our general plan and that of our first development, an island tourist-spa for the wealthy, where, because we will marry the bold machismo of the wild-boar hunt to the refined amusements of the baronial palace, our guests can live the life of the modern hereditary aristocrat in full enjoyment of all its comforts and privileges.' She bowed to her right. 'I present my friend and colleague, Philmer P. Swait.'

Actors find rôles in the myths of others; my associates find theirs in our own.

Phil stood, beaming the charm of his aristocratic-but-business-like blazer-clad self. Aimée smiled up at him. Different myths have different new-year dates, but most build meaning around the sun-guided, greening-browning, planting-harvesting, birth-death pattern. Phil told a joke that pleased them. Phil limned an image of lawns and woods and cotillions and castles and hunts and subsequent profits, composing in all a picture of large appeal to snobbery and greed. A good herald, indeed, of our ZTG myth – whatever that turns out to be. George, sitting there serenely digesting Virginia baked ham, will put guts into it, and the sowboy will impart the zestful ideals of youth. She'd been a woman fallen between illusions until Alexander moved in. No regrets there, except a flush of annoyance in remembering him accidentally smashing the china pig.

'And now, my friends, as the central phase of a very pleasant evening, we invite you to step into the adjoining ballroom, where you will find an open bar, and opportunity to socialize, enjoy music, and do business with our representatives.' These came mainly from the trading department of Aimée's broker's office, and thus brought an old and respected firm into symbolic union with inflating, upstart ZTG. 'And before we part, my friends, allow me to leave you with this thought, one which all of us in the securities industry share: it is blessed to give; it is blessed to receive ... and it is blessed to solicit funds.'

They applauded in polite contentment. Was that last bit too

much? No, Phil. Not at all. Fun and thrill, these should be the theme, but not the object, of the ZTG adventure. Back on Haight Street, a quarter-century ago, did any of the folks we fed tonight enjoy free sandwiches? Not bloody likely. Back then when I was trying to stop the war, their war, they were the ones who kept telling me to get a haircut and take a bath.

George stood, smiling, and shook hands. 'Those bastards wouldn't make a good pimple on a sow's ass.'

'Do you think they enjoyed my paean of capital gain and parvenu snobbery?'

'Did Mrs Lincoln make the theater give her money back?'

The next morning, soothed awake by fresh cool sunlight coming in her east windows, Aimée snuggled up to Billy and reached over his hips to cradle his jock, and she was holding a trembling, wounded bird. The clock radio sang sad blues. The bird stirred. Nowadays, real poetry is in song lyrics, and maybe always has been. She drew the covers up over their heads and cuddled and teased him awake. The bird reared in its nest. Billy let out a loud stinking fart and sprang out of bed, whooping: 'Time for your reality pill!' And he snatched off the covers and slid on to her and they made laughing love until, calm and happy, they sat smiling on the side of the bed.

Billy stood and went toward the bathroom. He turned in front of its door. 'A new day rises from the ashes of the old!'

'My favorite bird.'

'Try to make that canard fly in Arizona.'

He closed the door behind him and waters flowed. She opened her bedside dictionary and found *Phoenix*:

In Egyptian mythology, a bird of great beauty, said to live for five or six hundred years, and then consume itself by fire, only to rise from its ashes and live through another cycle, often used as a symbol of regeneration or immortality,

which is the way she read it to him through gurglings and flushings and the panels of the door. Is *that* a zeugma? Well, close. He came out, toweling himself. 'Hygiene time, honey.' She showered and shaved her legs and armpits and did a little more trimming and plucking here and there. Wet spots on the toilet seat! When she'd

105

finished, she sprang out and flung a bar of soap at him and he caught it.

'You pissed on the seat!'

They kissed and he said, 'What do we wear today?'

She scratched a bit of rime from the window. The Wacker-walkers had dressed in heavy coats and earmuffs and were blowing frosty clouds. Soon, clad in heavy coats and earmuffs and following breath-clouds, Aimée and Billy walked half a mile on slippery sidewalks to their office, as they always did, mixing exercise and business. Today, she would work on financial matters, and he would continue his study of potential islands. Late in the afternoon, in George's office, they were all to meet with their broker and hear how many fish they'd hooked on the banquet bait and what that implied for the future.

When Billy arrived at his desk, he spread out a map of Indonesia, and, from time to time referring to the federal government's *Area Handbook*, he highlighted islands which seemed to be the right size and otherwise geographically promising. When, eventually, he finished locating what Earth had to offer ZTG in this respect, he would eliminate such islands as cannot or may not be bought outright, and all those in countries with too many laws, or having regulations insoluble in graft. The phone rang. George.

'Bill, come over. I want you to meet our new security chief.'

Happy and joyfully alive, Billy ambled across the office floor, lavishing smiles and hellos and hi's and what's-happenings and how-you-doings, and walked into George's reception room, by his sexy chamberlain, and stepped through the carved wooden door behind her into the presence of the *Praefectus Castrorum* himself.

His Excellency, perched on his desk drinking cooler wine, waved a big hello.

Seated in a chair, feet on the desk, holding a glass: Tom the police sergeant last seen at the Battle of Pigville.

My Pig Spa Island is Portsmouth Naval Penitentiary!

'You remember Tom. He's an angel from Heaven.'

Tom saluted hello.

'Angel from Heaven! No. Cop from Indiana.'

'Deep cover.'

'Felon retriever.'

George has turned me in, that double-crossing sadistic son-of-a-bitch.

Chewing bubble gum and drinking wine at the same time.
'Fill your glass, Bill, and sit.'
Why not?
'Tom ain't a cop now. Welcome him to our team.'
'Welcome to our team, Tom.'
Up rises George's glass, offering wassail: 'Tom, Tom, the farmer's son / Stole a pig and away he run!'
'Fee fi fo, fun / I smell the blood of a po-lice-mun!'
Glasses clicked.
'Back there, when I talked with Tom alone, just before the battle, I told him he could keep all the pigs he could steal, and I gave him a signed, dated bill-of-sale, blank, so he could fill in the number, and take them to market, and sell them easy. The more he could steal, the better. The end of Pigville was written all over the fucking wall, so I figures letting my pal here get some good out of them sure beats the shit out of letting the fucking town get good payback from busting up my family.'
'Yes, Bill. And that hog money, plus my savings, plus selling my house, plus what I'd accumulated in the pension fund added up to enough to let me quit my job and go out and see all them places I've always dreamed about.' His kindly, flaccid face no longer spoke sadness.
'Fucking-A! Pigs and police. Pig *means* police in slang, yeah, like I say, pigs and police, and other people too, when they get too bored, they begin biting off tails.'
'I've never ever even been in Chicago before, and now, sonny, I'm Security Director of a big corporation, with *headquarters* in Chicago.'
'And don't that give him the hots! Headquarters in Chicago, but who the fuck knows where the *hindquarters* will be? Wherever the fuck we want. London, Bangkok, Rome, Hong Kong.'
At least, for the time being, Portsmouth, New Hampshire, had not made the list.
'Tom, believe me, I'm just as glad as George is you're on our team, and can chase your dream. So tell me, are they still after me? Are they going to extradite me?'
'They couldn't find shit about you down at the station or in the computer networks, but we didn't try very hard, either. In fact, we closed the case. You know, no harm done except a slew of dead pigs, and some ammo blown away, and the big profit they got from

selling all the pigs I couldn't steal. And, well, what the hell? We didn't know what your last name is. How do we go looking for a white male, about twenty-one, six-foot, light-brown hair, from Monterey, California, answers to the name of Bill? Shit. We had to put Bill Doe on the warrant, and that's a fucking fact.'

'But I told you. Burke.'

'Oh! Right. In all the hoopla I lost my notes, and I could not fucking remember.' He leaned back even farther and lit a cigar. Feet on desk, balanced on back chair-legs, he's a county sheriff on TV. 'George is a bad influence on me. Sonny, don't let him get to you. On the job, and around town, I never had a foul mouth. It ain't my nature. It's disrespectful to the ladies. But one hour with George, and, well – would you listen to me now?'

Because Tom wanted to start his long-delayed world tour with food, and the more exotic the better, they went to lunch at a Thai restaurant. Billy declined wine so as to remain sharp for the afternoon meeting. Four p.m. found him with Aimée, Phil, Janet, George, and their broker, sitting around George's conference table. A pitcher of cooler wine and some glasses stood in the middle. George's housebroken, bulldog-sized, pot-bellied pet mini-pig slept underneath. George poured a refill, then spoke in a loud voice, indicating chatter time had ended and business time was here.

'Me and Bill, we been looking at maps of islands, checking things out with the government handbooks to the countries they're in. As I go along, I been working out the pig-to-person ratio for each country. Yeah. The more welcome pigs are, the more welcome we are, if you get my meaning. Here in USA, the p:p ratio is one-to-three. America's pigs are a third as numerous as America's people. Expressed in weight? America's pigs and her people weigh the same. You rank the world's countries by p:p ratio, you find USA's way down the list. So who the fuck's number one? Denmark, that's who. With a stunning p:p of almost three-to-one! Now ain't that something!'

Aimée made a face. The broker smiled. Before the meeting, Phil had told Billy not to expect too much of him. 'That this broker graduated from Dartmouth business school means, in the words of the Dartmouth alma-mater song, he has the granite of New Hampshire, in his muscles, and his brains.' Looking at him, reminded of New Hampshire, Billy felt a panic spasm. Insofar as the feds are concerned, only death closes the case on deserters.

Can any of this be real? Three hundred thousand people in these office buildings right now, thousands at meetings like this, acting their rôles as usual in their normal daily theater of the absurd, where nothing is made and nothing is grown, where, to its quotidian practitioners, the surreal seems real, as natural and right as life for those in *All Quiet on the Western Front*, or for the Marine guards in Portsmouth, New Hampshire, or the atom bomb scientists at lunch in Livermore. Maybe the true purpose of all this inner-Loop activity is to support the pleasure domes that top executives have built on all the highest towers – here, New York, Dallas, Los Angeles, London – and networked by personal jets and helicopters. Aimée's nudging! Oh, yeah – the broker has begun to speak.

'For all of us, this is a real surprise.' He glanced at the papers before him, as if he could not believe what he read there. 'Never saw anything like it in my life. They bought it all – *all*; one million, two hundred and twenty-five thousand shares, every doggone share in the offering. Five different dealers, all men I know, were waiting for me when I came into the hospitality room during dinner to set up my table. They missed the banquet and the speeches, but they bought the entire offering, and at par. Let me tell you, when your guests came in after dinner to do business, and learned those early birds had eaten up the whole pie, the fur flew. Yessir, flew.'

'You're talking like we weren't fucking there!'

'My job at this meeting is to report what happened and my impressions thereof.'

'Okay, talk.'

'As you know, we had some mighty angry dealers there. And very, very curious, too. The fellows who missed the dinner and got the stock, they made enough on commissions to buy a lifetime of dinners, believe me. Thinking all this over, it means to me that unless you market the half-million shares you hold in reserve, buy them yourselves, somebody out there could put together a controlling interest. You can't market your reserve without going through a lot of legal rigamarole and red tape. So, well, how do you explain it? They brought cashiers' checks with them, already made out. The usual banks. They must have agreed about the purchase and the details beforehand.' He sat for a moment in silence. 'You have more money than God,' he said, 'but you may have lost control of it.'

'Well,' said George, breaking the hush of contemplation, 'don't that just fill the fucking drool cup.'

'Sir,' said Janet to the broker, 'have you any ideas about who the real owners are?'

'No. Except, from my knowledge and experience of these matters, I know this is most unusual and must, in some respects, be illegitimate.'

'Can we find out who the mysterious owners – or owner perhaps, who they are?'

'I'm afraid not. The law regulates the seller, to protect the buyer. Insofar as I know, the only regulation of the buyer relates to margins, or the kind of instruments used in payment, but here we have full payment by cashier's check.'

'And so, if someone has bought a controlling interest, and uses it to call a special meeting of the board, they could replace the current directors with their own. Right?'

The broker sat looking at Janet, tapping a pencil, and thinking. 'Well ma'am, I'm not a lawyer, of course, but, yes. I think they could do that.'

'So they could take the policy-making power away from us, and use it themselves?'

'In that case, yes.'

'And soon?'

'Relatively soon.'

'The Mafia is in the over-the-counter stock market, isn't it?'

'Profoundly.'

'That aside, the new owners, controlling the board, could buy their own stock back, and spend all the money my board members have invested on chinchilla farms and toilet paper?'

'Yes.'

'Right now, can ZTG buy our stock back with *their* money?'

'I suppose so.'

Janet left with the broker to deposit the checks and tell the business office to complete the necessary formalities and issue the stock certificates. The directors sat musing in a silence interrupted only by the sound of George chewing gum. Billy spoke first.

'Technically, our stock offering did not begin before Phil invited our guests to visit our broker in the hospitality room. If we have to, surely we can go to court and get the sale annulled.'

'My experience,' said Phil, 'leads me to agree with Ambrose Bierce's view that lawsuits are machines you enter as a pig and leave as a sausage.'

110

George's hand on the table clenched and Billy saw the wild-sow tattoo and *LEGIO DIX FRETENSIS* tremble.

'You dig deep down under this shit. You wonder why the broker didn't wait until after dinner when all the suckers were in the same sty. We could have got them fighting for stock and maybe sold it over par. That son-of-a-bitch broker kept saying he's on our side, and maybe we've been screwed. Me, I kept remembering, he represented us, in law he *was* us, and it takes two to fuck — for fun or money.'

FIFTEEN

'This game is getting more interesting every day,' Phil said to Billy, sitting in Phil's office, drinking beer, and rolling the cans out his door on to the empty office floor, where, if not stopped by a desk or computer stand, they bounded and clanked all the way to the elevator. 'I've been meaning to tell you, for relaxation, I've been reading Captain Streeter's book.'

After the meeting, and reviewing it over dinner, Aimée and George and Janet had gone home, and, on Phil's invitation, Billy went back to the office.

'What I knew about Streeter before is only what I'd heard people say. He's a Chicago legend I've always liked one hell of a lot better than those about criminal bootleggers. For me, his myth's up there with Darrow and Eugene Debs and 'Streetcar Bohemia. The spirit of it – I had that right, but I was wrong on details.' Streeter's captaincy, Phil explained, came not from the Civil War, where he'd served in combat as a boy infantryman, but from operating steamboats he'd built himself for service on the Great Lakes. One of these ran aground near the mouth of the Chicago River, and could not be moved. So he and his wife – a descendant of Francis Marion, the Swamp Fox, a South Carolina hero of the Revolution – on noticing the Lake was silting sand and mud around their boat, persuaded contractors to help nature along with wagon-loads of rubble, which, thanks to the Chicago Fire, abounded. From old maps and law books he learned the state of Illinois ends at the original waterline, so he claimed his new land, eventually scores of acres, and organized it as a federal district, à la Washington DC. Some of Chicago's richest families were building mansions along the Lake shore. The fill, and the view, and the captain, and his associates, seen together, set a tone grossly offensive to the sensibilities of these parvenu millionaires. So by means of hired goons, actions-at-law, and bribed politicians making bureaucratic obstructions and ordering police raids, they tried to evict the Streeters. The Captain, an amateur student of law, and his wife, and their friends, and a few honest judges, defended Streeterville for decades, until the old man died. Defense often took the form of ambush, shotgun blasts, and butt strokes with his trusty Civil War musket. On this downtown stage, for many years, acted out before the people of Chicago who mainly cheered him on, unrolled a dramatic allegory of the struggle between the Money Hogs' contempt for the democratic process and the democratic Pioneer Spirit.

'A man's house is his castle, Al. That ancient doctrine, and its conccomitant, no one may be evicted from their castle without a proper court order – those are the grounds he stood on, and defended, even against police, and are grounds we should defend with equal commitment, still.'

'All that power, and all those years, and they didn't get him. How come?'

'Because he was right. And everybody knew it. And he defended his place with dogged ferocity. Near the end they held him in jail for a long time, and he got out on a habeas corpus, but not soon enough, because this additional pressure killed his wife.'

Billy gazed at Phil feeling an ambience of comradeship.

Phil balled a fist. 'Whenever I think about that story, I draw strength from it, as in quitting my money-hog law firm. And I think of the classic quotation from Coke defining the principle which inspired it. Since the eighteenth century, Coke's book has been studied by law students like I was, and readers-of-law, like Abraham Lincoln. The quote goes something like this: A man's house is as his castle and fortress, as much for his defense against injury and violence, as for his repose, a refuge so strong in law that, in the absence of judicial warrant, all the forces of the King, without her leave, dare not enter the poorest widow's hut.'

113

From his perch on the desk, Billy watched Phil pace the room, and settle down on the window-sill, where he popped another beer can. Definitely something more on his mind than socializing. Definitely. Billy pulled off his tie and rolled up his shirtsleeves. Before Chicago and ZTG, he'd never been aware of his clothes, and now he felt tyrannized by the binds and discomforts of the business uniform, by having to *think about it*. Which suit? Which shoes? Shirt: white, colored, tinted, patterned? Socks? Tie! Choose one! How does it all look together? Visualize it. Go to the cleaners; go to the laundry. At home, living in California, the rule was be comfortable, and when necessary, select a tie and sports jacket from a rack of one. Marines? They tell you. Only thought there: Keep clean.

And when he finished saying all this to Phil, Phil said: 'For me, it's easy. I always wear a blue blazer, gray slacks, and black shoes. My dress blazer has brass buttons. I have a rack of solid colored ties, and a drawer of tinted shirts. Up in the morning. Shave, look out the window at my yard, at my outside thermometer. Hey, Phil, what color is today? Blue? Red? Black? This morning, I felt gray. So – dark gray tie, light gray shirt. Even so, though, I'd rather be back in Levis and pullovers. So that's how it goes, except I already know tomorrow's gray because I'm going to spend the night on my office couch. You should get one.'

'Why not? Except I'm only half a mile from home, an easy walk or run, and all this extravagance is getting to me, and you've beat me to the blazers.'

'But not to what matters.'

Billy felt a surge of trust and affection. Concern about Phil's hacking experiment broached. Can't *ask* him, though.

'Al, did you ever hear of the Hog Farm?'

'I don't think so.'

'It's a roving, idealistic commune I greatly admire. As a lad in Frisco, they asked me to join. I wish I had.'

'But you went to law school instead.'

'Yes. And for the same reasons.'

'Phil, I keep thinking about a leaflet I saw back in '89. It's a translation of a statement faxed to the States by the students in Tiananmen Square. They recognized the tremendous problems we all face, and at the risk of their lives, tried to work for a solution. They said: If we don't, who will? That's what I feel about myself. I have every gift, and no personal responsibilities. If *I* don't, who will? Who in hell will?'

'I used to feel like that, too, but I went off the track. I hope I'm back on now.'

'Those Chinese students, and Aimée from Canada, and me, and millions more, from everywhere, the young people, are the new team, the current embodiment of the farthest advance of history, the new team taking over from older generations. The captains of that team should be its best members, like the Indians had chiefs for different things – the best hunter leads the hunt. Like Jefferson's aristocracy of the able.'

'Which is you, Al, and me, isn't it? And Aimée and Janet.'

'George too?'

'Do pigs have wings?'

'Ask Alice.'

They raised their hands high and smacked palms in a big double high-five.

'My Uncle Bill called me a gentleman of the Third Millennium.'

'And you're proud of that, aren't you?'

'For sure. And I'm a director of the Al Foundation, a trust fund my father left to pay for a yearly party at Bill's place, the El Flaco Club, which really is a year-long party, as he endowed a bar stool with free drinks.'

'Consecrated to hilarity and genius.'

'That's it. *Hilaritati ac genio dicata*, George's favorite toast. Me, I like joy and genius better.'

'Me too.'

'Phil, I've been wondering what my politics are. I mean, a name for them. It's like trying to put words on a storm cloud and a rainbow. My dad and Uncle Bill, they called themselves New Deal Democrats, but – ? The best I can come up with is, me, I'm a Green democrat.'

'Small *d*.'

'Small *d*. Big G. My ancestors, my mind-ancestors, are from the New Deal and the Progressive Movement and the Populists and the Revolution. One of them is Abraham Lincoln. Yeah, and Harry Truman too. My body-ancestors are from western Missouri. Like Truman. From Jayhawker Quantrell Red-Leg Dalton Jesse-James Little Dixie. My people freed their slaves, and then fought for the Confederacy. Originally, they came from Maryland and Virginia and were on the right side in the Revolution.'

'That makes us mind-cousins.'

'Fucking-A!'

They slapped another high-five.

'I don't think we're body-cousins, though,' said Phil. 'My people could be body-cousins of Streeter. They went from Chicago into the Union Army, and go back through Ohio to Massachusetts. I wonder, did our grandfathers ever see each other over the musket sights? That war erased a whole generation of idealists. Those it didn't kill, it burned out. Just imagine! Our forebears survived. By luck. Had someone aimed a musket, or a cannon, a bit differently, you, or me, or both of us, would not be here.'

'Like my dad used to say: Life is a sequence of unforeseen consequences.'

'As I used to say, and still say, all living people are blood aristocrats. They descend from a long line of survivors, going back to Adam, my name for the first living cell.'

'I'll drink to that.'

'Thanks to Aimée's Alexander coin, and her saying, Phil, read this, I've been reading a book about Alexander the Great. What a legend *that* is. In a letter to Aristotle, he called Aristotle his mind-father. His body-father was crude old Philip of Makedon.'

'Aimée told me about that. Which accounts for what I just told you.'

'Now it's my turn to tell you something.'

'I knew you had more on your mind than drinking beer.'

'I have.'

'So, tell me!'

'I thought it might be too early to let you know, but, what the hell? I think I've done it! Yes, *done* it! I'm not certain-sure, but, yes, I think I've got you off the hook. The whole thing's against my principles, but it sure was fun. Thanks for the excuse. I hacked into the Department of Defense computers, and others too, and wiped the desertion off your record. I gave you a medical discharge called Under Honorable Conditions, which, I think, is the truth of the matter. They released you, as they put it, for the convenience of the government.'

Billy embraced him.

'Man alive!'

'And I changed your name to Alexander William Burke on your social security records, and on the DOD records, but kept your old number. So everything fits.'

'What can I say?'

'So now we test it.' Phil took two papers out of his desk. 'Here's a passport application, and a certified birth certificate from San Pedro in Los Angeles County. The application's typed out. You sign it in their presence. Take it to the passport office along with the birth certificate and two passport photos, and the fee in exact cash – thirty dollars, I think, but phone them and they'll tell you. You'll find photographers near their office. So, apply. Your passport should come in the mail within a fortnight.'

'Talk about making my day!'

'When the passport comes, we'll know we've done everything right, and you don't have to worry any more. If it doesn't? Leave town, and I'll get back to my hacking. This is a step forward for ZTG, too. You'll need a passport when you start traveling around to look at islands.'

'Lucky Al the Second, that's me.'

'Have you told Aimée you deserted?'

'No.'

'Anyone else?'

'No'

'That's good.'

'What you've hacked out for me – can anyone reverse it, or expose it?'

'Other than your Uncle Bill, I don't think so, but nothing is certain in this vale of tears. Write him, when the passport comes.' Phil bowled a can across the office floor. 'George. He could expose you. He could blackmail you. As in make you vote with him to open the spa on Groundhog Day.'

'Uncle Bill and George, they're the only ones. Right?'

'Well, you. Me. But I can't blackmail you. I'm as deep in this crime as you are.'

'Brothers in felony.'

'I don't like that.'
'I don't either. I feel like I've double-crossed myself.'

PART FOUR

OF RIDDLES

PRAEFECTUS
CASTRORUM

To me, living through all this, it's
almost as if George is the past; Phil,
the present; and Alexander, the future.
Aimée and and I are present/future
because women don't have to change as
profoundly as men do to become good
members of the world tribe.

Janet Ma
Pig Spa Island, 1993

SIXTEEN

In New York, going to the airport, the cab had carried Aimée and Billy through a weedy, junk-strewn trashscape, and now, just hours later, they were rocketing along ribbon rail, by a sun-sparkling sea, on the way from Marseilles to Nîmes. Of a recent design, reflecting the sophisticated aesthetic of France, the car carried two rows of bucket seats on each side of the aisle. Aimée, by the window, watched in utter fascination as the view unrolled. *France.* And on the first day of summer.

France! It really exists! 'The southern accent of the Midi is a long way from the hard sound of Canadian French,' she said to Billy. 'But I can understand most of it.' She only had a modest gift for languages. 'Everybody should have two languages because everybody *can.*' She'd applied herself to French with intense willpower. 'As a Canadian, I'm morally obliged to learn French. You Americans should feel the same way about Spanish.' Billy smiled, indifferent to Spanish, grateful someone could make sense out of the measured, musical, meaningless sounds surrounding him since Marseilles airport. He drew his passport from his pocket, and looked at the entry stamp: Police Nationale, Marseilles, 21 Juin, 1993. One year ago, on another hot and sunny day, clad in cap and gown, he'd graduated from UC Berkeley. An eventful year. Last week, George had phoned them from Paris, asking them to come to New York, where they found a message to meet him in Nîmes. This lovely passport! He examined it in awe and wonder. They still didn't know who'd bought all the stock. Five dummy companies – but who owns *them*? Feeling somehow at home in the

121

strange sound of French, Billy touched Aimée's shoulder. 'Here I am, still with my tribe.'

'You really think like that?'

'I sure do.'

She opened their guidebook, reread the page about Nîmes. 'They say the Roman past is a presence in Nîmes, because so many Roman buildings remain.' The city reached its highest point eighteen hundred years ago under the emperor Antoninus Pius. And that's well in excess of seventy generations ago. She gazed at the conductor. When she'd asked him about hotels, he told her as a native of Nîmes he would recommend the one by the station. She imagined – imaged – seventy pairs of his grandparents, that long line of begats, seated on both sides, two-by-two, the length of the car, dressed as in their times. The men all resembled the blue-clad train chief stepping down the car in his moment under the bright spotlight of the living now, the authority who passes along the aisle, asking his forebears for tickets, in a language progressively more difficult for them to understand, until, at the end of the car, grandparents contemporary with Caesar Augustus, who'd established the Roman veterans' colony in Nîmes, talk mainly by gesture. The train chief casts easily in the rôle of Latin lover. Would he kiss me all over? She vowed to investigate the Latin lover myth, but spoke to Billy of a less intimate idea. 'The Roman Empire was as big as the continental United States. Everywhere they went, Romans thought: Here I am, still with my tribe and its familiar servants. Clients. Slaves. Aliens. Mercenary German soldiers. To the conquered locals the Romans said: Worship your ancient gods. Your old stories are all true. Pay your taxes and keep order, and you have nothing to fear from us. We'll develop the infrastructure and keep the peace. You need not learn Latin or copy us. Doing so, of course, was good for business. So on the Latin side of the Empire, everywhere, establishment types of all the bloods and customs within its compass, fused together in the melting pot of Roman civilization.'

'And that was the dream of Alexander the Great.'

'To ask tickets of the conductor's grandparents contemporary with Alexander you'd have to go six rows into the next car. They wear trousers and long hair, wash every day, speak Gaulish, and worship oak trees and sacred springs and make human sacrifice.'

'Aimée, of all the qualities of Alexander, the one I admire most

122

is his ambition to unite all the tribes of Europe and Asia into a single state. With only one country, how can you have war? That's what drove him, the quest for universal concord. He would melt the tribes together. Kinship, commerce, and culture would provide the heat. During his ten years of conquest, from Egypt to Pakistan, he founded cities to serve as centers of commerce and Greek culture, and he organized political administration so as to produce intermarriage, and, thus, as the generations turned, an ever-strengthening common kinship. He did all this in ten years! And, no shit, some of it's still in place today. The alien conquered were to be equals of the Greek conquerors, and co-heirs of the new world. And lying there in Babylon, dying, only ten years older than me, with half the world not yet conquered, meaning united, his companions could think only of asking him: Who gets the Empire. Not one of his closest comrades understood his dream, attainable now, his heart's purpose. He looked at the familiar faces, one-by-one, then said: Fight for it. They did. But even so, that ten years had tilted his part of the world toward union through commerce, kinship, and culture.'

She smiled at Billy, warm in the thought that he understood, and would not have asked about the power, but the dream.

'Aimée! That's what's happening now! We have world commerce. World kinship? The new team travels. Intermarries. Exchange students and youth hostels. We're all cooking in the pot. And world culture? Music, art, science, they're shared by everybody, and now world culture is coming together around a single common tongue – English. English has passed the critical mass. History's momentum can affect it, but cannot overcome it. Eventually, people will speak their local language, and English, the world language.'

'That, dear boy, is the A and the Zed of it.'

'That, sweet girl, is it from farrow to finish.'

'When mustering the Greek armies to attack Persia, sowboy mio, Alexander went to visit Demosthenes, a philosopher in rags, who lived by choice in a huge clay pot, and had tried to arouse the Greeks against him. Alexander found Demosthenes sitting on the dirt before his pot and placed himself between the old philosopher and the sun. "Demosthenes," says the young prince to the old philosopher, "I am now so firmly in power I can give you anything you want. Ask, and it's yours." Demosthenes, seated there in the boy-king's shadow, peers at him in silence. "No matter what it is,

123

you have but to ask, and I will grant it." The old philosopher regards the young king scornfully and says, "Step out of the sun." Alexander does so. His sycophants and companions chorus derision at this old fool's contempt for opportunity. Alexander turns to them and says, "Were I not Alexander, I would choose to be Demosthenes."'

'Do you think George will be waiting at the station?'

'In Alexander's place, what do you think *he*'d say?'

Billy thought for a moment. 'I think he'd say: Were I not *Praefectus Castrorum* of ZTG, I would choose to be a Superior Certified Meat Sire.'

'Me, I'd say: Were I not Aimée, I would choose to be Amy.'

George was waiting for them at the station. There he stood, on the quay, under the sheltering canopy, in slacks and a pink muscle-shirt, a pack of Gauloise Bleu cigarettes tucked under the shoulder-strap, his cuddly sixty-pound potbellied purple-black pet Chinese minipig beside him on a leash.

They shouldered their baggage and alighted in Nîmes.

George, a big happy smile smeared all over his face, strode up and caught them both in an affectionate embrace. 'It's fucking happening!'

They said a joyful hello.

'I'm all fucked up.'

They walked through the station, across the street to the opposite corner, and entered a beautiful, old-fashioned French hotel. They checked in, left their baggage, and walked with a stumbling, drunken George up the main street leading from the station to a park. 'Keep going. Something I want you to see.'

They crossed the park and there, on the other side, to the left, in majestic beauty, stood an intact Roman amphitheater, four or five hundred feet wide, and seventy feet high. Billy and Aimée stopped, stared, stunned by the awesome immensity of it.

'I've seen some shit-kicking shows in there, you better fucking believe it. They can afford the best. A sellout is twenty thousand people.'

They stood there in wonder, imaginations inflamed, picturing street scenes of the previous and present millennia, Romans on their peaceful daily rounds, fierce wild Germans raping and looting, the place being made into a fort, more armies, a massacre of Catholics, huge fires – builders vs. wreckers – one of history's favored themes. George drew them away, along the rue de la République, to the terrace of a nearby café. 'I used to be stationed here in Nemausus. *Legio XX Valeria Victrix.* See that big tower on the hilltop? Many's the watch I've stood up there, looking down at four miles of thirty-foot walls, ten feet thick, with ninety towers and ten gates. Even up there, the town stunk worse than the Devil's armpit.' The waiter served them. 'Here's to hilarity and our guardian spirits.'

They clicked glasses.

'Here's to joy and genius,' said Billy, toasting back.

'No fucking legionnaire ever drank to that. We never knew joy. At best, we had moments of hilarity. As for the dazzling light of what you call genius? Forget it. We were pieces of a smoothly working mass-murder machine. A flame? Snuff it the fuck out. *Hilaritati ac genio dicata.* Consecrated to this moment of hilarity and each soldier's guardian spirit. I've seen some shit in that arena. They used to shade it with awnings extended on poles from the attic level. They still use it. Tonight, it's the Randy Hansen band, a rock band from Seattle, led by a guy who plays guitar with his teeth. Yeah. Them and Dada Commando. I went last night. Fucking pussy civilization you have these days. You're all wimps. No more gladiators. No naval battles; no chariot races or wolf hunts. No boar hunts, either. Sissies! We were tough. We got half our pay from the paymaster, and ground the other half out of the locals. That was expected. It was the system. As with Mexican police today. Sometimes, if we kicked ass in battle, the general would fling us handfuls of gold coins. *Legio XX Valeria Victrix.* The Twentieth. The good old Twentieth Legion Valorous Victor. Served with them in England, too. Chester, chiefly. On its standard the Twentieth carries its emblem, a wild boar. I got my tattoo in a stall right across the street, there. When I sobered up, I realized some clown-faced crotch sucker made them mark me for life with a *sow*. A fucking sow! If I'd caught that bastard, I'd have made him eat the flaming sword of death and destruction. Bet your ass I would have. You know something? *Roma.* That's Rome in Latin. *Roma* spelled backward is *amor.* Latin for love. Means love affair, too. *Amor – Roma.* Love spelled backward is Rome, and that's the fucking truth. *Oui,* mister, more wine. What's love backward in English? E-fucking vol. That's what. E-vol. I'll tell you an evil love story.'

He chugged his wine. 'So far as I'm concerned, a love affair is like stepping in dog shit. It's weasel breath. It's pigs' assholes. Aimée. Get that fucking mounzer over there to bring us a bottle. Good.' He poured some in a saucer for his pet. 'One of the shit duties they used to give us was crucifixion detail. We had to make felons carry their crosses to the crucifixion field, nail them on, set the crosses in holes, deep holes, packed hard, to make them stand up. Cold winter; hot summer. Oftener than not, the fucking ground was cast iron. When I made optio, I didn't have to dig anymore. But now that I was the sergeant I had to stay up all night by the crosses to make sure no kin or lover or dogfood-maker stole the bodies. Twenty-four hours on the cross, to make sure they croaked, to let birds eat their eyes, that was part of the sentence. If a body were stolen, the optio guarding it was nailed to the cross in its place. I hated that fucking duty. And they kept giving it to me. Crucifixion detail. Why? Because I'm a Jew, that's why. Born in fucking Palestine. That's why, with years of service, I never got farther than optio of the first cohort. I should have made *Praefectus Castrorum* at least! I am now! ZTG! Tell that fucking parley-voo to bring another bottle.'

He refilled his pet's dish. 'Pigs and people, they're the only animals who love booze naturally.'

'George, the love story.'

'Oh, yeah, Al – the fucking love story. Gets kind of mushy. Here, right here in River City, the crucifixion ground is a small hill in the necropolis. Cemetery, to you. It's a nice warm moonlit night and I'm sitting there with a big wineskin full of Falerian, happy as can be, watching the felons twitch and bleed, not a worry in the world, when I hear a sigh, and then weeping, coming from somewhere in the necropolis. So I go down, and look around, and glance back every now and then, to make sure it's not a trick, a diversion. What the hell, you can't rip a guy off a cross in five minutes. It takes time. You bet. The sighing and weeping leads me to an open vault, and I go in, and there on the slab is the body of a beautiful young man, looks a lot like you, Al, and weeping over it is an absolutely stunning broad, almost the clone of you, Aimée. I've got a thick hide, have to, but her sorrow and suffering got through to me, and she told me her story. They'd have been married the next day, but he'd been killed by a snakebite, and, believe me, she was keening and carrying on something awful. So

126

I hold her and comfort her and stroke her and croon to her and she begins to get the hots and one thing leads to another and we set the body on the dirt floor and make all kinds of love on the slab and I look out the door and see the sun's up.'

Lost in the memory, he kissed the rim of his glass. 'I looked up the hill at the crosses, and one of them was *empty*. Empty! the body'd been stolen, and if I didn't do something soon, I'd be croaking up there instead. Crucifixion's a bad death. Horrible. I've seen plenty of them and I know. You heave up to lessen the pain, and then you slump. Takes hours. I used to kill them when I could. I'd poison the water sponge we pressed to their mouths on the end of a long stick to make them live longer. And I told her all this and she held me and cried and cursed herself for having killed me by letting me comfort her. But, yes! There is something we can do. By the slab is a coil of rope they'll use when they close the tomb later in the morning. So we carry her lover's body up on the hill. We tie the rope around his chest, under his arms – right here Al, see how it fits under your armpits – and I heave him up on to the cross with it, and I tear out the bloody, meaty nails, and, using my short sword as a hammer, we nail her lover's body to the cross, and I'm saved.'

His head slumped to the table. They found a receipt for his hotel in his pocket, and walked him home, about a block away. On seeing him, and his drunken pig, the concièrge flew into a fury, screaming and yelling, and she put money on the counter, a refund, a preface to eviction.

In a cold, precise voice, Aimée said: '*Madame Gérante, ce monsieur, c'est un sergeant de la Légion Etrangère. Méfiez-vous.*'

The woman calmed, and they dumped George and his pig into bed. Outside again, going back through the Park of Général de Gaulle, Billy asked Aimée what she'd said to achieve such wondrous results.

'Madame manager, this gentleman, he's a sergeant in the Foreign Legion. Beware.' She laughed merrily. 'In France, the Legion's above the law.' She stopped at a kiosk and bought a French guidebook to Nîmes, and they sat on the terrace of their hotel's café, and watched the action in front of the station, and listened to a recorded warning coordinated with the stoplight telling *piétons* – pedestrians – not to cross against the red light, or saying cross now while it's green.

Aimée browsed the guidebook. 'Hey Al, here's one for you. What do you know about the pants you're wearing?'

'You mean my original designer pantaloons? 1849, goldrush Frisco, a miner asks a tentmaker, name of Levi Strauss, to make him tent-cloth trousers tough enough for the diggings. Result? Designer pantaloons, chicly riveted, we call Levis.'

'And of what cloth are they made?'

'Blue denim.'

'This book says denim begins here. It's a contraction of *serge de Nîmes* – serge of Nîmes, *de Nîmes*, denim. Now isn't that special. And here's another. Their most illustrious and influential citizen, since the emperor Antoninus Pius, at least to my way of thinking, is Jean Nicot, the man who in the Year of our Lord 1560, introduced tobacco to France.'

Billy raised his glass. 'Consecrated to Nicotine John.'

Aimée kissed his cheek and said, 'Sowboy mio, our George certainly has a wonderful imagination.'

SEVENTEEN

The next morning they joined George near the Arena in a bright and colorful café Aimée thought of as a manifestation of the current French aesthetic of color, form, light, and joy. They roused him by telephone. He came in, rubbing his eyes.

Billy stood to greet him, one hand squeezing Aimée's shoulder. 'Hey, you old sowpoke, you sure told us a lot about Rome last night.'

'Oh yeah? Forget it.'

'Where's your pal?'

'I left the little fucker upstairs.'

'So he doesn't get any breakfast.'

'Fuck no. He's too hung-over.'

'You're having guilt feelings about gilt feelings.'

'Kiss my ass!'

'You okay?'

George presented a massive arm, fully exposed by his singlet. 'Feel my muscle and decide for yourself.'

Billy grasped it and laughed. 'Okay, Chief, do your stuff.'

George sat down in disgust. The waiter brought coffee and a basket of crescents. George sent him back for a bottle of Côtes-du-Rhone. 'I've found our island.' He unwrapped some bubble gum, and, radiating paternalistic contentment, looked from one to the other, waiting for reaction.

'Where's it at, Chief?'

'It's on the border of Indonesia and Malaysia. Both countries claim it, a contradiction that lets us come in like a surgical strike.' George chugged some wine. Intensely, with sodden enthusiasm, he began giving details. The island is tropical, about two miles by three. It was among those Billy had selected in his research. Buildings? A ruined village we can rebuild. 'How'd you find it, George?' Study and inquiry, it seemed, had led him to meet with Indonesians at the UN in New York, and they put him in contact with colleagues in Marseilles. From these conversations an understanding emerged. The Indonesian government would sell the island to ZTG, and run a bill through their legislative process prooviding that ZTG and/or its assignees be granted clear title and be freed of regulations and restrictions that would otherwise apply to operating an enterprise like ZTG's spa. For this, George paid four million dollars in advance, and promised eight million more on delivery.

Wondering about the deal sounding too easy, and curious about how George could drink wine, chew gum, smoke, and talk at the same time, Aimée asked him about the native islanders.

'We're in luck. Nobody lives there any more. Both countries, and pirates too, have raided the place so often everybody fucking croaked or ran. Both governments say they own the island. So we buy clear title from both. Get it? And, yes, you bet your ass, most if not all of what we pay is graft, and – well, sure, dealing in big bucks like this, extreme caution *is* good policy, so that's why I told you to meet me here, not Marseilles.'

'So, Chief, what do you want us to do?'

'This morning I'm off to London to meet with assholes from Malaysia. We'll buy the rights from both them cunt-ries – get it? – and that will moot their border dispute, which then can slide down into the river Lethe and sink into the mud along with beaucoup other bygones. Fucking-A! As for you? I want you to hang in here for a few days. Stay in that same hotel so I can phone you. Then you'll join me in London, and we'll fly to Djakarta, and meet Phil there, and charter a seaplane, and visit our island.' He poured wine into their coffee cups. 'To the resurrection of Pigville!'

'Consecrated to Pig Spa Island!'

'You can say that again.'

'So, okay, Chief. Why must we wait here instead of going with you?'

'I have my reasons.'

'Why?'

'Just fucking do it.'

'Like what reasons?'

'Like someone may contact you.'

They promised to wait, then walked him to his hotel where they fetched his baggage and his pygmy suidic companion, and waved goodbye to a sullen desk clerk. A taxi took them to the station. Once inside, they crossed the concourse to an adjoining café set off behind a glass wall. Some of its tables were out on the main floor where you could watch the big schedule board whirr and flip as it announced trains and times and destinations. They sat at one of these and asked a waitress to bring wine. Might just as well go along with George's demented plan. It seems like a *fait accompli*, and, besides, there's plenty of money, and something has to be done to forestall the new stockholders, should they decide to take over. 'Right! We got to move fast, beat them bastards to the punch.'

They went through a tunnel to an eastbound quay, and studied the chart showing the composition of the various trains. The train came. Porters and passengers rushed about with baggage. Frantic folk questioned conductors in soft blue caps about destinations and tickets. George swung up into the doorway of a first-class car coupled to the diner.

'George,' said Billy, 'I just remembered, both those countries are Moslem, and it's a sin for Moslems to eat pork.'

'Don't worry. I told them ragheads we're going to raise goats.'

'*Goats!*'

'Why sure, our pigs will be honorary goats.'

The train began to move. George stepped down and gathered them both into a big affectionate goodbye hug, sprang back on to the steps, and was gone.

Watching the train diminish as it went down the tracks carrying George to his rendezvous with the resurrecting Pigville, Aimée said, 'He loves us. *Both* of us.'

'He always treats me like a boy.'

'To him, you are. He's the man. To me, it's the other way around.'

Billy took her hand and walked her back through the concourse out on to the busy sidewalk where the robot voice kept warning about crossing against the light. 'His pet, sowgirl mia. We forgot to ask its name.'

That evening, after talking at length over dinner about ZTG, they went to the amphitheater to hear the Randy Hansen Band. Some five hundred people had gathered in front near the stage, and they surrendered to the power of raw energy music, and Hansen flung himself in among them, and they held him aloft, and stroked his guitar, and a roady wearing a whole coonskin for a cap helped him back up on to the stage. And then the encore: screams for more, rewarded. And then the wait for Dada Commando. He really *had* played the guitar with his teeth. 'Al – can you play lute with your snoot?' Does the gift of music run in families? It must. The guidebook says in Roman times this arena seated twenty-four thousand. Some of the sections had been left in ruins, so now it holds about twenty. What if all Randy's ancestors had come to the concert? And brought their instruments and played along? How many generations of them would it take to make a sellout? Fifteen? At twenty-five years to the generation, that would be about four centuries worth of Randys and Randas, which makes how many, Alexander? How many? In excess of sixteen thousand grandparents in the fifteenth generation. Doubling each time, from Randy through the fourteenth, it comes to 16,385 more. They all could find seats, plus half the grandparents from the fifteenth. But how many would there *really* be? How about it, Al? How many?

'Going back in time, there's fewer and fewer people, so there must be lots of duplicate grandparents: doubles, triples, quadruples – more. So to fill the amphitheater with Randy's forebears, with yours, with mine, you'd have to admit the sixteenth generation, or part of it anyway, and that, Aimée, makes your four hundred years, 1593, Shakespeare's time, maybe even admits him, because, as a lad, Shakespeare ranged through southern Europe.'

'Yes, the 1500s. George once told me that the premier event of that century is the Spanish introducing pigs into America.'

The next morning, after coffee and crescents near the station, they walked back through the park and by the amphitheater to the Maison Carrée, a temple consecrated to Augustus Caesar's grandsons, alive fifty generations ago, an exquisite mini-Parthenon surviving from the previous universe, a stone screen on which to project romantic drama, odorless fancies, like the plays of Plautus, representing the street-life of ancient Rome. 'Aimée, almost right up to our wonky times this place must have stunk through and through of shit and piss and manure and livestock and rotting meat. I mean, that must have been the summer atmosphere of all cities, great and small.' Although silent as to the olfactory ambience of yesteryear, the guidebook deigned to lead them to the ruins of the public baths, rebuilt some nine generations ago into a series of pools and streams with bridges and walks and swards and gardens, watched over by a ruined temple of Diana and fed by the sacred spring of the Volcae Arecomici, a dominant tribe of Gaulish Celts who had founded Nîmes in this place, their holy wood, the scene of their tribal assemblies. Here, they'd heard their bards sing history and seen their Druids dispense justice and foretell the future, did these doughty Volcae Arecomici who, in 121 BC, surrendered to Rome.

After napping on a sunny lawn, the guidebook trail took them to a crowded square before a church with two stone towers. To one side stood the Augustus Gate – one of ten once piercing the Roman defenses – an ornate marble structure which in the previous century had been dug out of a castle wall then being razed where it had successfully concealed itself for many human lifetimes. Today, with the blessings of banners displayed on the church, and notices posted inside, a Druid Bard is urging the rallied citizenry to support an impending railroad strike. Aimée translates the speeches as best she can. She seems too fair to possibly be French, too Celtic, too Maeve-like.

'Why don't you call yourself *Amy?*'

'My Aimée's part vanity, part romance, part idealism. It reminds me we Canadians have to splice the Anglo and the Franco together.' She paused. 'I truly feel that way, Al.'

'What have you done today to make the world a better place?'

'Shown solidarity with the common man.'

For intimacy, he decided to call her Amy from now on.

After dining in their hotel restaurant, they spent a quiet night watching French TV and wondering what the Romans would have produced for the idiot box had they had the chance. Windy political debate. Surely, for divertissement, death sports, fierce armed combats, innocents penned with wolves and lions, and, yes, as news, sensational public trials and crucifixions, the scientific practice of torture, the massacre of successful battle, interviews with boyfriends of celebrated actors, and intimate details from the lives of illustrious freedmen and slave owners. Education? Features on poured-concrete structures and high stone bridges and on exotic places and wine-making and gardening and fashion and pricey art and myths. There'd be gurus of astrology and of necromancy and

133

the black arts. And charismatic preachers raising money for the eunuchs of Cybelle and the grottos of Mithra. And dull tragedy. And situation comedy supported by claque laughter. And endless soggy soapy serials of sex, power, money, treachery, ambition, egotism, and the high-life. And George's favorite entertainment, dirty pantomime. And pornography! Image the details if you dare. And Billy and Aimée slid from this fancy into a sweet evening of each other, of feeling and frolic soothed by the yodels and colors of Télévision-Française, of kiss me all over, of truly making the world a better place for one another.

The next day they rented bikes and rode out into the country to see the Pont du Gard, a huge aqueduct bridge surviving from the previous universe, and the day after that, still having received no message, they strolled around the city to see what they could see, and eventually found themselves among swarming school children in the anthropology museum, which they named the Stone and Bone Gallery because that's what was there, stones shaped and bones abandoned by the ancient Gauls and their strata of predecessors.

The following morning George phoned for Billy and told him to come to the station café between four and six p.m. and bring Aimée.

'Why, Chief?'

'Don't be so fucking inquisitive.'

'We're curious.'

'Just be there.'

'You're sending us from clue to clue, like a kids' treasure hunt.'

'Fucking-A!'

'What's happening?'

'Be there.'

'Okay.'

'I don't think you trust me.'

'I've always trusted you.'

'Sometimes I think you don't even fucking like me.'

'Come on. All that time in Pigville! Our swino colloquies! The swine fêtes! The Battle! Chicago! ZTG! You're still my *Praefectus Castrorum*. We're pals, and just as tight as ever.'

After discussing this, Aimée and Billy decided to spend the day visiting the watchtower atop Mount Cavalier, the one George had

134

pointed out, and then picnic in the park and go to the station. As they trudged up a street rising from the ancient baths to the Turris Magna, Billy said: 'George. He's fucking *brimming* with self-pity.'

'All males have a streak of poor-me, even you, Al, even you.'

'Did they call Alexander the Great, Al?'

'Poor baby.'

'I didn't mean it like that.'

'Sure you did. That's the poor-me streak. As in, Don't belittle me, Mom. Where are you, Mom, when I need you? Take care of me. I'm scared. Baby me. Hold me. Stroke my brow. Wipe my ass. Daub my tears. I can't pretend any more. Tell me I'm wonderful.'

'You silly girl!'

'We silly girls *are* the moms. We're not nearly as bad. The buck stops with us.'

The tower rears almost one hundred feet from a parking lot on the crest of Nîmes' highest point. A tour bus and some school buses stood there and a class of Catholic girls in uniform was filing in. The guidebook said this is the oldest structure in the city, and that it used to be taller. They paid their admission and mounted narrow stone stairs behind the girls, occasionally squeezing by people walking down. From the top, an immense and magnificent sunlit vista, much as seen by owners and builders standing here two thousand years ago. To the north: vines and olives; to the east, the Rhône Valley – where they'd gone on bikes – and the distant alps. To the south, the Mediterranean, and, westward: the Pyrenees. They looked down at the city, trying to trace the way to the station, and then imagined George's four miles of walls, with all their towers and gates.

'That George. Can you figure him out?'

Aimée leaned against the parapet, arms folded, and said: 'What I make of him is what I make of everyone else. Breed, nest, and survive to breed again. That's what it's all about. Everything else is illusion, delusion – romance. Yes. That's it. That's what it's all about, in essence: breeding and nesting and the survival of the species. Breed, wean, survive to breed and wean once more. That's the theme of myth and legend, old and new. All religions start there. The most successful of them boost the true-believer high above it, generate an illusion of grander purpose, of eternal personal existence. Talk about an ego trip! Breed, wean, survive, and pretend there's more because there should be. That's reality. That's where George fits. Just like you and me and all those ant-folk down there on all those little ant-farms.' She itched her back against the parapet. 'So what do *you* think of our favorite *Praefectus Castrorum*?'

'I think we're all trying to get along and keep smiling. Him, you, me, each one of us, you silly girl.'

'And that's all there is to it?'

'That's how I feel about things. I always imagine others feel the same as I do. But maybe other people's basic feel – feels are different.'

She kissed him and nuzzled him and did that scandalize any of the Catholic girls? 'So, sowboy mio, I'm wrong, and you're right?'

'Sure. Well, no. We're both right, only you're righter than me.'

They walked down the stairs and down the hill, the liquid flowing down-pace, a joy in itself making the upward struggle worth it. They bought bread and butter and various cheeses and Evian water, sat on some lumpy grass and ate. Then, off to the station. On the way, they exchanged stories about memorable treasure and scavenger hunts of their adolescence. Both their fathers had passed on to them these forgotten games from times before TV, adventures both fun and funny. Their fathers had written and placed the clues leading to the treasure or had composed lists which set groups of maids and striplings to combing Easy Street and Pacifica for items like cow bells, political buttons, white roses, canned lox, football tickets. After hearing the robot voice lecture the *piétons*, they crossed the busy street and found themselves before the station, ten minutes early.

'And now, sowboy mio, we get the next clue.'

He grasped her hand and walked inside. 'And some folks say life is just a game.'

'Recently, it's been a game of leaphog.'

Inside the station, a French Visigoth with a big blond moustache stood studying the master timetable of *Départs*, reciting what he read out loud. They crossed the concourse and went into the café. At the far end of the bar a cluster of idlers watched the Boston Celtics playing basketball inside the TV set. Atari and pinball machines, also speaking English, stood against the far wall. Aimée and Billy sat at the near end of the bar where the glass partition gave a full view of the inside of the station. Billy ordered wine from a robust young woman who tended both the bar and the tables. 'Did you notice that guy's reading the timetable aloud, not because he's stupid, but because he's drunk?'

'For sure. And that's what makes him a Visigoth.'

They sat in silent anticipation, scanning the main hall for the messenger; the Visigoth walked out to the left on to the westbound platform. Aimée said something in French to the barmaid and the barmaid smiled. Four soldiers in tan summer uniforms carrying shoulder-bags came in from the street and sprawled into chairs at one of the outer café tables. Here I am, watching the movie, when I'm in the movie. They wore spotless white hats resembling big coffee cans with visors. A silent movie. All I can hear on my side of the glass is the audience, Amy and the others.

'*Canaille!*' said the barmaid.

'What's that mean?'

'Rabble.'

'Who are they?'

'I'll ask.' Another rush of French. '*Légion Étrangère*, which is to say, French Foreign Legion. She told me all Legionaries wear those white kepis, and are little-boy proud of them.'

Roman soldiers!

They piled their shoulder-bags.

Still here in Nîmes!

They stacked their kepis on the greasy floor.

'She says most of them are Germans.'

German Legionaries defending France!

'And speak French with a German accent.'

One of them drew a wine bottle from his bag, pulled the cork with his teeth.

'Al, do they still have to train tame killers to defend civilization from barbarian killers?'

Laughing and shouting, they passed the bottle around.

Hilarity.

They loosened their tunics.

Where are the Visigoths of today?

The empty bottle rolled across the station floor.

Do they extort half their pay from civilians?

One of them rose, opened the glass door, and stepped out of the movie into real life.

Standing at the bar, he looked like George.

In a pleasant boy-to-mother voice he requested wine.

'*Oui, monsieur.*'

He stepped back. The barmaid filled four glasses, set them on a tray, and carried them into the movie.

She served the glasses while they laughed and pointed and said things which flushed her face with fury.

She came back with the empty tray.

'A book I read about the Legion, Al, says they like to sing.'

Aimée talked French to the barmaid, and she replied in a voice of suppressed rage: '*Quoi!* ICI!'

The Legionary came back inside and ordered a bottle. She followed him out with it on her tray.

'What did you tell her?'

'I said she might get them off her back by asking them to sing. And she said: What! HERE!'

Thus spoke the voice of civilization.

Out there in the movie, as she was collecting the money, one of them pinched her ass.

Grim-faced, she paced in.

She began stacking stools on the bar. 'We're closing early.'

. . . And then, tall and proud, on spiked heels, a shoulder-bag slung, onstage from the tracks came Janet Ma.

Janet Ma glanced around the concourse, spied her friends at the bar, and walked toward them passing close to the Legionaries' table. One reached out an arm and blocked her. Another stroked her ass. She turned and, bending slightly at the waist, glared down at them.

In a voice carrying the scorn of centuries, she said: '*Vive la Mort; Vive la Guerre; Vive la Légion Étrangère.*'

'*Pas mal,*' said one.

Another, in perfect Los Angeles American, said: 'That's right.'

Janet stalked out of the movie into real life. 'Let's get the fuck out of here,' she said.

The barmaid smiled at her.

They strode out to the street, where the robot lectured them, and crossed to the terrace of their hotel café.

138

'What did you say to them?' asked Aimée.

'I said Long live Death; Long live War; Long live the Foreign Legion.'

'You are one cool gal.'

'I am a great granddaughter of General Ma.'

'Who's that?'

'You don't know?'

'No.'

'You should.'

EIGHTEEN

Billy's dad, Al, the merchant seaman, had reared him on history books and sea stories. Consequently, Billy had a picture and a sense of how life used to be as seen and felt by Al all the way back to the 1920s, and, from what the books told, and other people's stories Al remembered, much farther back than that. Fine art, music, movies, and artefacts like the arena and baths in Nîmes, opened more dimensions. When Janet Ma delivered the message they were to meet George in London ten days hence, Billy felt an intense romantic excitement and the theater of his mind filled with images and stories and the surprise of *déjà vu* anticipated. For Janet, that day had been one of wake up in Chicago, eat an English muffin, take the El to O'Hare International Airport, look down at ant-life and oceans, have crescents and coffee in Marseilles; then Nîmes, to skirmish with naughty boys, dine and bed down. Naughty. Sure. Like the winsome, playful lads of *Legio XX Valeria Victrix.*

Today was the tenth day, cool and calm and clear. Billy stood on the boat deck of a channel ferry, the tricolor of the French Republic snapping at the stern, the rrrrrrrrrrrrr of the engines vibrating through him, and he watched Calais receding ten miles behind and daubed his nose with a sodden handkerchief. George would meet the boat train at Victoria Station. The deck rock-solid underfoot, Billy walked by life rafts toward the bow. He'd left the silly girls at the bar drinking cocktails whose colors matched their outfits, black Russians and crèmes de menthe, respectively. The sniffles had hit him during their week in Paris. An anticipated *déjà vu* fulfilled, a *now* now where he felt at home, much more so than in the gray shale formation of past nows, even when understood as family history. France keeps the old, yet pursues high tech. Past nows have been cleaned and colored. In Paris, the Roman baths, restored. Bronze statues, triumphal arches, graceful bridges, vibrant boulevards, gargoyles and bas-relief on the bright clean stones of antique buildings. Subway stations as art galleries. Musical groups playing in medieval churches. The two Parises coming together – the international pleasure dome and the city of the poor. Art everywhere. Happy, smiling people. The decorative arts at once their creation and their reflection. Bright colors and new materials in interiors, cafés and stores, and on façades, and on products and machinery, they are blended with the old, refined aesthetic sense toward the end of making people feel joy. Paris is back again. Back? Paris is finally achieving it, becoming Paris. What an immense change since the time when – as Al used to say, 'Paris is a great place, except the French Quarter's too big.'

Billy sneezed and gripped the rail, hocked phlegm and spit and watched the chalk line of Dover's cliffs, ten miles off, grow and take on detail.

> *When the lights go on again*
> *All over the world:*

With a good run downhill in Calais, I could jump from France to England.

> *There'll be blue birds over*
> *The white cliffs of Dover,*
> *Tomorrow,*
> *Just you wait and see.*

Today, it's gulls over.
Al used to say the war had brutalized his generation.
Man, woman, and child.
In all countries.
Exacerbating what economic conditions had already wrought.
Hitler had not managed the Calais to Dover broad jump.
Al once said, in Frankfurt, in bed, after a supreme moment, his lover had told him, good as this had been, the best thing that ever happened to her was when as a girl she shook the hand of Adolf Hitler.

141

> *There'll be love and laughter,*
> *And peace ever after,*
> *Tomorrow,*
> *When the world is free.*

Al had bowed to her and shaken her hand.

'Now *I* can say I shook the hand that shook the hand of Adolf Hitler.'

Then he shook Billy's hand. 'And now, son, *you* can say, and forevermore, you shook the hand that shook the hand that shook the hand of Adolf Hitler. And so, Billy, from now on when you shake hands, you'll be extending a chain of handshake infection, like syphilis, like AIDS, down into the generations, from now till the end of time.'

> *The shepherd will tend his sheep,*
> *The valley will bloom again:*

There's plenty of Garibaldi and Goethe Streets in Europe, but not even a single alley named Mussolini or Hitler.

> *And Jimmy can go to sleep*
> *In his own little room again.*

The brutalized Jimmy did, and he grew up to be a greedy stockbroker and vote for Maggie T.

> *New lights are coming on,*
> *All over the world.*

A more innocent generation living in the European Economic Community and carrying EC passports has achieved the economic union of 1992, and moves smiling toward political union, the US of E, as proposed so long ago by Garibaldi and Victor Hugo.

> *When the lights go on again*
> *All over the world,*
> *There'll be happy voices then,*
> *All over the world.*

Closest in Billy's experience to the lights going out all over the world was the San Francisco earthquake way back in 1989, a catastrophe not, like Europe's ordeals, produced by man, but by nature, and about all the Bay Area could handle.

142

World War III?

Terminal magnitudes worse.

An accident, or some fanatical submarine commander, or some malevolent dictator.

Hits without warning.

'Billy, ask yourself what caused the Great War? You know, World Wars I and II – 1914 to the atom bomb. Then ask, What caused the causes? Keep on asking. What caused the causes of the causes? Again. Experts, academics, policy-makers, most of them stop short, because they're afraid of what they'll find, and of its moral implications for them. Billy. You find the answer. So we can eliminate the causes before they take effect.'

Okay, Al, I'll try.

It's like asking why of why of why.

On October 17th, 1989, at 5:04 p.m., Billy had been in the undergraduate library of the University of California in Berkeley, working on a paper about this very question, when land became water and buildings shook like wet dogs and walls slapped in and out and trembling ceilings shed plaster-dust and fireplaces exploded and bridges collapsed and land slid down mountains and houses sprang from foundations and buildings sank down into terra abruptly infirma and folks reconsecrated themselves to Phoenix/Quetzalcuatl, ancestral bird-snake god of the City and County of San Francisco.

Without a thought of its scrabble value.

Billy swept his stuff into his backpack and walked across undulating floors out to the pedestrian street. The main library, Doe Library, was on fire, and Billy went in, and by waning sunlight and flashlight, helped fight the fire until it subsided and expired.

Outside once more, he found no light but that of the moon, and breathing the warm air of Indian summer he ran up the hill to a panoramic viewpoint.

The great arc of San Francisco-Marin, normally ablaze with light, winked here and there, while fires burned, and sirens sounded, and he felt himself in London, during the Blitz. Here I am, me, Bill, a member of what Al called the kinder, gentler generation, here I am, against my will, swept back fifty years into the midst of War. 'Billy, the last generation as human, as promising, as yours, the youth of the turn of this century, the cohort of the Wandervogel

143

and the Lapin Agile, was smashed in 1914–1918 on the Marne and at Verdun.'

Born in 1907, Billy's father had been one of the youngest of the pre-war generation. Of the military, he often said, 'When the fist begins to think, the country is in trouble.'

'Sitting at a café table on Omonia Square in Athens, Billy, watching swarms of young Europeans, long-haired, in shorts and T-shirts, come to visit the Acropolis, I imagined myself back into 1945, sitting at the same table, watching their fathers, men with the same faces, but in uniforms and steel helmets, carrying rifles.'

Billy walked in the moonlight, along College Avenue, toward his rooming house. He stopped to join a group gathered around a pick-up truck, its doors open, listening to the radio. Part of the Bay Bridge had collapsed. In Oakland, the top deck of a freeway had dropped on to the bottom deck. And at the amphitheater in San Francisco, tens of thousands were waiting for the World Series game to start when the quake struck. Had it hit two hours later, the game, in progress, would have been snuffed by darkness, thus subjecting the multitude to pandemonium.

As this passed through his memory theater, and the jetty at Dover drew close, the ferry became part of a fleet of boats large and small carrying the dirty ragged survivors of Dunkirk home to England, and airplanes fought overhead and fell flaming into the water, and then came the armada of transports and battleships bound for the invasion beaches of Normandy, and then huge bomber formations passed overhead, carrying catastrophe to Dresden.

His mind slid from past nows into the *now* now. He looked at his passport, a solid relic of a real miracle, and at the stamp the Brits had affixed in Calais:

LEAVE TO ENTER FOR SIX MONTHS
EMPLOYMENT PROHIBITED

And as they rrrrrrrrrrrrrrrd around the end of the jetty, toward the dock, his thoughts returned to the bar and the riddle Janet Ma had presented there.

What goes on four in the spring, two in the summer, and three in the fall?

'Some of us can solve that one, Alexander, but the Sphinx has posed others, unanswered to this day.'

144

NINETEEN

The Fly buzzed over the rooftops of Soho and up Greek Street to a green square, circled the pay toilet, then settled on a life-sized petrous replica of Charles II, whence from a distance he watched The Chief of the New Team, for the moment seated before a high house, #2 Soho Square, on a marble step worn down by the feet of sixteen human generations, draw a sodden blue handkerchief from a back pocket and blow. The Fly and his blood kin, aristocrats all, cousins to the South Carolina Flies of Beaufort, Parris Island, and Hilton Head, had prospered and multiplied sufficiently since swearing vengeance on the killer of the family's patriarch to fill all the flyspace in the amphitheater of Nîmes, and then some. The Chief of the New Team rose to let a woman pass in, then moved crabwise to a small shop window to look at the books displayed there. Curiosity aroused, his attention stuck as to flypaper on the cover of one called *SQUED*, a novel of promise, for it dealt with familiar subjects, like death, and displayed a skeleton, a barstool, a Buick blazoned on a black flag, a postage stamp depicting Warren G. Harding, another commemorating Daniel Boone, and a bronze statue of Nathan Hale, a man who, thought The Fly, would look much like The Chief had he been represented in shorts and a T-shirt instead of the garb of an eighteenth-century schoolmaster.

The morning commuters, thickening rapidly, aroused in The Fly a certain gratitude that the Creator had blessed him with wings. Numerous people were now detaching themselves from the stream of London Wacker-walkers to tread the step where Thomas De

Quincey had once sat writing fragments of *Confessions of an English Opium Eater*, and enter the house of Bloomsbury Publishing Ltd.

The Chief of the New Team, trembling with the excitement of being in London at last, had risen at sunup in Highgate and walked downhill between lofty rusted iron fences guarding an overgrown cemetery, fallen columns and broken angels, to the end where he caught a 214 bus and sat at the front of the top deck and peered in fascination at the streets of London being drawn toward him by furious bus wheels. He descended the spiral stairs and stepped out on King William Street, and, at random, roamed in awe and wonder as image after image, from books, from prints, from films, manifested in reality. The silly girls and their *Praefectus Castrorum* were sleeping still in Highgate in the house George had rented on Swain's Lane, a medieval passage yclept Swine's Lane in more basic times. As he, the Chief of the New Team, a disembodied hovering sphere of observation opening to one marvel after another, walked around in a golden aura of romantic feeling, he was on occasion shocked back into classical reality when traffic moving on, to him, the wrong side of the road, abruptly reminded him that stepping off a curb was not nearly as safe as his automatic pilot had assumed.

The pedestrian traffic moved in a kind of chaos too, because, as he saw, most people seem naturally to trend to the right, and then sensing their error, veer to the left.

On drawing away from the book display, The Chief strolled up Soho Street toward Oxford Street.

The Fly sprang from the head of Charles II and followed.

The Chief stood poised on the curb, ready to cross.

The Fly swooped down toward an eye.

The Chief shied back and jumped up to smack The Fly.

And felt a tremendous painful flash and fell into oblivion.

Images began to form and Billy swam upward in the dream sea and broached the surface.

He was aware of a sunbeam, and of having been asleep, and of a pleasantly painful throbbing, and then he saw the silly girls and George, and Phil, all arranged around him, in a deathbed scene.

A very premature deathbed scene.

He sat up.

That made him giddy.

'Where am I?'

Watching himself in this TV-soap movie, he cringed at having spoken such a cliché line.

'You're in the Royal Free Hospital,' said Amy. 'In Hampstead.'

'*Ham*pstead?'

'You fucking-A.'

'George thinks it's the best.'

'What happened?'

'You were struck down by the rearview mirror of a bus.'

He remembered worrying about them, the way they extended out beyond the buses' crimson flanks.

Smitten but not slain.

Call me Lucky Al the Second.

'You're going to be okay. As good as new, Sowboy mio, but you have to rest.'

'A close call,' said Phil, blazer-clad as always.

Today was a sky-blue Philday.

Billy felt faint and the TV serial clicked off and dwindled to a glowing spot, a white hole opening into the anti-universe of dreams.

The Chief of the New Team broached again and saw night windows, and Phil, seated beside the bed, reading *Time Out* magazine.

'Phil.'

'How you feeling, lad?'

He thought about this. 'Ready for action.'

'You had concussion. You know how it is with them. Either you come out okay, or you don't.'

'I'm okay.'

'I know. That's why I said it.' He moved his chair, so as to face the bed. 'No action for a while, though. You have to take it easy until the brain-bruise abates.'

'Did you fly here specially to see me?'

'Yep. As you no doubt notice, for me it's a sky-blue day.'

'How long was I unconscious?'

'From the bus until now? About three-and-a-half days.' He reached in his dispatch case and produced two beers. 'Time to roll some cans.'

Billy popped the top. 'Here's to joy and genius.'

They sat, sipping beer, smiling, silent, content.

'Al, my detectives have peeled back another layer of the onion. Five companies bought all that stock, but they're just fronts for *one*.'

'Meaning one group, or person, owns the controlling interest.'

'You've got it.'

'So what do we do now?'

'We move as fast as we can.'

The next morning, after a luscious British breakfast – prunes, herring, one egg, bacon, bangers, fried tomatoes, toast, tea – and the doctor's round, Billy found himself host to his colleagues and a notary public from the embassy. 'Hey hey, a royal levee, just like Louis XIV.'

'Fucking-A. Time to drive the hogs out of the creek and clear the water.'

Phil drew a legal document from his dispatch case. 'This is a power of attorney, written so you can rescind it whenever you want. It means you grant us the authority to act in your name in all matters concerning the ZEUGMA Theme Group.'

'So you guys can move fast while I lie here and vegetate.'

'That's it.'

'Okay. But how can you make it legal, I mean, signing it in a foreign country?'

'You sign it. We all sign as witnesses. And this gentleman from the embassy will notarize it.'

Billy signed in triplicate. He kept one copy and returned the others to Phil. The notary stepped outside.

'Now comes the levee,' said Janet Ma, giving him a sweet smile. 'We'll take advantage of your private room.'

'Yeah. Now we get down to fucking business.' Billy propped himself up on pillows and they all drew chairs close to his bed.

'I'll sketch out where we are,' said Janet. Although dressed for business and the street, Janet radiated a powerful, sexy aura, and Billy got an enormous hard-on under the sheet. 'As Phil told us, one company holds control, if not complete ownership, of the five companies which bought our stock. That means they can do anything with ZTG they want. But who is *they*? Why did they invest that immense sum in our stock offering? We don't know. We don't even know who they are. A consortium? One person? We have no way of guessing how they intend to use their power, but we do know they never would have bought control unless they plan to use that power somehow.'

'So we have to move fast, and get things done, before they dump us for new directors,' said Phil.

Janet tapped her knee. 'What you directors could do, is use their money, which is now banked in company accounts, to buy your stock back at par value, including the shares you gave yourselves free.'

'Yes,' said Phil. 'That would be perfectly legal, but it would be robbing somebody. What I propose is if that sneaky somebody tries to rob us by dumping us and using our money to buy his stock back at a profit, *then* we let him make us rich with his money.'

'It still doesn't make sense,' said Aimée.

'That's the fucking truth, bet your sweet ass it is.'

Phil drew some papers out of his dispatch case and passed them around. 'Here's what Janet and I worked out. We sign this affidavit confirming that here, at this formal board of directors meeting, which our *Praefectus Castrorum* will now call to order – thank you, George – we unanimously instruct our CEO, Janet Ma, that if any indication appears they're trying to sell stock, on such indication, using company funds, Janet buys all of our stock back for the company at a price per share not to exceed par value.'

They all agreed. He summoned the notary again, and, in his presence, they made a formal resolution to that effect, and signed the papers. Janet thanked the notary and saw him to the door.

'Prima!' said Phil, beaming. 'We're clear! When I get back, I'll file this with the Cook County Recorder. Now, if they walk into one of our meetings with their stock certificates and some new directors, and kick us out, Janet follows her instructions, buys our stock, and we're all rich, and we start a new company.'

'Yeah! Like Alexander! When he was eighteen, his father was murdered while walking down an aisle toward the dias where he was to conduct a meeting of the generals of the Greek forces assembled to attack Persia. Alexander stepped to the dias, peered silently over the assembly until the body was removed and the people hushed, and then he said: "Nothing has changed save the name of the king."'

'Yes!' exclaimed Aimée. 'We'll be Makedon Theme Group Associates, and other than that the only change will be all our free stock has metamorphosed into good old US money!'

'Fucking-A! Now that we've fixed that, we have to get as much done, as much committed, as we can. We'll spend the money. If we get all the other pigs running, *they* will have to run along too.'

Billy was now stone hard and aching.

'Tomorrow,' said Phil, 'we'll be back in Chicago. Except George, who'll secure the title from the Malaysians. I'll file the affidavit, and we'll make arrangements to put our money into a maximum state of liquidity. Melt it, so to speak. Janet will stay there and keep the home fires burning under the melting pot, and Aimée and I will fly to Djakarta, meet George there, and fly to the island.'

'We going to buy George's island?' Billy asked, drawing his legs up under the sheet, creating a snow-covered knee-mountain.

'Yes sir. Don't you like the idea?'

'I'm all for it.'

'Gather round,' said Aimée, embracing George and Janet.

They all embraced.

'Here we go!'

She led to the door, and out, and they followed.

Janet paused in the doorway, and turned. 'We'll keep you informed. I'll call you every day.' She came back, closing the door behind her, and sat on the edge of the bed, by the twin peaks of knee-mountain. 'As soon as the doctor permits, you'll fly from here to Djakarta, and go meet them on the island.'

What a sexy bitch!

Light gray stockings!

'I sure will.'

'I'll smooth everything out. I'll keep it *oiled*.'

Billy's suspicions kindled and flamed. 'Janet. There's something wrong with all this. Fishy. It doesn't make sense. I – I'm kind of wrought up anyway, I mean the way I'm feeling now. It's like being at the eye doctor, and he's testing your eyes, and keeps changing lenses, and manipulating your focus.'

'I feel the same.'

'As George says, we've been sliding around like a hog on ice.'

'It's much warmer than that.'

'I sure feel warmer.'

'I know.'

'Do you think I'm too naïve?'

'Why ask that?'

'I'm lucky. I always land on my feet. But, well . . . you know, me, I believe people's stories, and that they mean what they say, and I treat them that way.' He touched her knee. 'So what do you think?'

'I think you have bright eyes and a good smile.'

'So do you, Janet.'

'Almost time for me to go.' She stood, and drew the white curtain of privacy around the bed. 'Alexander, I like your funky smell.' She slipped her hand under the sheet along his abdomen into the corn silk and gently grasped him. 'I'm going to give you a little goodbye, get-well kiss.' She threw off the sheet and flipped the pillows on to the floor. She straddled him, pressed his legs down and apart, and slowly took his throbbing prick into her mouth.

PART FIVE

OF CHANGES

PIG SPA
ISLAND

Pigs remind people of themselves. Why?
We don't identify with cattle or sheep
or goats or even horses. Just pigs.
I ask you, why the fuck is that?

George Ahasuerus Baxter
Pig Spa Island, 1993.

TWENTY

Sowboys and Indonesians, that's the game I'll be in before the sun sets. The plane had stopped in Rome; it came down from low rain clouds on to an airport. It might just as well have been Chicago. Going to Rome without seeing Rome! Now, outside, five miles down, exotic romantic places packed with trouble. Syria. Soon, Saudi Arabia, and then the Indian Ocean. The plane hurtled high above rugged sun-burned land resembling the route of Alexander. Was it greener down there twenty-three hundred years ago? Alexander had the wrong travel agent. He should have gone via KLM Air instead of by horse and foot, and reserved a window seat. Would the Persians have granted him a visa? Another spasm! Despairing, Billy peered at the line by the toilets, at traditional clothing of Southeast Asia and the East Indies. For horse and foot, the whole world is a commode. He rose, struggled out to the aisle, and joined the line. In London they would call it a queue – a loo queue, a toilet tail. Haunted by images of sudden shame, writhing from bladder pressure, from regrets for his folly of waiting seated for the line to vanish, Billy braced, and suffered, and made it. After lunching on fish-of-the-sea, five miles above the sea, and finishing *Snail*, a satirical novel he enjoyed immensely, he gazed out the window at an endless white ocean of ossified waves, a scudding stormy cloud-sea, abruptly petrified under the sun, and then he watched cartoons and movies with his earphones tuned to classical music. Funny! In school they'd said: this piece is Napoleon's battle, that piece Humperdinck's pals, but in fact the music fits *Popeye* and BBC news just as well. The hostess announced impending arrival. Rocking and shaking as it sank through a deep cloud, still miles aloft, the plane seemed caught in an earthquake, an airquake, that drew him back to 1989 and the UC undergraduate library. Emerging in rain, the plane thumped on to the runway, Djakarta, Indonesia, another Chicago.

As it moved toward the terminal, a voice warned in English and in Dutch, and in Bahasa Indonesian, that passengers should remain seated and belted until the plane stopped at the gate.

All *right*. It's really *happening*! I'm really *here*!

Billy passed through the formalities, and, a bag slung from each shoulder, stepped into the terminal.

He was struck by the sharp odor of cloves from the local cigarettes.

There stood George, chomping bubble gum.

Smiling, happy to see one another, they embraced. George slung one of the bags. 'It's fucking together! We've got the show on the road!' As they walked the length of the terminal, breathing cloves, Billy felt himself at a masquerade party, and then on the stage of reality theater, the set of reality films, only more like being in myth theater, myth films. I'm playing a rôle where everybody but me has a script, and that's half the fun. 'This door, Bill, here by the Hertz counter.' Obscene yellow as always. 'Come on – let's go.'

They stepped out on to the airfield beside a security fence behind which men in red fezzes serviced a Quantas jumbo jet.

'There she is!' exclaimed George, indicating an amphibious twin-engined plane, white with a high wing. 'You are gazing at one growthy boar!'

Emblazoned on its side, a wild boar, winged, entangled in the letters ZTG, all done in olive green and brick red. They entered by an aluminum ladder and sat in the back seat. In front, a long-haired pilot and George's Chinese pig.

'I got two pets now. Him, and this titless wonder, Chandra.'

'I'm Al,' Billy said to Chandra as they shook hands. 'I'm honored to make your aquaintance.'

'Me speak not the good English.' She smiled a bright, even, filed-tooth smile. 'Hello Mister Al.' She wore a sweater and slacks and a headset and had tits, small but nice. She started the engines and it was all noise and tug. Alighting from the plane, she laid a candy bar on the tarmac, drew the ladder inside, sprang back across the pig into her place, and closed the door. 'Me like you, good boy Al.'

Boy! And you younger than I am!

'Allez-oop!' cried George in his trombone voice. The plane raced and roared, and reared up off the ground into the rain and soon it was grinding along in a gray cloud limbo, thus resolving once and for all what the Walrus and the Carpenter had so passionately disputed many many years ago: Can pigs fly? 'I advertised in the Djakarta papers for a pilot, and, yeah – lots of qualified shitheads applied – good job, good pay, bet your ass they did, so I cut out all the hot-doggers and mercenary soldiers and all the other fuckheads I couldn't trust. So I thinks, now, George, this broad's our best bet. And then, when she tells me where she's from – Bedulu on Bali, I'm sure, and I hire her. Yeah. *Bedulu*. It's a crossroads village now, but six hundred years ago it was a royal capital. She says she's a direct descendant of the last king of the Pejeng Dynasty, the pig-headed magician king pushed into the shit by an army from Java.'

'Pig headed?'

'That's the story. Seems his magic was so strong he could get his servant to cut off his head, then set it back on, and, *voilà*, he's okay again. So one day the servant cuts off his head to impress some rich assholes, and a dog grabs the head and runs off with it, and drops it in the river, and blub blub blub, goodbye head. So the servant panics. He chops the head off a nearby pig, and sets that on the king. Result? Pig-headed king.'

'So now you have two pets, her and piglet, sitting side by side.'
'Yeah.'
'Chandra, and . . .?'
'Waggles. I named my pig Waggles.'
'Waggles!'
'Waggles.'
'You named him after the dog that broke the back of Pigville?'
'You fucking-A! Waggles, reincarnated in a better form. A cur, upscaled. A nice Hindu touch, ain't it?'
'I'd rather think Buddhist.'

They reposed, musing, in their thrummmmming thrummmmming thrummmmming light-metal capsule, suspended in gray nowhere.

'So tell me, George, isn't it asking for trouble to have a Moslem sitting next to an unclean abomination like sweet Waggles?'

'She ain't no Moslem. That's why when Chandra said she's from Bali, I got serious.' George turned and reached over the seat's back into the baggage compartment. A bub-bub-bubbling burping sound emerged, as from an office cooler. With a flourish, he set brimming wine glasses and a wine dish on a folding table, then passed a glass and the dish to Chandra. She set the dish on the floor before Waggles who slid down and began slurping. 'You can have your phoenixes and quetzals, Al. Give me a pig-bird like this, any day.' He hugged Billy's shoulder. 'Our company plane's the origin-al, number one, deb-u-tante swino special!'

'Bali, George. Bali.'

'Oh yeah, Bali. They got a weird Hinduism there. Much better than the real stuff.'

'So Chandra's Hindu?'

'Weird Hindu.'

'Seems like a good pilot.'

'Nice little broad, eh?'

'Plump and spirited.'

'And respectful. Talks to me in High Balinese.' He gripped the back of her seat. 'She believes in spirits, evil and good, both kinds. Them invisible pus-eaters, they're everywhere, part of life, and you better believe it, you fuck with them and they'll roast your ass. Yes, they will! It's how she sees things. Her candy bar? An offering for a safe flight.'

'You go for her, don't you?'

'That titless wonder? Shit, no! The broad I want to fuck? You really want to know who? Janet Ma, that's who.' Impulsively, George reached in to the baggage compartment and drew out a tabloid, folded back to an advertisment.

'I bought some of this shit. It's coming. Express Mail! Right now, it's in the air somewhere, just like we are. I'm going to tell her it's mosquito repellent, and squirt it all over me, and fuck the hell out of her, up the ass, too.'

George was still babbling along when the plane burst out of the clouds into sunshine. Far below, in a gorgeous sparkling sea, hundreds of islands, large ones, small ones, alone, in groups, some hilly, some mountainous, dark green, ribs of gray rock, shorelines traced by white beaches, the whole, somehow, seeming flooded, the waters still rising, soon all would vanish save for a single post-diluvian ark.

'George, that's kind of what the California coastal region'll look like when the ice-caps melt.'

'This fucking country has about fourteen thousand islands, maybe six thousand inhabited.'

'So nobody will really miss our island.'

'Not until we've secured it.'

'How'd things go with the Malaysians?'

'Good. They went for the payoff like sows go for Boarmate.'

'Looks like jungle down there. Might be too hot for hogs.'

'Shit, no. They've got more varieties of wild boar in Indonesia than anywhere else in the world.' Again, the burble and belch of the cooler. 'But thanks to them fucking Moslems, the people-to-pig ratio sucks. I mean *sucks*. I just got some figures from our department of agriculture. USDA says in the States we only got about fifty-six million hogs. Five-to-one, for Christ sake! And me, all the time I've been thinking it's *three*-to-one. Canada has twenty-five million people and ten million hogs. *That's* close to two-to-one. In 1886 the States had forty-six million hogs – you got to go way back then to equal the Canucks.' He turned back to the cooler. Another bubble and burp. 'I tell you, Al, on Pig Spa Island we'll have a better ratio than that, or even than Denmark's three hogs per.'

The plane began angling down and everything enlarged and boats differentiated from their wakes and tiny people, ant-people, manifested on their decks.

'There she is, Al. Pigville reborn!' George pointed at a medium-sized island rising ahead, one shaped like a potato. 'That low mountain there in the middle, that's where we'll build our Bavarian castle . . .!' He spoke to Chandra. 'Now we'll circle, come down slow, and I'll show you what's what. See, Al, plenty of beach. And

159

down there! Our town rising on the ruins of the old village. We got people working down there already. Yeah! We'll connect the castle to the kampong – that's what they call village around here – by funicular, you know, inclined railway.'

'Hey. All right! You and me, we both act out myths, that's our life, everybody's, but you and me, George, we're dancing and eating our way around the whole smorgasbord.'

'Look at our town there, rising on wreckage, the resurrected Pigville! Lose the battle, win the war. No swine commissioners down there. No architectural review boards, or zoning laws, or building codes either. Not in our town.'

'Not in *Streeterport*.'

They high-fived.

'Yeah. Streeterport. Just look there at them stone quays, and the pier, and that jetty. We'll dredge inside for big boats.'

'Sure will.'

'And we'll fence off most of Pig Spa Island – PSI, and keep it wild, and import boars as fast as guests kill them, and turn goats loose for the boars to eat.'

'And the goats eat jungle.'

'Fucking-A.'

'PSI's our Treasure Island, and you're my Long George Silver.'

The plane skimmed on to the water and moved around the end of the jetty.

'I sure as shit wish Sir Ron were here to enjoy this.'

TWENTY-ONE

As they taxied into the harbor, George said, 'Streeterport reminds me of Caesaria Maritima before Herod made such a big deal out of it. Folks used to say it once was a little kampong like this.' Chandra reversed one engine, making spray scud, and the flying pig pivoted and drifted sideways up to a float connected to the end of the pier by a hinged gangway. 'We only get two feet of tide; we made it this way to accommodate surge.'

Aimée and Phil and Janet and Tom Kraemer, the security chief, waited on the pier waving and shouting, and Aimée held a big picket sign saying WELCOME HOME ALEXANDER. They secured the plane and lowered the ladder to its pontoon and Billy skipped down from the pontoon to the float.

'Sowgirl mia!'

'Sowboy mio!'

They kissed, and they all embraced him. Chandra passed Waggles to George. His hands on Phil's shoulders, Billy held Phil at arm's length and studied his new costume: a Cubs cap, green T-shirt, shorts, and boots. 'Sowboy boots, eh, counsellor?'

'No. Sowskin cowboy boots. And a green T-shirt for a very green day.'

Chandra passed Billy's bags down, slung the mailbag over her shoulder, and followed them along the short wooden pier to the stone quay. About fifty yards ahead the road crossed Streeterport's principal and only avenue, then went on between two squad tents to a large medieval-style pavilion flying flags and banners almost

161

as colorful as the birds winging about the sick green jungly ridge rising steeply behind.

'That,' said Phil, 'as you'll notice when we're close enough to read the teak wood plaque over the door, is the seat of G. A. Baxter, *Praefectus Castrorum.*' They stopped at the intersection.

'Yeah, it's executive style. I just use my initials.' George stripped the wrapper from a lump of pink gum. 'That's professional. If I was a Brit, I'd use three letters. Maybe I should anyway. G. A. M. Baxter. Has a nice echo to it. Why not more? I've plenty more initials where the M comes from.'

The tent to the right served as kitchen, the left-hand one as tool house and shop, and as shelter for water pump and generator. From the main power line conveying ionized electrons from the generator into the tents and huts hung an electrocuted bat with a foot-long brownish body and five-foot wingspan.

'We've got to insulate that fucker. Them *pteropi eduli* – flying foxes to you – keep roosting there and zapping out our power.'

'Coming in, looking down, George and I named our town Streeterport.'

'I like that,' said Aimée. Janet smiled and so did Phil.

'Beautiful! Then it's done.'

'*All* done,' said Phil. 'We named the streets. This one's Quetzal Way, and, as for our premier thoroughfare, we christened it Phoenix Road.' He drew in the dust.

<pre>
                        Q
                        U
        P H O E N I X
                        T
                        Z
                        A
                        L
</pre>

'See, it makes a cross, shaped just like the town is. And a challenge, too. We make a new street, well then, its name has to fit, both the abstract and the fact, and at the same time yield the highest possible Scrabble value.'

'Who named the streets?'

'Janet did. We thought George would go for Hampshire and Duroc, or something else equally suidic, so we beat him to it.'

162

'I like them birds. A new Pigville is rising on this island.'

Before George's dwelling, and under the dried bat, stood several tables with benches and candles set in perforated tin cans, Quetzal Café. A rank of thatched, olive-green, A-frame huts stretched along Phoenix Road, facing the sea, ten on each side of Quetzal Way. They rested on foundations fishermen's homes had occupied until razed by Indonesian soldiers crushing Communism, and then by pirates. Between the dust of the road and the stone of the quay spread the sward of a soccer field and courts for badminton and basketball. At the moment, in the lull before dinner, a leathery two-foot lizard sunning seemed to embody all life on Phoenix Road. A cloud of yellow butterflies swept by.

'Do you expect us to dress for dinner?' asked Billy.

'You can come bareass for all I care.'

'Our supply ship came last week,' said Phil. 'That's one of the reasons we were in such a hurry to get here, to supervise the workmen it brought. Most, it took back.' He gestured at their new town. 'We've got more now than Chicago did in its early days. Look at it, Billy. Aren't you proud? Back in Chi – halfway around the world – we used computers to mix our ideas and relevant data, and we made plans and contracts, and gathered all this stuff and more together in a warehouse in Singapore, ready for rapid deployment anywhere in the world. And now, lo and behold, here it is! And thanks to Chandra and George, we've a cadre of people to make things happen, and we'll fly in more as required.' He smacked Billy on the muscle. 'Sure beats rolling beer cans around an office floor!'

On the ridge behind George's pavilion, monkeys trooped, crickets crackled, giant yard-long ebony-and-red squirrels frolicked, and a blaze of technicolor birds wheeled and darted, roosted and called.

'Now for the guided, lectured tour,' said Aimée. 'We can do it all from the crossroads here, just looking. The huts on the corners are supply depots. Next, toward the mountain, comes the cockfight arena and across from it the movie house. In George's place we have a telephone connected directly with the Chicago system. It gives us everything we always get but the right time. TV? We don't have any, and won't, if I can help it. The other huts are all living quarters. Each has a chemical toilet, and a water tap connected to the water tank behind George's pavilion. We have a permanent team, all young, so that makes you its Chief. Right? One of the huts belongs to you and me. Our names are on a white board over the door. Phil has a hut. Janet has one. Tom has one. The two cooks share one; the mason and the carpenter share another. So do the electrician and the plumber. We have an architect, an engineer, a draftswoman, a surveyor, and an artist, each with a hut. We have a guest hut and a hut reserved for Chandra. Our eight boys Friday share two huts – six in one, two in the other. I call that our testament to the eternal nature of sexism and racism.'

'As in: Why no girls Friday?'

'Exactly.'

'Why?'

'Ask George.'

'Hey swino, how come no *girls* Friday?'

'Because we need a defense force.'

'Against what?'

'Pirates. That's what. You think the old fishing village here just flew up into the fucking sky?' He made a side-tooth snarl. 'I'd rather swim in a puddle of hog piss than rely on girls to fight.'

'You've seen too many movies.'

'As soon as the pirates notice action here, smell our riches, you'll be *in* one of them fucking movies.'

'Oh?'

'Right now, what's to stop them? They see our lights. They land way down the beach, sneak up with automatic weapons. Your fucking head's in their collection and they play soccer with it on our own fucking green. What you think the first soccer ball was, anyway? A hive? A stone? A stuffed piglet? Believe me. We need goons, and fast. But where the fuck we get them? Advertise in *Soldier of Fortune* magazine? Don't have time, and even if we did, them mercenaries are about as trustworthy soldiering as hungry hogs babysitting. So when Chandra goes to recruit the Fridays, I tells her to get adolescents who don't hate pigs, lads I can trust, boys I can train as the nucleus of our Praetorian Guard, our Foreign Legion. So what the fuck's she do? Guess! She hires fucking queers, that's what! She says pansies'll be loyal, and work with us as long as we want them, instead of always mooning off after broads.' He smacked a fist in to his hand and side teeth flashed gold. 'Damn! Why the fuck did God invent women, anyway?'

Janet burst into ringing laughter. 'Chandra tells me she was lucky to get them. She noses up six Balinese, but she can't find any more, and, despairing, standing in the street looking for a taxi to take her to the airport for her daily flight here, she spies these two pale ragged wimpy Anglos spare-changing passers-by. Students from Cleveland on their grand tour. Spent most of their money, were robbed of the rest. So she hires them on the spot, and brings them straight to us, and, the next day, flies in her Balinese. And that's going to be George's trained army. That and Tom! And his militia? The rest of us, including me and Aimée and the draftswoman and the cooks and the architect too – all of them, every one, is a mere blood-dripping broad!'

'Ma. You will show me respect.'

Janet spit on the ground, peered at him, then replied in a steel voice. 'You give me those Bali babies and those Anglo wimps and old Tom, too, and automatic weapons, and ammo, and I'll show you some action. *Ma* action. I'll make shit into soldiers.'

'And then you'll build a fucking opera house for them to campaign in.'

'Watch your mouth, asshole. You're talking to Janet *Ma*.'

'In Chinese, babe, Ma means Horse.'

'Yes. And it also means General Ma Changshan, who took the money the Japs offered him to ally his army with theirs, and spent it all on his army, pay, ammo, and weapons, just as he'd promised – then kicked their ass so hard the chief Machiavelli who'd told the Emperor they could buy General Ma killed himself.'

'Okay, horseface, as *Praefectus Castrorum* I'll consider your broadass fighting qualities.'

Billy broke in. 'George. You sure you don't want me to dress for dinner?'

George snarled and strode away.

'That, sowboy mio, concludes the lectured tour. Time to check in at our new home.'

Amy walks at my side, arms folded, sweating under her still fresh light-blue cotton frock. In our hut, she's spread a big futon for us to sleep on. Some crates and boards serve as shelves, and more as stools. She has a big table with a typewriter, a basin and bucket by the water tap, a soap dish and a mirror, some luggage, a tall filing cabinet with a vase of orchids on top, and a sturdy generator crate on which she's set up her computer. I drop my bags. I touch her shoulder, turn her to me and kiss her gently, all the time aware

165

of sweat sticking our skins together. 'You silly girl.' I said.

'I'm going to kiss you all over.'

'Not 'til I unpack.'

'And not until the Fridays call us to dinner.'

I drew her down beside me on a crate. I like it here. Where would I be now had The Fly not make me desert from the Corps? We look into each other's eyes, sweating and smiling. Happy.

'Sowboy mio,' she said in her love voice, 'George is jealous of my taking his place in your heart.'

'I can believe that.'

'George is as amoral as money.'

'And as tough as boiled warthog meat.'

'And horny! A couple days ago, honest to God, just after supper, he called on me, sat right where you are now, and showed me his mail-order catalog of rubber sex-dollies.'

'I guess he goes for you, Amy; how could he help it? But the one he truly lusts for is Janet.' Now to tell Amy about Attractant-10.

She shrieked with joy. 'I've been keeping something for you.' She sprang up and rushed to her luggage and dug happily in a suitcase. 'Brought it from Chicago.' Flinging out clothes, she found a newspaper, and, still laughing, came back. 'Look at this! George's ad – see – the one you're telling me about. Attractant-10. Right?'

'That's it.'

'I thought so. and in this same issue of the *National Examiner*, the *same* issue . . . ! This news story!'

Sex spray won't drive the women hog-wild

ATTRACTANT 10, a spray that's supposed to lure women, only works on pigs, reports a British magazine.

Sold for $17 a can, the spray is actually repackaged Boarmate, a sex-attractant spray for hogs which sells for one-fifth the price of Attractant 10, writes the magazine Which.

The makers of Boarmate admit: "We do supply Boarmate under a plain label to other companies. What they do with it then is their affair."

166

They whooped and wept with laughter, and they heard pounding on the flimsy screen door, then George's voice.

'Come on out Al, I want to talk with you.'

Billy came out, cheeks wet with tears.

'What's so fucking funny?'

'Oh, it's a private sex thing we have.'

'Well, feast your eyes on the sex thing *I* have.' George drew a spray can from a paper bag. 'It came, my Attractant-10, it was in the mailbag. Talk about fast service! Express Mail to our PO Box in Djakarta.' He handed it to Billy for him to inspect and admire. 'Bet you wish you'd thought of sending for some.' Returning the can to the bag, he drew Billy aside, stepped on a slug. He scraped it off his sole. 'Fucking slug! But what the fuck do I care? It's my day.' He gripped Billy's shoulder. 'Janet's going back to Chicago. Flies out of here tomorrow night. I want you and Aimée to invite us on a picnic tomorrow morning. We'll go way down the beach with a basket of good food and wine – the cook'll fix it, and we'll eat, and then you two make an excuse and leave Janet and me there alone. Okay?'

'Glad to help.'

'And this little baby here'll take care of the rest.' He smiled a huge, happy smile. 'Janet. I'll wash her and worm her, you can bet your ass on that.'

Billy walked back into the hut.

'What was all that about?'

Billy told her, and, choking with mirth, virtually hysterical, they planned the picnic. Then, as they kept on talking about George, elation faded.

'Alexander. As time goes by, I feel I know him better and better, but what do we know *about* him? There's plenty more down in the depths we don't even suspect.'

'Yes. It's like looking at the surface of Monterey Bay, then swimming down thirty feet, and trying to imagine what it's like a mile and a half deeper, where no one's ever been.'

'And his security chief? What do we know about him?'

'He says Tom is an angel from Heaven.'

'Phil says his detective agency – and he's given them an open purse to work with, Phil says they can't find anything about George, not even in New Orleans – no vitae, nothing. They don't know where he was born or how old he is. It's awesome. He rules us, so to speak, but we don't know anything about him. Something's going wrong for him. Lately, he's been depressed.'

'He's *Praefectus Castrorum* now. Maybe he's feeling the emptiness of ambition fulfilled.'

'What's the next level?'

'I don't know, Amy. I don't know any more about him than you do. What I *do* know is I never know what will happen next, and that's fun. I know all this is interesting and exciting, and that down in my depths, below my diving range, something's happening I feel good about.'

She stood and strode to her computer. 'I don't care, either. I'm getting what I want. Eventually, I'll have a computer room here, and then I can run all the world's myths through it, and recombine them into new ones, mesh these into a new mythology, one suited to the new world, a shared reality myth, a master myth, an armature, to form morals and meaning for the worldwide tribe of man. Alexander, I believe it helps belief when myth finds confirmation in historical truth, and – for sure, in experience. Personal experience. And it helps when myth is consistent with probability. Like the Alexander stories. They are secular myths the ancients believed. The master myth for the new world will be the ultimate product of the science of chaos. Today's cacophony will transform into tomorrow's harmony, a worldwide, mythological foundation of meaning. *The* mythological *emotional* foundation of meaning. And *I* am going to be able to do it. *We* will be able to do it. We *are* doing it! Right here in Streeterport!' She threw her arms around his neck and kissed him. 'And Pig Spa Island provides the perfect cover!'

A gentle knocking agitated the screen door.

She opened the door, admitting an impish Anglo Friday who formally announced: 'Dinner is served.'

They walked to the Café Quetzal where at the largest and most substantial of the tables, the one directly before the open front of the pavilion, they joined George, and Phil, and Janet. Other diners sat around lesser tables. Bustling Fridays set a wine cooler, à la champagne bucket, by George, its electric tail reaching back to a plug in his tent. The Fridays scurried about in the dusk, serving pork curry, and malaria pills, and a blushing assortment of strange, soft fruit, while giant bats flopped and wheeled overhead. Waggles cuddled against George's leg. Doubtless, Waggles had imprinted on

168

him. 'Just like the good old days in Pigville, Al, just like Pigville. We maintain command and control by isolating ourselves and keeping the others in ass-sucking subservience, by symbols, by intimidation, by making them carry out missions, some sensible and necessary, some absurd, dangerous, and stupid. When they fuck up, you shit on them. Like they forgot to order pig food for poor sweet Waggles here. Our Fridays of whatever rank, they got to remember their responsibilities. They forget, in all innocence maybe. But now, what's Waggles going to eat?'

'Feed him garbage, like always.'

'Garbage! You think garbage grows on trees?' George filled a German beer mug with wine and drained it. 'You know what that fucking Chandra did? She pinched Waggles on the cheek, and told him, in low Balinese, at her yearly temple festival they roast dogs and pigs for everybody, and he's invited this year, to lie on the table with an apple in his mouth. He understands low Balinese. She scared the shit out of him.'

'George,' said Billy, 'why do you keep calling Waggles *he* when we can plainly see that *he* is *she* – a *her?*'

'Because I fucking feel like it.' George sipped wine and a benevolent expression spread over his features. 'Got a riddle for you. What's black and white and red all over?'

Aimée made a face. 'A newspaper?'

'Thought you'd say that. Well you're wrong. *Red*, not read. R-E-D. A pink-skinned Hampshire.'

'Once upon a time,' said Phil, 'there were three little piggies who moved from Chicago to San Francisco. One was very lazy; one was indolent; and the third, intensely industrious.' Phil paused, to fix attention. 'Listen carefully, there's a moral here. Very well. It soon came time for them to build their houses, for they were homeless. The first little piggy supped wine and slept under newspapers on a park bench. That was his living accommodation. Along came a violent cold rain and soaked him and he died of pneumonia in SF General Hospital. The second little piggy built his house of cardboard and old packing crates and boards with galvanized iron for a roof, and cooked over an oil stove. He ate steak and drank wine and stayed dry and healthy through the whole rainstorm. But the next day a high wind whooped in through the Golden Gate and huffed and puffed until his house fell down and the boards knocked him cold and caught fire and he burned to death. Now the third little piggy, the good little piggy, had taken no time off to drink wine and eat steak and laze about. No, not him. He stopped work but once a day, and that to eat at McDonalds. He struggled and slaved and built a wonderful house, all of brick, with the best tile roof money could buy. When he heard of the fate of his two colleagues, he smiled and raised a glass to himself, another to virtue. Then, in autumn, not so very long ago, along comes an earthquake, and seizes that house, and twists it, and shakes it, and wracks it until it falls down and crushes that piggy flat.' Smiling, Phil poured himself some wine, and sat back.

'And that's it?' asked George. 'That's all?'

'That's all. Now it's time to talk business. Chandra brought us news in today's mail. We heard from Kuala Lumpur. In exchange for our money, Malaysia has waived its claim to our island, a claim they had already decided is too weak to press further, and they transferred all their rights, proprietary and otherwise, to ZEUGMA Theme Associates. Malaysia is honest. The deal is thoroughly legitimate. But Indonesia is awesomely corrupt, and we have the pot boiling there. Indeed we have.'

They agreed, as Aimée put it, to spin wheels, keep refining plans and acquiring tools and supplies, but not to invest large capital until they had clear title from Indonesia.

'This week, we're going to take that fucking surveyor, and architect, and draftbitch, and work out plans for a golf course.'

Suddenly, *deus ex machina*, a huge dazzling flash exploded overhead and they all looked up and saw a blazing bat and all the lights went out. Scurrying Fridays lit Coleman lanterns and candles. George chugged another mug of wine.

'Yes,' said Phil, 'the golf course. We can't build it until we can bring in backhoes and loggers. But we can lay out the world's best, something even better than Spyglass at Pebble Beach in California.'

'No, we ain't sitting around with our thumbs up our ass. Not me, anyway. I'm bringing in a spray plane to soak this whole fucking place in DDT to kill all the mosquitos.'

'No we don't,' said Janet. 'And I'm beginning to wonder whether it's ethical to call this place a spa. I know we have spectacular cataracts of pure water. But when people hear spa, they think of medicinal waters, waters which can cure, and even prolong life.'

'That's *why* we call it spa, you tit-licking cretin. Telling them so – making them suckers believe drinking our waters preserves their youth – *makes* it true.'

'George. I see it now. I *know* you. You are *Pigsy*. I don't know where Sandy or Monkey or Tripitaka are, but I do know you are Pigsy in his most revolting manifestation. I'll bet your rake is hidden right over there in that tent.'

'You fucking dildo plunger, you can take your Pigsy, and your Monkey, and your Sandy, and your Tripitaka, and your rake, and your idealism, too, and roll them up into a nice neat ball and shove them up your ass! I ain't no pig! I'm *me*, G. A. M. Baxter, *Praefectus Castrorum* of Pig *Spa* Island. I like pigs because they're practical, like me. None of your piss-complected idealism for *me*. Hell no! I'm practical, through and through. Like I wear brown underpants, and always have, and if you have any sense, you do too.'

'If your aunt had balls, George, she'd be your uncle.'

TWENTY-TWO

Jamie! Jamie! Time to get up. She cuddled and massaged the warm, smooth muscular back on the futon beside her, but it's not Jamie, and this is not Montréal. Soon he'll have snow on his head and shoulders as he walks to his classes at McGill, and we'll have sweat on ours as we live here in temperatures hovering always between seventy and ninety. She kissed Billy's shoulder and sat up. *The picnic.* 'Up! Up! Billyboy! Picnic time!' Remembering she'd named him Alexander, because of the ideal to surpass human limits, she watched him walk naked to the chemical toilet and close the door behind him. Farts and gurglings, and he came out, and dressed in cut-off shorts and T-shirt and a big floppy Australian hat, and she put on shorts, and a thin blouse, and her beret. They sprayed each other with insect repellent, then walked to Quetzal Way where they stopped at the crossroads to adjust to a new day. A blue painted sky, and the sick green ridge with all its fancy birds and butterflies and the fringed pavilion tent with its limp banners, and in the café a tired-looking Phil, alone at their table: all of these abruptly slid out of mind when her eyes focussed on the dead bats.

The first, though dry, remained brown – but last night's sacrifice to progress and development and to rich-tourists-to-come-mainly-from-Japan resembled a giant slice of bread, burnt black in some diabolic toaster. Somehow the metabolism of bat A had been more commensurate with a 220-volt surge than that of bat B.

'Watch out life!' yelled Aimée. 'All living things beware! Here come people!'

'Must humankind die so life can live?'

172

She grasped Billy's hand and ran him to their table.

Phil gave them a wan good-morning smile.

'Hey, sport, how about a big happy grin?' No response. She knew he would be working all day on the terrain model of the island and supervising the erection of a pole soon to display the ZTG flag eighty feet aloft. 'You're pissed because I didn't invite you to the picnic.'

'Oh, no. I'm thinking about why I hate doing business with Indonesians.' He sighed. 'Shortly before I was giving food away on Haight Street, the Indonesian army, and the Moslem fanatics it controlled, murdered about half a million people. They call it the Great Killing. Bodies clogged the waterways. Headless torsos rotted on the roads. Our Embassy and CIA had infiltrated the government and army at the highest levels. The Embassy and CIA compiled a list of five thousand Communists, gave it to the army, then checked off names as the army caught and killed them. And you know what? It still goes on. They field death squads which kill subversives and suspected criminals, as they put it, by the thousand. Jails are stuffed with prisoners. Torture is routine. In any travel agency you can get brochures celebrating Beautiful Bali and Romantic Java and Seductive Sumatra.' Grimacing, he scratched his brow. 'In 1975, Indonesia invaded Timor, a quondam Portuguese colony recently granted independence. When the UN condemned the invasion, USA abstained from the vote, then lobbied against UN efforts to make Indonesia leave Timor. What of Iraq and Kuwait? Do you hear an echo? Indonesia killed 100,000 of Timor's 700,000 people. USA gave Indonesia weapons and advisors who, the Timorese say, engaged in directing the campaign, and even in combat. And me, I thought I could do some good giving away bologna sandwiches. Yes. So what now?'

Yawning and stretching, George came out of his pavilion and hollered for Fridays. They came running, all eight of them, and brought his cooler to the table. He grunted acknowledgment. Aimée spoke to an albino Friday, and, soon, two backpacks containing picnic solids and picnic liquids lay beside her chair. Coffee and muffins and soft pastel fruits appeared on the table. Janet came whistling 'C. C. Rider', and sat in her place. They could see George had already established a table protocol, mainly psychological as the table was round. At this moment, unknown to each other, they all decided to sit in different places at each meal. 'Boss swino,' she said smiling, 'where the hell are our silver napkin rings?'

A shrieking sound came from the pavilion.

'Waggles fucking knocked the phone off the hook! He likes the dialtone, even after it turns into banshee wailing.' George fetched Waggles, set her on his lap.

'Ain't he cute!'

'She, George. *She.*'

'Go ahead,' said Phil, 'be adolescents. Play. Enjoy your picnic. And as you walk the beach and let nature divert you from brick-house building, and while you listen to the mocking birds sing their mocking songs, remember, basically, we are in show business and still in trouble. As we produce the movie, we have to stay in control. I think of TV baseball. Of my hopeless Cubbies. Baseball is showbiz – NFL football too – except that the people you see are really doing what they're doing, and really do what they do. That's how we've got to be.'

'It ain't that fucking easy.'

'One thing we're not on top of. Who bought that stock? My detectives can only push it back to five companies representing one. And they are the best in Chicago. Twenty percent of being a lawyer is being brother to the best detective agency. Another twenty is knowing how to make the jury laugh.'

'Fugitive Hong Kong money?' asked Aimée. 'It's bought half of Vancouver.'

'Or,' said Janet, 'Japanese capital seeking a vacuum.'

'Maybe. Or some drug cartel shopping for a laundry. Or US Mafia. This dimension does not make sense, so it's what we must understand before we can feel confident. You tell me where that money came from . . . and I'll tell you where butterflies go in a storm.'

'I know where,' said George, finger-digging ear wax. 'But I ain't saying.' He wiped it on his khakis and got a gallon thermos from his tent and filled it with wine and put it in a pack. 'Our supplementary rations.' He slung the pack. 'Let's go picnic.' Billy slung the other. Waggles romping and larking behind, they walked down Quetzal Way to the quay and then out of town on to the beach. The sea at their left, they followed the hard wet path of surf-washed beach, sand colors and sea smells. On their right, thirty yards across dry sand, rose a wall of jungle colors, of jungle smells and

174

sounds. Somewhere in that batik green curtain sat orange-coated orangutangs – Malay for the wise men of the forest – watching.

'Maybe it *is* Japanese money,' said Aimée to Billy, as they followed along behind George and Janet. 'During the war, tens of thousands of Japanese lived on these islands and over on the Malay Peninsula. Maybe one of them waxed rich and sentimental and wants to come back.'

'Or wants to bring them all back.'

George in his maroon shirt and khakis, Janet in her dark-green shorts and halter, both wearing olive-green ZTG caps, marching ahead, suddenly seemed to Billy, obscene. 'People out in nature – in city clothes anyway – look like gross intruders.'

'So do orchids and parrots.'

'I told Janet the whole story.'

'That makes it even more fun.'

When they came to the end of the island, where the beach sharply circles to the east, George led around to the other side, then stopped. They spread their cloth and unpacked and bantered and ate and drank. Billy gathered the trash and stuffed it into his pack. He stood. 'Aimée and I have to go early. We promised to help Phil build the model.' A beaming George and merry Janet embraced them goodbye, and they walked the beach until out of sight, then doubled back through the jungle to a clump of ferns through whose fronds they enjoyed a perfect view. 'Hey, look,' Billy whispered, 'he's getting the can out.' He clapped her shoulder. 'We can't hear, so I'll invent the dialog: Okay, Janet baby, here's some hot-shit bug repellent, something new, worth a try. So I'll just lie down here on my stomach, and you shake it up good, and squirt it on my back. *Yeahhhh*, that's it, thicker than flies on dogshit!'

Waggles uttered a plaintive squeal.

Suddenly, bleating shrilly, Waggles leapt on George, and began furiously rubbing her privates against his rump. They snorted with wild but suppressed laughter as George sprang to his feet and kicked Waggles away. Waggles dashed back and rubbed against his leg. 'Amy, Amy! Young love in action! What a wonderful and delicate emotion!' George kicked Waggles again, and Janet, gasping mirth, drew George into the surf, where Waggles could not follow without getting salt in her eyes.

'As George once advised me: Always remember, Al . . . bliss rhymes with piss.'

175

Janet turned George's face to hers.

Gently she put her arms around him and hugged him to her.

And gave him a long kiss.

Suddenly, having caught the scent of another boar in his territory, a huge long-legged hairless hog with four curling tusks – antlers, burst from the jungle and sped at George, dragging a chain attached to an iron stake, and he ran right over a squealing Waggles who tried to defend George and didn't stop until shoulder-deep in sea water, where he stood snarling at his rival. George confronted him, hog to hog. 'You fucking babirussa!' They both weighed about two-fifty. 'You gangrened diarrhea-drinker, I'm going to tear out your tusks and shove them up your ass.' The babirussa boar uttered a drooling snarl. Janet moved slowly aside, then splashed to the beach.

'Al, I think she's going to grab that chain and drag him back.'

'Let's go down and help her.'

They loped down and met Janet and slung the chain over their shoulders, tug-of-war style, and heaved, but the babirussa seemed set in concrete.

It lunged at George, dragging them back two feet.

George growled, side teeth flashing gold.

The huge hog lunged again.

George balled a fist.

The babirussa had moved in so deep it had to hold its head high to clear the water.

George struck it a mighty blow right on the snout.

It blinked, and gasped, and backed away toward shore.

'Well,' said Janet, 'I guess we know who's top hog now.'

George came out dripping, and comforted Waggles with hugs and pats and caresses.

The babirussa sat down on the sand and wept in shame.

'Al! Look! Ben Gunn!'

A man had stepped out of the jungle.

Five more stepped out behind him.

All carried Arisaka rifles; all wore the leaf-green jungle uniform of the Imperial Japanese Army. They worked their rifle bolts, clicking rounds into place.

'Now we know who owns the hog.'

'More sowboys, Amy.'

George spoke to the strangers, respectfully, in Japanese.

'What did he say Al?'

'Beats me. My only foreign tongue is Igpay Atinlay.'

The soldiers looked confused, then bowed deeply.

'Bow,' said George. 'But not quite so low.'

George bowed, and they bowed too.

'Attractant-10!' said Aimée. 'Seven attracted, three to go.'

George spoke quietly, and at length.

They drew the bolts of their rifles, thumbed the rounds back down into the clips, clicked the bolts shut, then, by means of swivels, stacked their rifles, which soon stood on the sand like the poles of a small cone-shaped tent, a wigwam.

'Who are they?'

'They're quartermaster troops, left here in 1944, as an advanced party of guards who were to protect and maintain a supply dump – a whole year's supply for an infantry regiment, all stored in caves. Their comrades never came. Torpedoed, maybe.'

George and the soldiers conversed for a while in civil but formal tones.

'I'm going to introduce you. But before I do, I have to tell you to remember three things. One: always be polite. Two: Japanese hate to be touched, so don't shake hands or slap backs. Just fucking bow. And, three: they'll do what we tell them. Winners are always right. Losers join the winners or kill themselves.'

'If you can be so polite to them,' asked Aimée, 'why is it you're never polite to us?'

'Why the fuck should I be polite to you? You're feminists; you're Americans.'

'I'm Canadian.'

'What's the fucking difference?'

She began protesting, but he told her to shut up, and she did.

'From birth to death, Japanese have to belong to something. And they have to know everyone's status and rank within that something. It's like always being on some team, day and night and even asleep. I'm going to tell them about ZTG, that we are the Board of Directors and I am the *Praefectus Castrorum*. Then I'll introduce you, Al first, even though he's the youngest, because with them it's ladies last.' More rippling Japanese, and then, one at a time, the soldiers stepped up to the ZTG chiefs, and bowed low as George spoke, and acknowledged the return bows with more. Thusly, sergeant first-class Takada, sergeant third-class Takamori, privates first-class Yoshimura and Oki, and privates third-class

Kumiyama and Mamoru prepared to join the ZEUGMA Theme Group.

When this rite was consummated, George told everyone to sit in a circle.

'George, they've been here since 1944, yet none appears to be over fifty years old. How can that be?'

'I don't know. We'll find out in due time.' He produced his thermos of wine, passed it to sergeant Takada, and it circulated among them in order of rank and seniority. Soon they were smiling and at ease as they visited with George. 'I'm the first stranger they've talked with since 1944. They tell me their pig broke loose, went crazy, they don't know why, so they chased him here. They say he'll just sit there until they're ready to take him back to their caves. They saw the pirates destroy what the Indonesian army left of the fishing village; they've seen ships and planes, but they have no radio, so fifty years of history is missing from their heads. Food and clothes? They've got plenty – enough to last five hundred years. Beaucoup weapons and ammo, too, but last week they ran out of booze. They're *happy* to see us. I shit you not! Because they're Japs, they have to belong to some group dedicated to an art. Mass-murder, tea drinking, judo, Toyota building, flower sniffing – it don't matter. What does matter is they have to know everybody's rank, function, and seniority, so as to know their unique place in a sophisticated hierarchy, and, hence, what to do and how to treat others to preserve harmony. Reciprocity. A fossilized parody of Confucius. Japanese are play-actors. Each one has a part in some *belong* play. Our asshole pals here are well rehearsed for their rôles in the army play. I'll give them all better parts and let them shit on the Fridays. Even though they've never been blooded, I'll cast them as real soldiers. They haven't been paid or promoted for fifty years, nor have they seen a woman close up. Yet they're all mama's boys. I'm going to swear them in as our Praetorian Guard, with me as Praetor, naturally. The chain of command goes up their ranks through Tom to me to Janet to the board, and back to me as maximum chief. We'll bring them women from Japan. Geishas. Be butt-fucked if we don't.'

He spoke to them again.

They all rose and repeated something after him, then bowed.

Their new colleagues bowed back.

'Me, I'm happy, because we have our army. Them? They're

happy because they have wine again and won't have to spend their declining years drinking piss-warm tea.'

'Don't they want to go home?'

'No. And I don't know why. Maybe because the homefolk believe it a total disgrace to surrender. Like the Spartans. Come home with your shield or on it. Like the captain goes down with his ship. But they didn't surrender. They still have their guns. I just reassigned them. So why expatriate? Beats the shit out of me.'

The wine was doing its work.

He raised a toast.

'*In vino veritas*.'

'*Banzai*.'

'These little fuckers live in a wish-world, a world of myth-reality and make-believe history. They're masters of Double-Think. They invented the Thought Police. In an instant they can turn around completely, become their own opposite. They ignore what they choose not to see. They're emotional. They're infinitely pragmatic. They create their own reality while they live in it.'

'George,' said Aimée. 'Everybody's like that, more or less.'

'And they're slobs, too.'

'Yes, those uniforms do look sloppy.'

'Japanese have no sense of humor.'

'George. George.'

Irked, he turned away from her to drink with his troopers. Billy studied them. They wore soft cloth caps with chin-straps and visors, each cap embellished with a five-pointed star. They had sweat-wet short-sleeved shirts with a dark-blue M-like emblem over the right pocket – the color code for quartermasters – and red patches on the collar points, some with stars indicating rank. They were dressed in breeches exposing bare calves where wraparound leggings ought to be, thick belts with brown-leather cartridge boxes, and brown shoes. Clean, they were, from hot daily baths, but slovenly – baggy pants, buttons undone, even a fly.

Suddenly George gazed at his friends. 'How about *this* shit? They've vowed to stay here because they don't want to leave their hogs.'

'Why's that, you old swino? They can get hogs in Japan.'

'I don't know, son. I do not fucking know.'

'Dedicated sowboys,' said Aimée. 'Devoted members of the Imperial Lotus Hog Sniffing Society.'

Billy raised the toast to joy and genius, and pressed on with conversation.

Abruptly, George slapped his hands together. 'So *that's* it. Do you know why they've aged only ten years in fifty? No, you fucking don't. It's because of an esoteric elixir they get here. One of their comrades, long dead now, could speak Malay, and learned about it from the fishermen's witch doctor. And what, you might ask, *is* that esoteric elixir? That esoteric elixir, my friends, is fresh babirussa sperm. *Fresh.* Sucked directly from the source. Makes me sick to think about it.'

Amiée began to giggle. '*George*. I read something like that in the *National Examiner*. Yes. East Germany's hog steroid miracle youth preservant serum made from rare suidic semen.'

'Pig cum, hot from the pizzle, the fountain of youth.' He took Janet by the shoulder. '*Pig* cum.' His grip tightened. 'So you see, don'tcha Ma – we *have* been telling the truth. I've been right all along. Rejuvenation through waters? Fuck no. Through boar semen. This is indeed Pig *Spa* Island.' He kissed her cheek tenderly, and added: I'm going to give you a chance to make soldiers out of them fucking Fridays.'

TWENTY-THREE

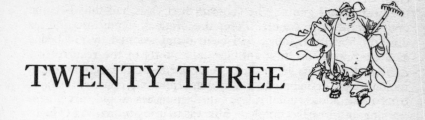

Chandra Ramgolin, circling slowly at five hundred feet, guided the flying pig over the land and water of Streeterport. Every now and then she reached into the space behind her, took a cardboard carton from a pile, and thrust it out her window to fall, drifting and turning, toward the harbor below.

For a fortnight, beginning at noontime, she'd been pushing cartons out into the aether. As the days went by, fewer and fewer reached the water intact, a circumstance producing in her immense gratification, for, baiting with candy bars, she had lured evil spirits and invisible demons into most of them.

Today, she banked and looked down on the grand panorama of Streeterport spreading below bright and clear under the sun, at the ZTG flag flying high above the crossroad, at Phil's hut where he and Alexander were at this moment completing their topographical model of Pig Spa Island, at Waggles and the babirussa family frolicking on the greensward, and at George, dressed in Roman armor, pacing back and forth behind quondam quartermasters and fragile Fridays, all of whom, paired off, were taking turns at blasting cartons out of the sky with air-cooled Nambu light machine guns while Tom, clad in the uniform of a major of infantry in the Imperial Japanese Army, flourished encouragement with his samurai sword or marked the chart on his clipboard.

George had enrolled seven of the Fridays as privates third class and uniformed them accordingly. The albino, he appointed private second class and placed in charge of the second cohort. The troopers of the first cohort George had transferred to the infantry, which meant red had replaced dark blue on the M-like emblem over their right shirt-pockets, and he'd promoted each to the next higher grade. The sergeant first class had thus become optio of the first cohort. Tom, the original significance of his uniform notwithstanding, had been commissioned by the board as centurion of the first and second cohorts of the resurrecting *Legio Dix Fretensis*. When Janet returned from Chicago, an event momentarily anticipated, the metamorphosis of ancient supply troops and adolescent Fridays into legionaries would, except for training, be virtually complete. She was to bring bronze ZTG logos to replace the stars on their caps, then spend a week running them through the wallows and pigsties of her choice.

'*Cran et élan* – spirit, comrades, will drive your lives, and pride will warm your hearts. Could any man ask for more!'

Thus spake George in peroration, before the time of Nambus, to the first muster of fledgling legionaries. Tom dismissed them and, along with George and Janet, watched them disperse to their regular duties: the Fridays to general service, the Japanese to gather around the wine cooler, set up on the green – the Campus Martius – whence they were to watch over the frisking hogs and provide such suidic services as might be required.

'George,' said Tom, chewing on a dead cigar and spitting on to the grass, 'do you really think we can make fighters out of them smarmy sissies and warehouse clerks?'

'Fucking-A! When you muster them, always say to yourself: Tom, before me parade the ZTG Superior Certified Military Meat Sires of the future. They ain't blooded yet; I'll grant you that. But they ain't mercenaries, either. And they ain't politicals out to pull down their betters or to restore Queen Boudicca.'

'Yes, but . . .'

'Art, spirit, duty – and faith, Tom, *faith*. Those are the qualities every legionary in *Legio Dix Fretensis* will manifest, including you.' His voice took on a more intimate tone. 'Yes, Tom, these qualities will prevail. I personally will supervise the entire program, from farrow to finish.'

George's teeth crushed down on a fresh lump of gum.

'Oh, yes. Take hogs for example. With them, the object is to achieve maximum efficiency in converting feed into pork. If you buy it, feed costs are over seventy percent of overheads. Cattle are poor substitutes. In bovines, one needs eleven pounds of feed to make one pound of meat. But pigs! That's another story! When managed properly, pigs need but *five* pounds to make the conversion. And that can be garbage. They have more prime cuts, too. Do you wonder why farmers call them Mortgage Lifters? Art, duty, spirit . . . and faith. What sustains faith is knowing the average family of six – we have data for America – eats two three-hundred pound hogs per year. That breaks down to one hundred pounds apiece, babies and all. The challenge is to raise that figure slightly, until we reach the happy state where every year the American people eats its own weight in pork. Yes! So much for hogs and cannibals. As for the trainees here, my dear centurion, never once neglecting the principles of efficiency, our mission is to transform them from cowardly sullen civilians and saucy thieving can-counters into maximum killers, loyal to command. And what sustains our faith? Our certainty that since time began there's never been a year without war and, scarcely ever, a country without an army.'

Barefoot, clad in shorts, wearing lavender T-shirts fresh from Chicago, shirts displaying SOUVENIR OF STREETER-PORT beneath the blazon of ZTG's winged pig, Phil and Billy stepped back to admire their model, a rasp of machine-gun bursts echoing in their heads. 'That should do it, Al.'

'Sure is a beaut.'

They'd just limned-in the golf course. It spread up jungly slopes, over forested plains, and down on to and along the beach. 'There, my boy, lie the best links in the whole world. Perfect weather, plenty of rain, two-foot tide letting us include natural sand and ocean water, plenty of Fridays to keep it impeccably groomed – no problems at all, save for driven balls striking cockatoos in flight.' Phil had found an enthusiasm. Maybe if I'd learned golf, I'd feel differently. Plan the links for PSI; plan the showers for Auschwitz. What's the difference? Take pride in complex problems finding sophisticated solution. Engineering triumphs! 'Chandra brought my scuba gear yesterday. My small tank, mask, and flippers. Janet got them from my flat and sent them Express Mail. Presently, I'll go see what's in our part of the big South China Sea fishbowl.'

As the flying pig droned above, they stepped outside to stand in the shade by the flagpole and watch the blasting smoking Nambus and their tenders. His sky-blue plume undulating in the breeze,

George strode back and forth behind the gun pits, sunshine flashing on his armor and helmet, on occasion dazzling so brightly the plume seemed a bird aloft, in all a living testament to the Fridays' devotion to duty. Emperor Hirohito himself, George had told the troopers of the first cohort, had planned it this way, precisely as it was now developing. Henceforth, his sublime majesty had decreed, no man in *Legio Dix Fretensis* will appear in uniform without neatly wrapped leggings, nor under any circumstances, appear in public clad only in cap and loincloth. Moreover, the imperial rescript enjoined, orders will be given in the new world language, English.

'Phil? Remember when I made you promise to go with me and run before the bulls?'

'Uh – no.'

'Drinking beer in our empty office?'

'And rolling cans to the elevators.'

'*Nambu Team Six*!' cried the albino Friday as a carton came tumbling out of the sky. A blast of bullets shredded it.

'Oh, sure. Hell yes! About us trying out the perfect male sport, the Pamplona bull run.'

'Janet packed my gear in *Chicago Tribune*s. In one of them I read Volkswagen has opened a giant factory in Pamplona. So, we're absolved of our vow, and have to look for something else.'

'*Nambu Team Two*!' cried the optio of the first cohort. Another carton reeled to the water and disintegrated as it shuddered away in spray and splash.

Waggles and the babirussa family sported on the grass while Billy and Phil gazed at the scene and its dramatis personae.

'Alexander, lately I've been thinking about history. How's this? Economics is the engine, culture the helmsman. And the latitude and longitude of its destination are determined by necessity and myth.'

'Me, I've been thinking what we're building here on PSI is like a cathedral – a tumor of history: teeth and fingers, flesh and an eye, all growing in the same lump.'

Nambu Team Four ripped out its statement.

'A long time ago, shortly before you were conceived, I was sitting on Haight Street, giving food away, and planning to master the masters, and steer history on to a better course. So I went back home to Chicago and mastered the masters sufficiently to influence the course, but perhaps for the worse, and then I shifted to the

184

ZTG mode to deepen and broaden my influence. So here I am now, with you, overseeing this comedy.'

'And thinking about golf.'

'When you get the power to do right, you lose the passion to do right.'

'Passion! Caring! I judge others by myself, Phil. Passion seems natural to me. It's my nature. But does it truly seem so to others? Phil, trying to imagine life without passion is like trying to imagine life without knowledge. I mean being as ignorant as all those college students back home who can't show you where Chicago is, let alone where we are now.'

'I set out to master the masters. I knew I could, and I did.'

'I set out to master my passion, to discipline it, so I could concentrate on fulfilling its object: the realization, worldwide, of liberty and justice for all.'

'When you get the power, you'll forget the passion.'

'Look out there, Phil. They all *like* to be mastered. And they all want to believe whatever happens, no matter how bizarre, was planned beforehand by some leader or divinity.'

'Because you know that, and are robust, and spirited, I concur with Aimée's belief, like it or not, you are destined to be – as she puts it, Chief of the New Team.' A tremendous blast from all the Nambu teams made Phil shudder. 'I think George likes that better than pigs.'

'I was hiding out with pigs. And I often thought George was doing the same. Whatever he does, though – he puts himself into it one hundred percent. Otherwise, he says, life would be insufferably boring.'

'What is he really? A dope dealer on the run?'

'You mastered law and business, but can you master George?'

'Beats me.'

'Why the hell don't you! He's not really trying to make the world better for pigs. No. That's a cover for something else. He says he's the Wandering Jew, whatever that means.'

'You want me to master the Wandering Jew?'

'Why not. No one else has.'

'I'll start by putting all the WJ legends into a computer.'

'It's not only George, Phil. We're *all* hypocrites.'

'And so you think we should manifest the absolute hypocrisy of pretending to no hypocrisy.'

185

'For *all* of us, Phil, ZTG/PSI is a cover story. Building it is camouflage. It's instrumental. The real purpose is something else. You want to play golf and monkey around with computers. Aimée wants to make the worldwide myth. Man alive! There's a challenge for your computers! Janet? What's *her* game? Money? Career? After all, she's a paid employee. Me, I think our motives ought to be what they seem to be.'

'Bullshit! I know what you're really doing, Al. You're adventuring, and hiding out until you're certain we've saved you from Portsmouth Naval Penitentiary.'

TWENTY-FOUR

Having filled his tank, Billy slung his scuba pack and emerged from the supply hut where the air pump was kept. He glanced toward Café Quetzal. Aimée and Phil, the only clients, sat fanning themselves and sipping from tall glasses of juice, chilled by the product of the ice machine. Five bats, a row of ragged decaying three-dimensional signal pennants, now hung from the wire. George had set the legionaries to work. Clad in pale red winged-boar T-shirts, hiking shoes, jungle-green army caps with shorts and wraparound leggings to match – the fatigue uniform of *Legio Dix Fretensis* – and directed by the electrician, they were scurrying about with aluminum ladders, stringing wires from tree to tree. These would soon be connected to a cassette player in George's pavilion, and speakers would be mounted on tents and huts the length of Phoenix Road and Quetzal Way, likewise on poles along the quay and on the jetty.

Catching sight of Billy, George waved hello, and approached. 'This here's the anniversary of the Battle of Pigville.'

Billy slapped his back.

'How can you wear armor on a day like this?'

'Never complain, never explain. But for you, Bill, I'll break my rule. I have to preserve distance, and set a mood and an example of fortitude for my ladder monkeys there.' He sighed and smiled. 'Them boys are shaping up, ain't they?'

'That's a fact.'

'Reminds me of the old days.'

'Me too.'

'Sure is nice to have someone around who remembers. You better believe it!' Sun and shadow sharply articulated the steel fish-scales on his breast and shoulders. 'You remember, Bill, as I always said about garbage: One man's trash is another man's treasure. Well. Just look at them trash people, old or young, don't make no difference. Pretty soon everybody will see they're really treasure. Same as sausage lovers re-eating garbage and tasting treasure. No magician, nor even a saint, can pull off a trick like that. But a master hogman can.'

'Are you going to paint murals showing the reborn garbage people what lies ahead for them in the inalterable cosmic plan?'

'Yeah. I been thinking I could make false fronts on them A-frame houses like in a Wild West movie set. Twenty-five feet high. Right now, that'd give us ten big panels. Shit! From here, on Campus Martius, pigs and people alike can get a first-class view of the whole fucking thing.'

'For sure. And you can show the garbage people in their original depravity – petty theft and prostitution – their rebirth as legionaries, and then their rise to glory. Yes. And afterwards, their inevitable decline and eclipse.'

'I knew you'd understand. Art! *There's* the stuff. The *difference*. No one knew that better than Hitler. The Nuremberg rallies with all the arts combined. Architecture! Music! Pagentry! Oratory! Seen as a living painting, sophisticated form and color. And male musk odor! And all of it choreographed into a single masterwork. Fucking-A! Bill, you understand! Didn't waste my time training you, no sir. Finding you there on the road was the best thing ever happened to either one of us! You came to me a sowboy, and now you are a true hogman! You deserted to a better Corps. I'm talking *Legio Dix Fretensis* now. Art! Poetry, too. We'll teach our legionaries English, just as the Japanese Emperor commanded. By getting them to recite and learn poetry. You and me, *we* write it. We'll teach English to them Americans, too. The albino and his pal. Americans are as illiterate in English as Japanese and Balinese, but the gooks have got a refined literary sense from their own languages.'

'And feed, George – feed!'

'Oh, yeah, only here we call it food.'

'We'll put brass rings in their noses so they can't root up inferior nourishment.'

188

'Sure. And those rings'll represent the rings we put in their minds to keep them from rooting up bad ideas.'

'Our A-frame huts, George. They remind me of Pigville.'

'Auto bodies! Yeah! But we can't have them here, and we'll have to rip out the A-frames too. Eventually, Streeterport will be a medieval fishing village on the Rhine. *Straßerhafn.* Peasant huts. Thatched roofs. Wood-and-plaster inns. You know, exposed beams. *Gasthofs! Weinlokalen! Wirtshausen! Die Diernen!* Medieval whores – you bet your ass I know what *they* are, yeah, and Rhennish fish boats! Fix it so our Jap guests can really feel like Kraut robber barons when they go boar hunting.'

'And a market! Fish and flea! Medieval German souvenirs! Whips! Crossbows! Shrunken witch heads!'

George whacked him on the shoulder. 'Boy, you really are something else! I want you to join my Legion and help me fine-tune it.'

'I tried that once.'

'I'll make you optio of the second cohort right now! *Principale* grade, so you don't have to work. Fucking-A! It took me eight years to make optio of the sixth. Because I'm a Jew. You'll be optio, and you can tell that albino second-class private what to do.'

'I don't like to take orders, and I don't like to give them.'

'When I am emperor, Bill – you can be *legatus legiones* of *all* the legions, and wear silver armor with an embossed breastplate.'

'Thanks, George. But that's not for me.'

'So what the fuck else can you do with your life? Hang out in Uncle Bill's saloon, playing the fucking lute? Worm around in library stacks and get terminal emphysema from book dust? No. I'll soon be emperor, and you'll be my prime companion.'

'That hot helmet must have baked your mind.'

'Don't give me shit, you tit-biting snot-eater.'

'George, would it seem inappropriate, would it hurt your feelings, were I to call you pig-headed, or to remind you we're friends?'

'Oh. Sorry.' Affectionately, he slapped Billy's cheek. 'Think it over.'

'Okay, Long George Silver. I've got to go now, and look for Ben Gunn, and check out the tropical fish.'

Billy walked away, toward the quay and the pigs frisking and gamboling o'er the green. Downright pastoral! Waggles came wiggling up to him, oinking greetings. A sudden guilt at having gone along with the Attractant farce came over him. How adolescent! He should have told George and let the practical joke remain in the realm of fantasy where it belonged. The movie reran on the screen of his mind-theater and he exploded into laughter and sat on the grass, weeping delight. Waggles crawled on to his lap and looked love at him. What wonderful blue eyes she has! He kissed her cheek. If you ever get out to the Monterey Peninsula, babe, we've got a date. I'll buy you lunch in Carmel at Clint Eastwood's Hog's Breath Inn. Waggles squirmed and squealed. Pure bliss. No doubt of that. Can pigs smile? Yes! Wish you weren't all black. You should have some white, like Farnsworth. 'I could really go for you, if I didn't know mankind caught all his sex diseases from domestic animals.'

Waggles cuddled and sighed.

'People make fun of you, don't they?'

Her moist eyes became wet with tears.

'I haven't been very friendly, have I?'

No. But she's used to it.

'I think you're quite attractive, and at least as smart as George!'

She snuggled.

'But what is intelligence? A male standard, for sure.' He told her the perfect woman cannot possibly be the same as the perfect man, and she agreed. 'So what did you do today to make the world a better place?' Took care of the babirussa children. 'Me? I helped lay out a golf course. Progress? A better place for whom?' Progress, babe. In towns all over the world, pigs used to roam the streets. Charles Dickens wrote at length about their wandering around in New York City. First, pigs are outlawed. Then goats. Then cows, then chickens, then horses. What will be next? 'One thing for sure, Waggles, and you can count on it, pigs will never be outlawed in Streeterport! I'll get the board to appoint a Swinereeve, like they used to have in England. You like that, don't you? I thought so. When George tires of you he'll eat you, but the Swinereeve of Pig Spa Island won't let him.' He sensed a wave of gratitude.

Better for whom?

'Better for tourists, babe. Tourists.'

Tourism, he explained to her, reinforces myths – nostalgia for a past that never was. It projects a history with no suffering or shitstink where everyone was a lord or lady – where every tired Japanese businessman can be a robber baron. 'We live in a time of colliding myths, babe.' The collisions focus in places like Beirut, Iraq. 'How can people raise their families on a stage like that? How can they go to work every day? And send their children to school, and put food on the table?' At least pigs don't need myths to make life mean something. 'Me, I'm a focus, too.' Of myths and history. 'How about you?'

She nuzzled him in rapture and it made him randy and he gently pushed her off his lap and stood.

'I've never seen a coral reef, but pretty soon I cannot in truth say so again.' He told her of the wonders he'd read about in the Cousteaus' magazine he received monthly as a member of their society. He described what he expected to find. 'Imagine, a water baby like me, and I've yet to swim into that fishbowl.'

He turned and walked away across the grass, and Waggles, all sixty pounds of her, came dashing after.

He bent and stroked her head. 'I wish I could take you, but I can't. I promise – cross my heart and hope to die – I'll rig you a scuba someday, and take you on a skin dive.'

He stood.

In an echo of George's voice, he commanded: '*Stay.*'

He walked across the grass and along the quay to the beach. He'd told Waggles what to do, and she'd done it. Next, the albino Friday, then the whole Tenth Legion, then all the legions, then he'd wrest the imperial throne from George. Today, Waggles; tomorrow: the World. Soon he was walking a swinging stride on surf-washed beach, all alone. Life must have looked like this before man. Attracted by the leached-green wall of jungle, he plodded through soft sand to get a better look. Tall trees, there, interlaced with vines and plants of a poisonous green, too thick to enter, so I'll go along the edge. Suddenly afternoon crickets begin their raucous clatter, the Nambu bursts of nature. Colored birds and flowers and clouds of butterflies and a rich rotten smell and hoots and squawks and cries and trills. And there's a gigantic squirrel, embellished brick-red and ebony, and now, aloft, out of sight, the crashing and shrieking of remote monkey cousins, trooping through the trees, screeching: 'Ow! Ow! – a sound soon to be replaced with cries of 'Fore!'

It's the first day of autumn, but, here, no fallen leaves.

He trudged back to hard sand, and walked along through the gentle wash of surf.

A dump bird planed down and settled on some driftwood.

He soaked his Australian hat, so the sun would cool his head.

And now, underfoot, mini-geysers of squirting clams.

Dropping to his knees, he began digging with his trusty counterfeit Swiss army knife, his last connection to the Corps.

Will these turn out to be quahogs?

Just the thing for George.

Too small. No hog clams here. Littlenecks, maybe.

He took off his shoes, and splashed along in his swinging route-march gait. Ahead, a towering black raincloud. From this solitude in the midst of life he drew a joyful sense of blood-warm peace.

Hermit crabs scrambled out of the way.

Abruptly it darkened and the air was solid with rain.

This is what I call one hundred percent humidity.

This September shower could be in my bathroom in Pacifica.

With the water temperature perfectly adjusted.

What's a shower without a song?

He began singing a Cockney ballad, a favorite of his father.

> All the dirty kids
> Down on our block
> Calls theirselves a gang;
> They all went to the copper's house,
> And this is what they sang!
> Never take a bath 'til you need one;
> You know what I mean.
> Never take a bath 'til you need one;
> It only makes you *clean*.
> Way out West on the prairie,
> That's where men are men . . .
> They never take a bath 'til they need one,
> And they don't even take one then!
> . . . the dirty *dogs*.

Old Al liked to imagine the Vikings, who never washed and never wiped, campaigning against Irish Celts who bathed every day. For the Vikes, laying ambush would be imposssible, but they would have advantage in close combat. All things considered, it probably balanced out evenly.

192

Had the Vikings arrived here, nature would have washed them. Columbus tried to get here, but he only made it half-way.

And Billy walked out of the torrential shower into the sun. 'See, world – even though I don't know what I'm going to be when I grow up, I do know enough to come in out of the rain.'

And he sang along with his footfalls, two-beat five-meter, and then remembered another of his father's songs.

> It's the same the world over,
> It's the poor what gets the blame,
> Whilst the rich has all the pleas-ure,
> Now ain't that a bleeding shame?

Which brought his thoughts back to Pig Spa Island.
As he progressed toward the coral reefs.
Today, a jungle;
Tomorrow: The Fifteenth Hole!
Progress.

One reason he'd gone to the Monterey Peninsula after Al died was what Al used to say it was like in Ohlone times: thick with life, vibrant, both land and sea, immensely more so than today. Huge clouds of birds; steelhead runs; butterflies; elk and bear and deer in profusion hunted by agile Ohlone wearing antlers and buckskin to camouflage their approach.

The shore trended sunward and Billy tugged his hat down to dim the brilliant dazzle of coral sand.

He'd walked the woods and beaches of the Monterey Peninsula to sense the past abundance of life, to share the spirit of ten thousand years of Ohlone living that had left no mark, and to feel the presence of his dead father.

The gentle scud of the surf produced water music; it invoked the spirits Chandra found everywhere, the good favoring mountainsides, the evil dwelling on desolate beaches, in woods or in the sea, calling out to him: Water Baby.

This water baby, carrying his limited supply of air, would go around the northern end of Pig Spa Island to the east side where, in contrast to the smooth beach underfoot, the photos and the model show promontories and points. Maybe the mountain had once puked lava down that side and into the sea where it produced a base for coral reefs.

Abruptly, across the beach, he spied the place where he

193

and Aimée had entered the jungle to double back and watch Attractant-10 confront the Tenth Legion.

He trudged through soft sand to the precipice of flora. The leaves cascade thinner here, so break through like Monkey traversing the waterfall – into a dusky land thatched seventy feet overhead by hardwood branches and vines. Here in the perpetual shade are only a few shrubs and flowers, and, in the canopy above, the ceaseless cacophonic clamor of aerial beings. Do they hear each other? Could I speak to them with music, even as jazz speaks to mankind? Do they hear music when their own voices sound along with others?

All right! Here it *is*. The trail to the Japanese caves.

And now a rapidly rising slope, huge spider webs with birds in them, and bamboo; a scramble and struggle upward to a clearing: giant butterflies, birds-of-many-colors, and, to him, all of them as nameless as the insects, and flowers, and chromatic blazes hanging aloft from tree bark.

Ahead, low tables and mats, and a fire pit.

And cut into a lofty cliff, a portal, plugged by a steel door heavy as a bank vault, airtight, placed there to confound naval gunfire, tear gas, and flame throwers.

On the door, in red letters:

朝早くメイトサーヒス
を お願いします。

Wary of hazards, alert to perils, yet wonderfully elated – leaping and bounding and turning sharp corners to evade the spirits, Billy loped back down to the beach.

George had said this supply depot, quarried from lava by slave labor, was part of the plan that sent Japan's last fleet against Okinawa.

By any measure the Japanese had been intruders.

So why had the fishers' *dukun* told them the babirussa secret?

By means of what George called guru grease, the *dukun*, whom George called the witch doctor, had seduced the youngest Japanese soldier and instructed him in the art of fellatio, which this pretty boy soon performed so skillfully, so lovingly, the *dukun*, who secretly took the serum twice a week, taught him how to draw it from the source and deliver it with a kiss.

The pirates killed the *dukun*; the disciple shared the secret with his mates, who then killed him for having shamed his *iemoto* master by betraying his confidence.

All things juxtapose.

Some so wonderously as to scandalize even George.

Now, around the end of the island, and over these rocks.

A small beach, alive with leatherbacks.

From tunnels to turtles.

Some of them ten feet long, and heavy as the massiest hog, straining with their flippers to force themselves across the hard sand and along and along through soft sand well above the high tide-line to bury their eggs. What an awesome source of green turtle soup! Take a turtle ride! No! In his own body he feels the effort, the struggle, the painful ache. Agonizing to fulfill their destinies these cousins bear too great a burden to suffer a rider. Pig Spa Island, from end to end, is *alive*. It's the world before man; it's *alive* as the world before man, the primeval uninhabited.

How can ZTG own turtle beach?

Can we buy it from the turtles?

Must we deceive them or corrupt them first?

How can *I* be part owner of turtle beach?

They come home from afar to lay their eggs.

We, strangers, come from afar to take what we will.

Can a freed slave buy his mother?

The sun flames down on landsman and sea turtle alike.

Are these sisters sweltering like me?

What happens to them happens to me.

The man, who had precedent from the whales, and no eggs to lay, decided to return to the water. He traversed the beach to a low, rocky point, crossed over it to an empty beach, stripped off his shoes and pack, donned his scuba gear, crushed his hat flat and left it on the sand weighted down by his other stuff. With a whoop he ran into the water and slid under its surface into another world as remote from normal everyday as Heaven.

He glided over bright sand inclining down to fifteen feet, came to lava sloping up, and soon found himself gazing, as from a balloon over jungle, upon a blue-green coral forest. On seeing him the fish dashed away or drew back into holes and tunnels, all of them except for a few bold hand-sized territorials, dull yellow and blue, who defied him to trespass their cubic yard of private property. He passed over miniature canyons, hills, valleys, towers, archways, caves, living yellow stalks and other small planted animals, a bright-blue giant clam shell, all in all a summer garden brilliant with bloom, but here, on the coral reef, where save perhaps for rain forest, life on Earth has achieved its greatest variety and density, the water baby, a free swimmer in a tropical fishbowl, can see no fish other than insignificant though valorous territorials.

Should he see some, he could not name them. He would not even be able to recognize the Spanish hogfish George spoke about sometimes back in Pigville when speculating on farming hog mullet a. k. a. *hypentelium nigricans*.

So, water baby, sit on the coral, motionless, and wait for fish to return.

But would they? Perhaps they'd heard that in the interest of War-Is-Peace, humans sacrifice reefs like this to nuclear weapons tests.

Coral makes a rugged seat. What if something crawls into my cutoffs? Crabs, worms, stinging anemones, prick leeches, asshole sliders, and ball biters.

He pushed off and wafted slowly along.

Ahead, a large, smooth paddle-shaped object, protruding from the coralscape.

He kicked over to it and sat near its end.

An airplane wing, scoured bare by sand!

He gripped a machine-gun muzzle to hold himself in place.

Go limp; rest perfectly still.

The wing vanished into a big coral lump.

The rest of the plane?

The coral reef, that profuse garden of color, had enveloped most of it.

What emblem did this dead bird flaunt when flying free in its ethereal dominion?

The sun of Japan? The US star? The British target?

If only I'd built airplane models!

But the water baby'd been a boy without a hobby.

Is the pilot still in there? Do frightened fish find refuge in his skull?

Sitting as immobile as the wing itself, thinking of world wars, Al's voice echoed in memory.

'To this day, I cannot believe the authorities allowed them to happen. In those wars, what they'd been doing to their colonies for centuries they began doing to themselves.'

A sunnyside egg swam by.

Then came some fancy Christmas cookies, followed by a troop of undulating orange pencils. Suddenly, all around, hovering, drifting, wriggling, paddling, sculling, stroking, swimming, appeared a golden spearhead, an ace-of-spades, a cigar, some cheap platters, a school of shiners, a lone George fish, an octopus, a blue Philfish, a spiny balloon fish, a bubbling Amy fish, some spotted coasters as in Uncle Bill's El Flaco Club, maple leaves, some blue butterflies, a fierce orange Janet fish, and then a Farnsworth fish, piebald in black-and-white, and a Waggles fish, positively porcine, and then an immitation parrot, and then a real bird trailing bubbles, and they all dashed away, and after a while they came back, in ruby, green, gray, white, bright yellow, barred and spotted and striped, and they were moving to music he could play on his lute, or his guitar, but what would go with the banjo?

And what will go for air if I don't leave soon?

He glided back to shallow water, stood wet in the sun, soaked his hat, packed his gear, and set out for home so as to arrive before dark.

Walking along, he sensed the immense age of life on this island, and the presence underfoot of the ashes of folks who had over the past thousands of years lived here, only to be erased by disease, war, and piracy, themes dear to history. As he crossed turtle beach and remembered that some tribes believe leatherbacks created the world, as he went on toward and by the spot where George had prevailed over the babirussa, he fell into a poor-me, a lethargy, a vacillating indecision, a terrible despair.

Why not desert again?

We're doing the worst for the right reasons. Or is it even that? After ten thousand years of *our* stewardship, here, on the Monterey Peninsula, in San Francisco, Berkeley, and Pacifica, what will the world look like?

Time to desert again?

Sweep all this aside and replace it with . . . a castle, a funicular, a phony village, a golf course! This life and our life have a common destiny. So what? To hell with posterity. Let the new team pave it over.

Beginning with turtle beach.

197

Time to desert.

Destroy all this so tired businessmen can recreate, re-create. The intravenous boar-hunt fantasy, the all-powerful robber-baron mind pill! Recreation! Help them re-create . . . *themselves*. Greed, ambition, the powers of exploitation re-juvenated! How was it juvenated in the first place? Show-and-tell about parents of throw-away kids; Barbie and GI Joe; emotional advertising; the package worth more than the content; selfish exemplars, bottom-line ethics, and TV! What has never vived, *re*vived!

Raze Pig Spa Island to build a pleasure dome for the rich.

Fore!

Maybe monkeys will steal the golf balls.

Sure. Giving George a reason to stage a monkey hunt, or put a bounty on their heads, as was done with Californian Indians.

Reward vice and punish life!

Go ahead!

Desert.

We eat the green world, and digest it, and blast it out, as eternal, plastic, radioactive, diarrheic stool. Forsake joy and genius and consecrate life to consumption and its excrement. Under *our* stewardship, how long before this island and the rest of the world is one vast kitchen midden.

Make America the Brute America the Beaut.

Should all life be our toy?

Go home and get drunk.

Cogito ergo poto.

I think therefore I drink.

Striving to form specifics and arrange them into plans, he came to Streeterport, and saw Phil standing on the quay, looking fat in shorts, sad in a gray-day T-shirt, gazing out to sea. Phil turned, waved hello, and approached.

Desert.

'Hey, Phil, what's happening?'

'Janet's back. She and Aimée and George are going through the mailbag. We have some papers from the Indonesian government. I'll go through them shortly. Then, at dinner, we'll have a board meeting. And, yes – George received some heavy boxes from Chicago – cases of Attractant-51, doubtless.' Phil rubbed at his cheek. 'Look at how high the tide is! I've never seen it so high, and it's still flowing!'

Billy glanced at the flying pig floating almost level with the pier. 'But that's not what's on my mind, either.'

'So what *is* on your mind, counsellor.'

'I think I need love insurance. Dammit! Me getting close with a good woman seems about as likely as a Sox-Cubby world series.' He hitched up his shorts. 'You're not going to believe this, but I've got a crush on Chandra.'

'Did she squirt you with human pheromones?'

The Streeterport speakers burst out with 'The William Tell Overture'.

'She's great. Sexy. She flies planes, she's simple, and sharp, and I like her filed teeth, no *shit*. They're ground flat because witches and demons have fangs.'

The speakers shifted to a Roman arena steam-organ ode, an amphitheater caliope cantata, George's version of *Testing-Testing.*

'What became of *George*'s fangs?'

'Al, I was standing here, looking at sea and sky, thinking what I'm really doing is, well . . . looking for future memories.'

'Memories that delight you.'

'Memories I can live with.'

'Phil. I've been thinking too. My dad always used to say I should try to make the world a better place. About college he said, Don't study to make money, but to help people less fortunate than you. Coming along the beach, just before I saw you, I decided ZTG's over for me. I'm going to sell my piece for what I can get, and go back home, and see what I can do. If your cover-up worked, great. If not . . . well, we shall see what we shall see.'

'That's what *my* father always used to say.'

'This may sound crazy, Phil, but I'll take the money I can get, and my chances along with it, and go home, and run for Congress as a Green Democrat.'

PART SIX

OF CHAOS

MITHRA

I've been waiting eighty million years
for this, since He bungled his last try.
The Great Extermination is now in progress.
I watch the incidents accumulate, and your
follies proliferate, and I love it! This
time, you're all dead!

The Fly
Washington DC, 1993

TWENTY-FIVE

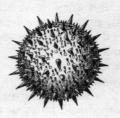

Janet walked up Quetzal Way and sat at the café table, under decaying bat banners, next to Billy, across from Aimée. Phil was at home studying the documents from Indonesia and George had yet to appear.

'When I was a girl,' said Aimée, 'meat was still forbidden on Fridays. Mom used to give us fishsticks if we'd been good, or macaroni-and-cheese – jailfood – if we'd been bad.'

Alexander, thought Janet, ever since I sat next to you at that banquet long ago, I never could get enough of your sex smell. 'I think we're having lamb curry,' Janet said. Sensing the presence beside her, she saw before her the dinner guests back in Chicago; then, picturing Billy's hips and jock on that blanch hospital bed in Hampstead, she recalled the musk, the taste, the passion. 'It's cooled down some,' Janet said.

'Would you look at that!' exclaimed Aimée.

George had emerged from his pavilion, resplendent in golden armor, fresh from the factory in Kansas City. Like a heroic statue of Augustus Caesar, he stood there, oozing immense satisfaction. Abruptly, he came to the table and sat.

'They wanted me to buy plastic, but I insisted on the real stuff – gold-plated steel.'

'It sure is fancy, swino, but what does it signify?'

'This masterpiece of the armorer's art is commensurate with the dignity of your *Praefectus Castrorum*.'

'Which,' said Janet, 'if I'm not mistaken, means Castle Commander. In this case, one still waiting for a castle.'

George motioned, and a scurry of slavish uniformed Fridays wheeled out the wine cooler and set the table. 'We'll start informally while we wait for Phil.' With a pinky, George dug some wax out of his ear, and wiped it on his steel skirt. He seemed confident and paternal, almost benevolent.

'Why do women have legs?'

No one answered.

'Give up?'

They nodded yes.

'So they won't leave snail tracks.'

'George,' said Janet, as the Fridays served them curry, 'do you think I would be too severe were I to describe you as a swineophile, or, even, as a male chauvinist *pig*?'

'We're in the game now,' he said, 'the shit's hit the fan, so we have to get ready to take on Club Med and the rest of the competition. How do we do that? Well, first, we have to analyze the market, which, if I may say so, is the same as probing live hogs to determine backfat depth. And we have to develop a public relations campaign, sticking to the truth, of course, but showing it in its best light. Did you ever wonder why almost all hog pictures taken from the side have a feeding dish in them? No, I guess not, you suckers never notice what's going on. That dish, my friends, is tied to fishline, and, just before the picture is snapped, somebody off camera pulls the dish away and the hog stretches. It looks longer in the picture than it really is, but, all the same, it's still the real hog. No airbrush work. So tell me, is that picture deceptive, or true?'

Phil laid a folder on the table and sat down.

'As your attorney, George, I'd say the picture stretches the truth somewhat.' He still wore a gray T-shirt. 'I think our spa here, with its Tourist Attractants Innumerable, will prove to resemble the Blarney Stone. By day, the tourists kiss it; by night . . . the locals piss on it.' He smiled at George. 'Aren't I right? Yes. Now let's get down to business.' He opened his folder and rubbed his jowls. 'I've been studying these papers, considering them from all angles and perspectives, and, what we have here, on our island – believe me, I've thought it through in every direction . . . what we have here is not just a theme park with a clear title free of annoying regulations, no, not just that. What we have here is a sovereign state!' Phil peered at Janet, at Billy, at Aimée, at George. 'It would seem that by accident we have founded a new nation.' He began to chuckle.

'Now don't that just beat all. It's awesome, wonderous.' He glanced down at the papers, and back to his companions. 'You remember, Malaysia vacated her claims to sovereign right in our island and vested all rights, property and otherwise, established or implied, in ZTG. These documents here transfer all Indonesian rights in this island, sovereign or otherwise, to Malaysia. Although they just came to us, these documents are dated nine days *before* Malaysia conveyed her rights to us. That means all of Indonesia's rights had been transferred to Malaysia before Malaysia transferred all her rights to us. Because Malaysia vacated sovereignty, sovereignty devolved on ZTG – *us*.' He rubbed his cheek and smiled. 'The Indonesian Republic comprises almost fourteen thousand islands, six thousand of them inhabited. I think maybe we bribed them to do something they wanted to do anyway. This island was one of the last disputed areas on their border. Personally, I think *both* countries are glad to be rid of our island, and thus come one step closer to achieving a stable border, most of which, of course, is laid out on water.'

'So now we got our own fucking country! Just like the Sultan of Brunei.'

'Yes, George. It would seem we are the ones who caught the greased pig.'

'So we can declare war on Sweden if we want to.'

'Yes. We are an independent country owned by a stock company, rather like the East India Company in the eighteenth century, or the Merchant Adventurers of Plymouth Plantation in the seventeenth. Our articles of incorporation and our by-laws are now our constitution and our statutes.'

'We'll junk that shit and adopt the hogman's bible as a guide. I mean Baker and Juergenson's *Approved Practices in Swine Production*.'

'That wouldn't be legal.'

'What do I care about the law? Ain't I got the power!'

'Now, my dear Founding Mothers and Fathers,' said Phil, 'we need a name for our country.'

'How about Saturnalia?' said Aimée.

'How about Zeugma?' said Billy. 'In celebration of this all too superficial equation of hogs and people.'

'*Plutonia*,' said George, striking the table making dishes jump. 'Plutonia! We'll buy some plutonium on the black market and become a world power.'

205

'George. Plutonia also implies rule-by-money. So why not direct you ambitions toward its peaceful pursuit. To commerce. To industry. The Japanese did it, so why not you? Perfect and market babirussa juice. Build us up in to the world's foremost producer of pheromones – sex sprays. Attractants for all sexes, species, and occasions.'

'I do know something about that. Studies suggest the pig sex pheromone five-alpha-androst-sixteen-N-three-one may function as a human sex pheromone. Two hundred male and female college cretins were assigned to one of the four odor conditions – androstenone, methyl anthranilate, skatole, and a no-stink control – and were asked to rate photographs of a male stimulus and to rate their own mood in the presence of each odorant. There was a significant overall sex-by-treatment-condition interaction. Bet your sweet ass there was. Men in the androstenone condition rated the stimulus male as more passive; broads in the androstenone condition rated themselves as less sexy. Fucking-A! You think you're so smart! Well, tell me what happened when a series of behavioral bio-assays were conducted to determine the aggression-influencing properties of urine and other fluids when subjects were prepubescent castrated male and female domestic pigs from commercial stocks. Yeah! And what do *you* know about pheromones occurring in humans and truffles! What do you know about *that* shit! Eh?'

'In the Republic of Saturnalia,' asked Aimée 'who is the Chief of State?'

'I am,' said George. 'I'm the *Praefectus Castrorum* of the United States of Plutonia.'

'Hey, swino. That title isn't nearly grand enough. I move we make George our Pharaoh, so we can call his army the Pharaoh Gnomes.'

'The *Praefectus Castrorum*,' said Phil, 'is our Head of State. That means George is the Chief, unless, of course, we elect a new PC.' He frowned and shook his head. 'The mystery stockholder can come out of the closet and elect a new PC whenever he pleases.'

'Don't fucking worry about that.'

'Why not? Don't you?'

'No.'

'Why?'

'Because *I* bought all that stock.'

Laughter detonated in Billy, and he whooped and gasped until tears came.

'What's so fucking funny? A little more of that and I'll be all over you like stink on shit!'

'You made it! You're Emperor! Monarch of about thirty-five people, and who knows how many hogs.'

'That beats the shit out of Pigville.'

'Congratulations, swino mio. You're rising in the world.'

'And you rise with me. I hereby appoint you Military Tribune of all the armed forces in the United States of Plutonia and *Centurion Primus Pilus* of my Praetorian Guard. I'll have them make you some silver armor.'

'I cannot accept. I'm not even a citizen.'

'You can be a Father of the Country.'

'I don't even plan on being a member of the country.'

'One boar can sire twenty thousand pigs a year from stored semen. Well, Bill – just like Pigville. Anything a boar can do, we can do better.'

'I'm leaving here tomorrow.'

George showed his side teeth like an angry dog, and, flashing gold, growled out: 'I own this fucking country and you will do what I tell you or suffer the consequences.'

Janet glared ice at him and spoke in a steely voice. 'Well, Pigsy, you are mistaken. You don't own this fucking country. You don't own any stock, either. At our central office, on Wednesday, acting in my capacity of Chief Executive Officer of ZTG, because I smelled you hiding behind those sham buyers, I invoked the agreement and bought back *all the stock* at a rate favorable to the company. Remember, in *Ham*pstead, you signed the agreement? Do you remember that, Pigsy?'

'Yeah.'

'So,' said Phil, 'now we have a Frankenstein – a Georgestein monster. A rich company that owns itself. In law, corporations are fictitious persons. Now isn't that just wonderful!' He burst into laughter, rocking back and forth and slapping the table. 'A company that owns itself is as rare as a ninety-yard field goal or a triple play unassisted.'

'Where's the fucking money?'

'In an escrow account in Chicago.'

'Janet,' said Phil, 'the stock? You bought it *all*?'

'Yes Phil. *All*. Every single share.'

'That means the ZEUGMA Theme Group has become a country, a sovereign state. The company is a country that owns itself.'

'So who makes the laws?'

'Nobody except the fictional El Supremo – the in*corporated* company once again embodied, has that power. We'll have to be like the Moslems and get along with what we've got.'

'Who administers what we've got?'

'Here's how I see it. The company owns all of its stock, including the reserve stock it never issued. It cannot sell either kind of stock without authorization by the board of directors. But excepting the ex-officio Chief Executive Officer, one must be a stockholder to serve on the board of directors. So you, alone, are now the board. You are the *Praefectus Castrorum*. You are at once the CEO and the PC, the executive and the legislature. And you know what? On second thought, I think *you* can decree new laws. If you make yourself Chief Justice, you can also interpret laws, and resolve disputes. Yes. That places all the powers in your hands, and legitimately so. That makes you the absolute monarch of our country. Our emperor, our *führer*.'

Phil glared contempt at her. 'Young woman, I think you planned it this way, and have long been fully aware of what I just told you.'

'So?'

'I think you've double-crossed and betrayed us.'

'Sandy. What else do you expect of the Monkey King? Would you rather submit to the will of George? To Pigsy? To rule by force and fear?' She turned to Billy. 'How about you, Tripitaka?'

'Mine is not to reason why.'

She stood. 'I hereby decree that henceforth, at my pleasure, George will be Chief of Staff of the Armed Forces of the Plutonian Empire with the rank of Imperial Legate, and that Alexander Burke, a. k. a. Tripitaka, will be Assistant Chief of Staff with the rank of Military Tribune. George, you will assemble our forces here, tomorrow, at sunup. We will all meet here and plan our next move.'

'Janet,' said Phil, 'I am deeply disappointed in you.'

'Don't be. When engaged in administration, excellence – rule

208

through the force of virtue, is achieved by emulating the North Star.'

Billy and Aimée walked down Quetzal Way toward the flagpole. The tide had engulfed the pier; the flying pig floated as if anchored, not moored.

George came running up behind. 'Al, I have to talk with you.'

Billy kissed Aimée's cheek. 'Sowgirl mia, see you in a bit.'

He walked with George down to the quay. Hog musk wafted from the speakers. The ocean level had risen within a foot of flooding on to the playing field.

'That tide's kicking ass, eh? A little more, and it will drown out the Campus Martius.'

'Looks that way.'

'I'm glad you're staying, and so is Janet.'

'I'm leaving tomorrow.'

'You going to swim?'

'If necessary.'

'You'll drown.'

'There are plenty of islands close by. I'll be a secret sharer.'

'You're not going anywhere. You are going to stay and help me and Janet.'

'Put the Emperor first, George, or I'll accuse you of *lèse-majesté*, if not of treason.'

'We need you.'

Billy offered his hand.

'Shake.'

They shook.

'You just shook the hand that shook the hand that shook the hand that shook the hand of Adolf Hitler.'

'What do you mean by that shit?'

'I mean you're my pal, but it's time for me to move on.'

'Boy! Back in Pigville, remember – at the Suidic Saturnalia, you told me your secret.'

'I was playing the part of Joe King – you know, *jo*-king.'

'The hell you were. I've looked into it.'

'You didn't see much.'

'Enough. Plenty. I'm going to turn you in as a deserter, then you'll *have* to stay.'

'You can't scare me George.'

209

'In Portsmouth Naval Penitentiary, asshole, the punishment *is* the crime.'

'So I've heard.'

'You leave here, and they've got you.'

'They never got the secret sharer.'

'We're sovereign with no extradition treaties. You're safe here.'

'Forget it, George. I'm leaving tomorrow; I'm going to San Francisco.'

TWENTY-SIX

Billy and Aimée slept fitfully on their futon, without rest, made love and talked at length. He told her about deserting the Marine Corps and about his determination to leave the island, and she kissed him all over to make him feel better. 'Sowboy mio, you are perfect.' She declared herself determined to stay. 'I'm established here. I'm cooking a bouillabaisse of meaning, a myth-stew composed of all the leftovers, which I'll serve as the master meaning-myth of the new world.' She cited peace-and-quiet, and the help of Phil, a proven computer genius, as good reasons. 'But deeper than that, beneath what I *know* are my reasons for being so sure I should stay, is what I can't *know*, a solid certainty I can *feel*.' She explained she believes it's a feminine trait to feel one is right and to be so sure of it as to firmly hold to that feeling, regardless of evidence and/or experience. They dozed off, and he cuddled up to her back, and, in the dawn's early light, awoke and slid on top of her, kissed her, called her silly girl, and they began to make love.

'Ride 'em sowboy!'

George!

There he stood in golden armor, a sky-blue plume on his helmet.

'You're late. Emperor Janet I bade me come and get you.'

As George watched, they visited their chemical toilet, dressed, and stepped outside.

Two ranks of legionaries in duty uniform, the Fridays and the Japanese, armed with Arisaka rifles, bayonets fixed, stood at attention, waiting. The morning high tide had submerged the quay and was washing over the edge of the playing field – the Campus Martius. George told Billy and Aimée to walk behind him.

'All right girls,' he growled to his troops, 'we will conduct these people in to the royal presence.' Billy and Aimée following, he paced to the crossroads where the flying-pig flag drooped from the pole, and turned to the troops. 'Left *face*! For-*ward* – Hoooo!'

They all marched in ragged step toward the Quetzal Café.

'Sowgirl, I feel more like we're going to our hanging than to our breakfast.'

Janet and Phil waited at the table under rotting bat banners. Phil wore a black T-shirt. Has anyone else noticed he color-codes? George ordered the Japanese to stand ranked before his pavilion at parade rest. After dismissing the Fridays to serve breakfast, he popped a lump of gum into his mouth and sat.

'This sure brings back memories. When I joined *Legio Dix Fretensis*, Tiberius was Caesar, and the Tenth was stationed at Cyrrhus, a crossing of the Euphrates on the road from Antioch to Zeugma. Zeugma! How's *that* for coincidence! We had twenty-five legions until Quintilius Verus lost three of them to the Germans. That was in Augustus's time. He formed the Tenth during the Civil Wars when he was still Octavian. In its first battle, as infantry aboard triremes, the Tenth crushed Sextus Pompeius's forces. That happened in the Straits of Fretum, now called Messina – hence our cognomen. *Fretensis*. As time went by, we became, you might say, the foreign legion of the legions, *la Légion Étrangère Romaine*.'

The Fridays rushed up with the wine cooler.

'*Carpae vino!*' He glanced contempt at them, and then glared at Phil and Billy. 'You two girls wouldn't make a pimple on a legionary's ass. Fuck no! The best part of you ran down your father's leg – you'd have about as much chance in the legions as a bucket of piss in hell. Better believe it. *We* never rode around. We always went by foot. Once, on detached service, I walked from Vienna to Paris and then shipped over the Channel to England and hiked to Chester to join *Legio XX Valeria Victrix*, and then back to *Legio IX Hispania*. We had to carry everything. Armor, saw, basket, spade, hatchet, an edged hook, a chain, three days' rations, some kit, our shields, and our weapons – two swords and a javelin.'

He spat on the grass.

'You think you got it rough? Once I lived for a month on nothing but human cheese. Mull *that* over. I earned my torques and armilae, all right. I deserved a phalara, too, as much as anybody, your Congressional medal, but they never gave me one. And discipline! You two can't tell discipline from pig shit. Let's do it here. You fuck up real bad, and I can't find out who's to blame, I punish the whole outfit. *Decimato*. Decimate! I line you all up, and take out every tenth person. It comes out Aimée, a Friday, and Chandra. The rest of you have to stone or beat them to death. We were cops as well as soldiers which helped us extort half our pay from the locals. But our centurions used to extort us! The sons-of-bitches!'

He smiled, having found a sweeter vein of nostalgia.

'Oh, there were good things, too. Legions were composed of ten cohorts. The first was double strength, maniple strength, an élite force that could operate independently. Me, I was an optio in the first, and should have been at least a centurion pilus prior, but they were prejudiced against me. Each cohort was made of six centuries, and each century of ten squads of eight men each. They shared a leather tent and a mule to carry it when in the field, and two rooms in the barracks. The *contubernia* were our mess units, too. Believe me, we got real close. Companionship, comradeship – mateship, now there's a value . . .'

'Shut up!' commanded Emperor Janet I. 'We have business.'

His face flushed with restrained fury.

'We have commanded your presence at the promulgation of our first decrees.'

They received this in stoic silence, awed, perhaps, by her use of the imperial *we*, which, thought Phil, resembles the editorial *we*, or the sports fans' *we*: We sure kicked ass in the Super Bowl.

'We, Janet I, Emperor of Plutonia, do hereby command that all military forces in our empire be dissolved forever.' This she said directly to George. 'We further decree that the defunct Board of Directors of Z E U G M A Theme Associates be reconstituted as a provisional government to rule our empire while a committtee, led by Philmer P. Swait, drafts a constitution embodying democratic principles and providing equal suffrage for our subjects, including all the Fridays but excluding pigs and other subhuman fauna.'

She rose to her feet, the very model of *gravitas* and *dignitas*. 'We now abdicate our imperial throne and order the abolition

213

of absolute monarchy and the establishment of a democratic polity.'

She sat down.

Phil embraced her and kissed her cheek.

George sprang to his feet, bellowing: 'Legionaries, fall in!'

The Japanese came running, and formed a rank behind him; the Fridays snatched their rifles and formed behind them.

George peered down at his companions.

'Have you ever heard tell of *coups d'état*?'

They glared at him in silence.

'Well, girls, you just lived through one.'

Silence.

George sat. 'Now that's settled and I've established my rule, I wish to extend an invitation to all of you to serve on my council. Life will go on as before. You can do whatever the fuck you please, invent myths, build the perfect golf course, it's no skin off my ass. We will complete Pig Spa Island and I'll run it like Rainier runs Monaco.'

'I'm leaving today,' said Billy.

'Stay,' said Janet. 'The day you got here, George reported you to the Marines.'

'Be that as it may,' said George, 'we'll now go into my pavilion – the temporary Capitol, where we can converse in private.' As they walked in, he said to Billy, 'Did you know, the first structure in San Francisco was a tent like this erected at Grant and Jackson by a British sailor who'd deserted his ship?' They found themselves in canvas-filtered sunlight. George set his helmet on a stand. Billy saw low tables and Roman couches, on one of which sat Tom Kraemer, dressed in his Japanese major's suit, a dead cigar in his mouth, Waggles dozing at his feet. Tom rose to greet the ladies. George snatched off Billy's hat. 'Don't you have no fucking manners?'

To one side stood an armoire, and a rack of wine bottles, and at the back, a grotto, about eight feet deep, made of styrofoam rocks, George's Mithraeum. The back of the grotto displayed a life-sized plastic statue of a crazed young athlete, wearing long underwear, a liberty cap, a cloak, and a short dress, stretched on top of a boar, one foot pinning its trotter, one hand gripping its snout and heaving its head back while the other hand drew a staghorn-handled, double-edged, flame-blade Black Forest boar knife across its throat.

214

Abruptly, when George became aware of them looking at it he ran back, armor clanking, and drew a curtain across the entrance. 'It's sacrilege for broads to see the sacred form of Mithra, or join in his mysteries.' George selected a bottle of wine, opened it, and came back to sit on a couch. 'When I get my way, I'll put all the broads in the world in their proper place: Pregnant in summer, barefoot in winter.'

Aimée shook her head in disgust. Janet said, 'And now that you're the Adolf Hitler of Pig Spa Island, you'll make us wear corsets, and veils, and bind our feet.'

'Would you listen to her, Al. She and Phil planned this whole thing. *They* reported you to the Marines. They fixed it so ZTG bought back all the stock at half price, so they could rob me. All they had to do was turn you or Aimée or you both against me, then they could fucking run me out, and ship you to Portsmouth, and take over the whole thing for themselves.'

It did sound plausible.

George poured wine. 'It's Saturday. A drink to Saturn!'

'You should invoke Pluto,' said Janet.

Billy toasted and they followed his lead.

'Mithra was born during the Saturnalia, December 25th. With comrades, together, in His warm grotto, representing a cozy world in cold space, you feel as one with all mankind, all of us brothers in the same family under the stars of fate. You take comfort from knowing the brothers, even the fatal stars themselves, are under the sway of the supreme imperator, our lord Mithra, source of light and truth, master of fate.'

'All that,' said Phil, 'is for white males only. Which is one reason we must move you out before we can build a model state. What scares me is that now the whites are at last getting together, ending their family feuds and cold wars, they will soon truly rule the world, with Uncle Tom overseers directing the dirty work, the slave labor of third-world proles. Hitler's definition of whites was a little narrow. He left out the Jews and the French and the Poles and the Russians and the Italians and that caused trouble. He made the Japanese honorary whites, doubtless meaning to rescind that distinction later. Look around you today. The family fight is over, and the master race is refining its solidarity, consolidating its dominion over the lesser races, the fish of the sea, the birds of the air, the plants, the animals, and everything that creeps on the earth.'

215

'George,' said Janet, 'Mithra is supposed to be killing a *bull*, not a hog. The bull, Taurus, represents the constellation, Taurus, the Age of Taurus, starry fate, and Mithra's mastery of fate, his shifting the age when four thousand years ago he killed Tauric dominance to admit Aries the ram, the Age of Aries, whom he later killed in favor of Pisces. So now, in our times, your idol should show Mithra killing a *fish* to open the Age of Aquarius, not a fucking hog!'

'Killing the hog opens *my* new age.'

'But there are no hogs in the Zodiac.'

'There fucking well ought to be!'

'Why!'

'So Mithra could kill their dominance over civil life.'

'I thought you like pigs.'

'I hate pigs!'

Waggles came squealing over to George and George gave her a savage kick. Weeping and gasping she ran over to Billy and leapt into his lap.

'George,' said Billy, gently stroking Waggles's brow, 'how can *you* hate pigs? Have you forgotten all your passionate soliloquies about suidic rights? As for me, before I moved into Pigville, I had no special feelings about pigs, one way or the other. But now I've kind of come to like those brainy bags of loose guts.'

'I want you to step outside and look around, and come back and tell us if you see anything unusual.'

Billy went to the front of the tent and out through the split in the flap. Presently he returned.

'It's amazing. The tide has covered the playing field and it's lapping at the foot of the flagpole. The architect and some of the others are trying to get in here to see us, but your troops are holding them back.'

'Wouldn't you say something strange is going on?'

'Yes sir.'

'Sit down.'

He sat. George now had their full attention.

'You really think I give a shit about pigs?' He showed his side teeth and gold flashed anger. 'Fuck pigs!' He clenched fists. 'You think I'm dumb. You think I'm fulla shit, don't you? A fine state of a-fucking-fairs when what I'm trying to do is save you.'

'Salvation through George,' said a scornful Janet.

'Listen you pus-eating cuntface. Of course I'm deep into pigs. Pigs are my cover story, and they've done it too, covered what I'm really after.' He gulped his wine. 'I'm trying to avert an absolute catastrophe. Yes. Now open to what I'm saying.' He chugged more. 'Okay. Like I've told Al, and the rest of you too, Tom here, Tom's an angel from Heaven.'

'Is that really true?' asked Billy.

A smile passed over Tom's slack but kindly face.

'You bet, sonny.'

'Tom's been under deep cover. He's my mole. He's an arch-angel on Jehovah's imperial council. Over the past few centuries Jehovah's been waxing so angry at mankind that he has finally decided to send a second flood. For years, Tom's been keeping me informed of the preparations. This time, arks won't help. No fucking Noahs. Jehovah has decided to drown *everybody*. All the animals too. And start over. Try again with a better pattern. He'll send Jesus to recolonize after the natives are exterminated, the same as the whites did after killing all the locals on Tasmania.'

'Kill everybody?' said Aimée.

'Fucking-A. He's been using the Near East for a laboratory, trying different methods. This has led him to change his mind about fire next time. He's staying with the tried and true. Water.'

'So the Great Extermination will soon be complete.'

'Yes,' said Tom. 'He says He's going to do it before they do it to themselves – you know, atom bombs and nerve gas and germ war and poisoning the land and the air and the sea. He's going to do it Himself, and, as He says, with *style*. But don't believe for a minute He's thinking about anything but Himself. He'll do it all right. You can bet your last loving cup on that. He *is* doing it. Right *now*. Today. But He ain't doing it out of love of life, or for art. Not Him! He's doing it for fun.'

TWENTY-SEVEN

Flying high, high, very high, The Fly, resurrected patriarch of Beaufort and PI, risen from ashes, obsessed by revenge, stealth-shield blinding radar, planed down from the sky, circled the White House, and buzzed through President Quayle's office window to settle on a pen holder.

'Expecting me, aren't you, Mr President?'

The distressed chief executive nodded assent.

'No poor me's now. No whining. I made you President as per our contract. I let you keep your miserable defective Republican soul. And you liked that. But you knew there'd be a payback. Today the payback begins.'

'I named our new secret attack Hu37x helicopters Beelzebub in your honor, didn't I?'

'Yes. But that doesn't count. Kissing my ass expressed your desire, not my request.'

'So what do you want me to do?'

'First, you can kiss my ass for real.'

The Fly rose and buzzed backward to touch moist presidential lips.

'Put a little tongue into it.'

President Quayle put a little tongue into it.

Satisfied, The Fly flew back to his perch.

'I've located a deserter from the Marine Corps. I want you to call the Commandant and order he be apprehended and jailed at once.'

The President called an aide, who got the Commandant on the phone.

'Commandant, we've located a Marine Corps deserter who I want arrested and jailed at once.' He asked The Fly for particulars. 'Recruit William Alan Williams, number 902-10-6251, deserted from boot camp on Parris Island in the spring of last year.' The Fly provided the latitude and longitude of Pig Spa Island, and explained it had by some ghastly blunder recently become an independent, sovereign nation. 'What forces do we have in that area? The *Carl Vinson*? Order them to send a force immediately to the island to apprehend the deserter, but not to kill anybody. What! The details are up to you ... Yes, yes, it's independent and sovereign. Rationale for invading? Hmmm, let's see. Okay. We'll say it's a center of communist subversion for all of Southeast Asia. No, wait. *Drat!* We can't use that any more. Let's say it's a drug distribution center.' The Fly told him six Americans and a Canadian were on the island. 'We've got a hostage situation here. Renegade Japanese drug dealers and their Balinese confederates, all heavily armed, are holding George Ahasuerus Baxter, Thomas Landon Kraemer, Philmer Prentice Swait, Janet Mun Ki Ma, and two unnamed students from Cleveland, all of them Americans – and a woman from London, Ontario. Amy Olsen Jones. What? Yeah, go rescue them. Good. No casualties. Yes. Semper *what*? *Fi*? Rhymes with *fly*, you say? Remember, no casualties. Yes. You work out the details. Okay?'

He hung up.

'The Commandant says nobody deserts and gets away with it.'

'*Carpae Deus*.' said George. 'Seize God. That's what I'd fucking *like* to do. But when I tried it in Frisco, He opened an earthquake fissure, and we both fell in. I thought I had His ass, but no such luck. Everybody watching must have thought we were crushed dead, kinda like Sherlock Holmes and Professor Moriarty, but no. When the fissure closed, we were on the level of an old sewer main. I was stunned, and when I came to on my back in the dark, He was fucking *gone*.'

'I didn't know you'd been to San Francisco, swino.'

'There's a lot about me you don't know.' Waggles slid off Billy's lap and snuggled George's leg. George kicked her aside. 'The water will stay at that level for a couple hours – Al, go have a look.' Billy glanced outside. No change. 'It's going to recede some, so people think it's a tsunami, you know, a tidal wave. Then it will rise again,

fast, and high enough to cover fucking Everest! Yeah! Forty days
and forty nights and no one survives save for males in submarines.
But all the broads are gone, so we drones live on canned goods
and seafood and eventually croak and the ocean will be the womb
of His new man, and His Son, Jesus, will be the model.'

'So what's our move now?' asked Janet.

'We take the Fridays, and follow the high trail to the caves, and
lock ourselves in. There's plenty of food and drink, but we have
to breathe the air that's there, and there ain't enough of that. So
nobody else goes in. Just us. The Fridays will carry our baggage,
and we'll leave them outside, on guard.'

'You are one ice-hearted cold-blooded reptilian swino!'

'Twice as idealistic, twice as practical. That's my motto. Remember, we're doing this to save mankind.'

'How about Mithra? You going to bring him along? He won't
breathe anything.'

'Fuck no. He can take care of himself.'

'I though you believed in him.'

'I believe in *all* of them.'

The Lord Chief Air Marshal of The Flies led his swarm across
the international date line, where Thursday bordered on Satur-
day, losing Friday utterly, and proceded over the Pacific through
Saturday to alight on the flight deck of USS *Carl Vinson*. A
Beelzebub assault helicopter was being readied for a combat
mission. The Commandant of the Marine Corps had caused
Billy's name and number to be run through Pentagon computers.
No record of desertion printed out, but it found the roster of
Billy's platoon on Parris Island, with Billy's name and the names
of his DIs. The Commandant asked for the chief drill instructor's
record. He'd been promoted to platoon sergeant and assigned to
lead a reconnaissance team based on *Carl Vinson*. While this was
going on, satellites photographed the island, and Streeterport,
and eavesdropped on the conversation in the tent. Intelligence,
interpreting, said Flood and Great Extermination were being used
as coded names in some sinister conspiracy; it reported sixteen
soldiers armed with antique Arisakas, and a score of civilians.

The Commandant spoke directly with the recon team leader,
Billy's old DI. 'You will arrest Recruit Williams, and bring all the
Americans and the Canadian out with you. You will take four fire

teams. Under no circumstances, short of dire emergency, will you engage in combat. If serious problems arise, contact command for orders and backup.'

'Aye aye, sir,' said the team leader.

A sudden whuff whuff whuff sounded, pervaded, and the tent canvas rattled and George sprang to his feet and said, 'What the hell is that?'

As they ran outside, he snatched his helmet and tugged it on.

An evil black helicopter slowly settled toward Quetzal Way and bat banners flapped and George said, 'Shit! You fuck with history, and history fucks with you.'

The café furniture went scooting and skidding and George told his troops to stand at parade rest in a single rank before the pavilion.

George posed motionless in front of them; dust clouds dulled his golden armor, his plume whipped and snapped.

Having sucked the maximum drama from its entrance on stage, the helicopter settled on Quetzal Way and stopped spinning. Out of it sprang armed men disguised as leafy plants. One of them, three chevrons and a rocker on his shoulders, lined up the rest facing the legionaries. He about-faced and, unarmed, tapping a swagger stick against his leg, he marched over to George. 'You are holding seven hostages and a deserter. I am under orders to take them back with me.'

A swarm of flies settled on the helicopter.

'You are invading a sov-er-eign state, so I give *you* orders to get the fuck *out*.'

'We are United States Marines, op-e-rating under *di*-rect orders from the pres-*i*-dent.'

With a sudden cold shock Billy recognized his old DI.

George about-faced, gave a command, and the legionaries in unison aimed their rifles at the Marines.

'Let us talk this over, sergeant. I suggest you and I order our men to stack arms.'

They ordered their men to stack arms.

The Fly watched Billy with an evil leer.

'I am the *Praefectus Castrorum* of the Empire of Plutonia, the Chief of State, so you can work this out with me.'

Trained by recon to expect frequent manifestations of the bizarre

221

while on missions, the DI felt perfectly at ease in the presence of a Roman field officer. 'You are holding seven hostages and are harboring a deserter.'

'And your information is fucked up. Do you have names?'

'George Ahasuerus Baxter, for starters.'

'That's me.'

The DI gave the other names, and George beckoned his companions over, and they identified themselves, and said they were on the island by choice.

'And who is that?' The DI asked, pointing at Billy.

'That is Alexander Burke, optio – sergeant that is – of the second cohort of *Legio Dix Fretensis*.' George motioned Billy to approach. The DI did not recognize him. 'Optio Burke's off duty today.'

Billy returned to Aimée. 'Talk about resonance,' she said, 'those two seem in perfect harmony. Takes one to know one.'

'We will stay until you deliver the deserter.'

'You will leave my territory instanter.'

'We Marines will do our duty.'

'*Baby* Marines. What do you know about the *old* Corps? Fuck-all, that's what. Me, I used to drink with Lou Diamond.'

'And I used to drink with J. H. *Christ*.'

'*I* nailed that crybaby to the cross.'

The DI made a thin smile, and tapped his swagger stick against his palm.

George gestured at the helicopter.

'I never saw a bird like that before. What do you call it?'

'Beelzebub subvisual airborne attack vehicle.'

'No *shit*?'

'Yeah. I don't know why. But what I think happened is nations have invented so many new weapons they ran out of terr-*i*-fying meat-eaters to name them for. So now they are o-bliged to select among ruminants, devils, and insects.'

George sent a man into the pavilion to fetch the wine cooler. On returning with it, the workman set up a table and two chairs.

The warriors sat down, filled their glasses.

'*Hilaritati ac genio dicata!*' said George.

They toasted.

'*Poto ergo sum*,' said the DI.

They toasted.

'Arisaka rifles, ain't they? said the DI. My father brought one back from Iwo.'

'What do you think of my boys?'

'Runts and wimps. Sloppy, too.'

'It's like with pigs. They get sexual early. Before he's trained, the young boar may mount the sow at the wrong end, or even go for the anus.' George swished wine in his glass, chugged it. 'Any hope for them?'

'Yeah. Jogging. Make them sweat off some of that gour-may fat.'

His patience at an end, The Fly buzzed over to Billy and hovered; he sent his swarm to the table to attract the DI's attention and bring him to Billy.

Suddenly, a cloud of flies enveloped George and his guest.

'Alexander, go get the Attractant-10 pronto!'

With a whoop of glee, Billy dashed for the pavilion. The water level began rising fast, advancing up Quetzal Way. Billy handed George the spray can. 'Good boy.' He turned to his companion. 'This shit'll fix them flies.' George shook the can, released a mighty spray directly at the flies and the DI. The flies dropped to the table and began a frantic fuck session. Waggles came running and began rubbing her twat against the DI who tried to beat her off with his swagger stick.

Then the babirussa hog came dashing to confront the Marines. The DI backed up into the water, George following.

'You,' said George, 'should have sent your mother in-stead.'

The DI burst into laughter. 'You,' he replied, 'are the kind of knucklehead who'd fart upward bound on a crow-ded escalator.'

They'd soon have been mired in the no-flinch game.

Had not the water reached the helicopter.

Suddenly aware of it, they ran to the bird.

'Get in,' said George to the DI, 'and I'll take you to the deserter.' He beckoned Billy and the others in, then summoned Chandra and the architect. The two men told the troops and workers to climb the hill. Then, water now knee-deep, the DI and George clambered into the helicopter and shut the door.

'Get this piece of rectal mahogany into the air!'

The DI spoke to the crew and the bird spun and rose.

He smacked a fly.

'The Corps has always had a fly problem.'

223

'Yeah? Well now you have a flood problem. Just look down there.'

The beaches had all vanished; the coast, marked by treetops thrusting from water, had become a swamp.

George explained to the DI what was going on. 'By miraculous alchemy, He's melting the ice-caps and converting air into water. Nobody on the surface will survive. Your aircraft carrier? All the ships at sea? You think they're arks? When the water covers Everest, He will treat the biosphere to a surge of nerve gas. No ark or airplane or mine is designed for that. Fuck no! Except for men in submarines and space stations, nobody will survive. And us? Because we're going to ride it out in airtight caves, dug into a cliff. *We*'ll survive. Because there's no women on submarines the race would die, as He intends, were it not for us.'

'The Soviets have women on their subs.'

George started, as if lashed.

'If only I knew that for sure, I'd do everything differently.'

'He would, too,' said Janet. 'He'd push Aimée and Chandra and the architect and me out the door, right now.'

'Fucking-A! Then we'd have eighty days of air.'

George showed the DI where the landing zone was, and the DI passed the information along to the crew. 'Hey,' said the co-pilot, 'here's something you should listen to.'

He switched the radio from earphones to loudspeaker.

The voice of President Quayle pervaded.

'Two hours ago, carrying out my orders, armed forces of the United States landed in the island empire of Plutonia, a notorious drug distribution enclave, freed seven hostages, six Americans and a Canadian, and apprehended a Marine Corps deserter who was in possession of top secret documents intended for sale to the People's Republic of China. Our superior forces swiftly overcame light resistance. The *Praefectus Castrorum* of Plutonia, who is at once Chief of State and kingpin in a worldwide drug network, has been taken into custody. My heart swells with pride at the ability and courage of our servicemen and women who have made this action a complete success.'

The radio urged its listeners to stay tuned for further bulletins.

'Yeah! About wet feet in the Oval Office.'

The helicopter settled down into the clearing before the

224

caves, sending mats and tables tumbling and disintegrating giant butterflies. The DI ordered all passengers out. He turned to the crew. 'I am staying here to reconnoiter. You will locate our men and the residents of Streeterport, and carry them back to the ship. I'll keep in contact with my pager.'

He leapt out and the Beelzebub reared up into the sky.

The Fly, alone now, planed down to alight in a bamboo thicket.

The DI studied the crimson Japanese characters on the armored door.

'What the hell's that say?'

'It says – and stop me when you catch it – it says: *Zimmer bitte früh aüfraumen* or *Fare subito la stanza per favore* or *Por favor mandar la criada temprano* or *Prière de faire la chambre de bonne heure* or *Pozhalvysta, uberite komnatu rano* or . . .'

'Please make up the room early!' The DI dropped his pager, adjusted its position on the ground with a foot, and stomped it to bits. George tugged at the airtight door, and its massy weight, ponderous but perfectly balanced, swung out, revealing a narrow tunnel going back into the mountain. The DI walked over to Billy; The Furious Fly saw his chance. He would make them look at each other; he would trigger their memories. And justice would be done. He swooped to them and buzzed around their heads, narrowing his spiral until he was going around and around the DI's scalp.

Jubilating, he sensed Billy's apprehension, impending success.

Abruptly, the DI reached up and smacked his hands together, crushing The Fly.

He extended his palm to Billy.

On it lay the tiny corpse.

'Boy.'

'Yes sir.'

'*I* killed it this time, so you can bury it.'

They burst into laughter.

Billy opened his counterfeit Swiss army knife and excavated a tiny grave. 'Do you think it will *stay* buried?' He pushed dirt over the cadaver with the heel of his hand, stood, and with a foot ground the earth flat.

'Alexander Burke,' said the DI, 'I am *utterly* devoid of mem-o-ry as to what that guy Williams looks like. My mind raises images of Pruitt and Sergeant Warden instead, and, mysteriously, they are intensifying.'

'*From Here to Eternity*?'

'Yes.'

They all moved to the entrance of the caves.

'We've got a big generator, and submarine batteries,' said George. 'Power will be no problem.'

'But air will, because we broads breathe too much of it.' Aimée was standing with her arms folded. 'Right?'

'Our pal George here,' said Billy, 'is really the Wandering Jew. He nailed Christ to the cross and supervised its erection. Then under the cross, he rolled dice for His clothes, and won. That so exasperated Him that He said to George: I go, but thou shalt tarry 'til I return. George told me all about it back in Pigville at the Suidic Saturnalia where we got so drunk on brandy we were conversing with the citizens and crawling around naked in their excrement. George says Christ can't come back until all the current humans are dead. Jehovah is recalling the defective model that looks like Him, and wants to replace it with a better one, patterned on His Son.'

'So *that's* it,' said Janet. 'As long as people survive, Jesus won't come, and Pigsy can keep on living.'

'Exactly.'

She exploded into laughter, and, when she regained control of herself, she said, 'Wonderful! George can't live *with* women, but he sure as hell can't live *without* them. And in this case, *them* is us.'

'Don't believe everything you hear.' George waved everybody away. 'Get inside. We have to lock up before the water comes.'

They all went in but Billy.

George, and then Aimée, came back out to him.

'I'm staying here.'

Aimée embraced him, kissed him, whispered that he should stick with her, and help with her project.

'I'm going back to Frisco.'

'Why?'

'I can't be part of this any more.'

'But you'll drown.'

'I don't think Jehovah can make more water than he has so far. To cover Everest he'd have to make the sea thirty thousand feet deeper – a quantity of water beyond imagination.'

'Miracles! Loaves and fishes!'

'If I drown, I'll drown swimming.'

They kissed, and Billy pushed her inside.

226

'George, old swino mio, you know, it's a fact. We males just aren't what ladies want us to be.'

'I'll miss you.'

'Can you go forty days without bubble gum?'

'I'll soon find out.'

'If your life didn't depend on it, would you still try to save all of us, or any of us?'

'I don't fucking know.'

'Were I in your place, I wouldn't know either.'

'You came to me, a callow sowboy. You leave as a true hogman.'

'Thanks to your instruction and example, the hogman's Trinity – art, weight, money – has become my North Star.'

'You could be right. Maybe he *can't* make enough water. If that happens, it's no skin off my ass. I'll be okay either way. And so will that Marine. He's figured out how to desert without deserting.'

'He recognized me, but he didn't choose to say so.'

'You trust me with that? You still trust me?'

'You're my pal. Of course I trust you.'

'And you don't think I turned you in?'

'You wouldn't do that.'

'You think I'm fucking dumb, don't you? You think my IQ is room temperature. So maybe I *don't* understand everything. But one thing I *do* fucking know, and I've been everywhere, everywhen – one thing I *do* fucking know is any year, any place, there are haves and have-nots, masters and slaves – rich, poor, and starving. It's always been like that and it always will be, yet you think – you *believe*, you can change it, don't you?'

'I'll sure as hell try.'

'Don't you?'

'Yes,' said the Chief of the New Team. 'Yes, I do. Yes.'

ILLUSTRATIONS: CREDITS AND SOURCES

ABOUT THE AUTHOR

Richard Miller describes himself as an independent social philosopher who writes. Jobs he has had include merchant seaman, foreign correspondent, grave digger, peace campaigner and college professor. In his mid-sixties, Richard Miller lives in California; he has written three previous novels, *Amerloque*, *Snail*, and *SQUED*, and a history, *Bohemia, the Protoculture Then & Now*.